PAPER CUTS

Also by Ellery Adams:

The Secret, Book, and Scone Society Mysteries:

The Secret, Book & Scone Society
The Whispered Word
The Book of Candlelight
Ink and Shadows
The Vanishing Type
Papers Cuts

Book Retreat Mysteries:

Murder in the Mystery Suite
Murder in the Paperback Parlor
Murder in the Secret Garden
Murder in the Locked Library
Murder in the Reading Room
Murder in the Storybook Cottage
Murder in the Cookbook Nook
Murder on the Poet's Walk
Murder in the Book Lover's Loft

PAPER CUTS

ELLERY ADAMS

Kensington Publishing Corp.
www.kensingtonbooks.com

KENSINGTON BOOKS are published by

Kensington Publishing Corp.
119 West 40th Street
New York, NY 10018

All Kensington titles, imprints and distributed lines are available at special quantity discounts for bulk purchases for sales promotion, premiums, fund-raising, educational or institutional use.

Special book excerpts or customized printings can also be created to fit specific needs. For details, write or phone the office of the Kensington Special Sales Manager: Kensington Publishing Corp., 119 West 40th Street, New York, NY, 10018. Attn. Special Sales Department. Phone: 1-800-221-2647.

Library of Congress Control Number: 2022950822

The K and Teapot logo is a trademark of Kensington Publishing Corp.

ISBN: 978-1-4967-2647-6

First Kensington Hardcover Edition: May 2023

ISBN: 978-1-4967-2649-0 (ebook)

10 9 8 7 6 5 4 3 2 1

Printed in the United States of America

This book is for every parent of a neurodiverse child. You are your child's tireless advocate, fiercest gladiator, selfless hero, and loyal friend. Parenting is hard, and no one does it perfectly, even though social media makes it seem like some do. When things get tough, remember that your perfectly amazing child is crafting their own perfectly amazing story.

Always, Ellery

When people hurt you over and over, think of them like sandpaper. They may scratch and hurt you a bit, but in the end, you end up polished and they end up useless.

—Chris Colfer

Paper is more patient than man.

—Anne Frank

The Secret, Book, and Scone Society Members

Nora Pennington, owner of Miracle Books
Hester Winthrop, owner of the Gingerbread House Bakery
Estella Sadler, owner of Magnolia Salon and Spa
June Dixon, Guest Experience Manager, Miracle Springs
  Lodge

Relevant Miracle Springs Residents

Sheriff Grant McCabe
Deputy Jasper Andrews
K9 Handler Paula Hollowell
Sheldon Vega
Kirk and Val Walsh
Kelly and Tucker Walsh
Gus Sadler

Relevant Visitors to Miracle Springs

Justine James
Lawrence Townsend
Colton Fieri
Dana Kopinski

Chapter 1

What is better than wisdom? Woman. And what is better than a good woman? Nothing.

— Geoffrey Chaucer

"I loved this book." Hester Winthrop stroked the paperback on her lap as if it were a cat. "I underlined a bunch of passages, but my favorite line was when A-ma said, 'Always remember that food is medicine, and medicine is food.'"

The perfect arch of Estella's left brow rose a centimeter. "Your food is more like therapy than actual medicine."

Hester laughed. "Come on. Does broccoli make you feel better when you're down? No, it doesn't. Certain times call for donuts and chocolate cake and pecan pie with ice cream. If comfort food isn't medicine, then I don't know what is."

"Maybe I should shelve a few baking books in the Health section," said Nora Pennington, proprietor of Miracle Books.

June Dixon, Guest Experience Manager at Miracle Springs Lodge, a high-class resort frequented by guests from all over the world, peered at her friends from over the rims of her reading glasses. "All I can say is that I'm glad to be living in this era of body positivity. When I was in school, back in the Stone Age, girls were always trash-talking other girls. I don't know why, but we all did it. From the top of our heads right on down to our toes, we were too big, too small, too pointy, too wide. No one wore the right clothes. And don't even get me started on hair. You don't know nasty until you hear what some folks say about Black hair."

"That kind of thing doesn't stop when girls become women either," said Estella. "Every time I put two ladies of any age, race, or class under the blow-dryers together, they start picking apart the celebrities in *People*. I don't know why all women can't just be happy when other women succeed. Why can't we tell another woman they look good without worrying about how *we* look?"

Hester smiled at Estella. "You *always* look good. And June? You're channeling Etta James with that new do."

June passed a hand over her head. She usually kept it close-cropped, but Estella had convinced her to rock a teeny-weeny, icy-blond Afro. "Which tea would Etta order?" she asked as she studied the paper menu on the table before her. "Beau-Tea-Ful or Feeling Flir-Tea?"

Nora removed her copy of Lisa See's *The Tea Girl of Hummingbird Lane* from her bag and placed it on the table. She was ready to order and get their book discussion going.

"I'm going to try the Flir-Tea," she said. "I've never had tea with hibiscus and apple before."

"I've never even heard of flowering tea. I might be in the food business, but I—"

Hester was unable to finish her sentence because Estella suddenly grabbed her by the hand and said, "You're not wearing your ring. Did you forget to put it on?"

Color rushed to Hester's cheeks, and she lowered her eyes. "It didn't feel right to wear it. Things are weird between Jasper and me right now, so I gave it back. The ring belonged to his mother, which is why he should hold on to it."

"But you're still together, right?"

"Yeah. We're just . . . taking a step back. Being engaged put too much pressure on our relationship. It's easier to tell people that we decided to put off the wedding than to explain that we're in couples therapy because I have trust issues. Luckily, no one's asked me why we postponed the wedding. Without that ginormous event hanging over our heads, we can focus on us without feeling like there's a clock ticking down the minutes to a wedding."

Nora searched her friend's face. "Are you okay?"

Hester seesawed her hand. "I'm getting there. This is going to sound awful, but I feel lighter without that ring on my finger. Our couples counselor asked us to pretend like we've just met, so that's what we're doing. We're going out on dates and getting to know each other all over again. It's strange and super awkward at times, but it's also kind of sweet. Last night, Jasper walked me to my front door and kissed me good night. He seemed almost shy."

"Maybe you can bring him here for a lunch date. Everything on the menu sounds good, but Tastes Like Royal-Tea was made for me, don't you think?" Estella tossed her auburn hair and cupped her chin in her palms.

"Yes, Fergie, it does. I'm getting a Cuppa With My Best-Tea." June put her menu down. "Looks like we order at the counter. Is everybody ready?"

The four women maneuvered around tables and potted trees on their way to the counter. It was their first visit to Tea Flowers and there was so much to take in. The newest business in Miracle Springs was an eclectic blend of café and garden shop. The large space was divided into sections, with the tea shop on the left and the garden shop on the right. A checkout counter sat in the middle.

The limited menu offered flowering teas, sandwiches, and a selection of macarons. After ordering at the counter, customers could sit at one of the tables in the dining area. The tables were laid with chintz cloths featuring pink roses on a field of pale blue. The floral centerpieces, which were in teapot-shaped vases, were all for sale, and the salt and pepper shakers looked like real blossoms.

The tea-shop side of the business was confined to the counter and dining area, but most of the building was dedicated to gardening. The front section was full of waist-high tables featuring potted herbs, houseplants, flowering plants, and hanging baskets. The shelf space in the back half of the store was stuffed with whimsical pots, gardening tools, bird houses and feeders, and a selection of small statuary. Spinning racks stood like sentinels at the end of every aisle, their pockets stuffed with seed packets, work gloves, and plant labels.

All the potted trees and plants in the café side were for sale, and as Nora and her friends got in line, they heard the customers ahead of them debating over whether to buy the plant on their table—a maidenhair fern in a Ruth Bader Ginsburg face pot—or the snake plant in a llama pot from a neighboring table.

"Can we really pick a llama over RBG?" one man said to the other.

"We can't. Let's get both. RBG for us and the llama for your boss. Remember the Christmas party? She was spitting mad when I stole that white elephant gift."

The first man put his credit card on the counter and gave his partner an affectionate nudge. "She *still* talks about that! I'm going to give her the llama so I can think about *you* every time I'm in her office."

"We should come here more often. Tea makes you extra sweet."

According to her name tag, the middle-aged brunette behind the counter was Val. She was short and apple-cheeked with blue-gray eyes and a quiet manner. After telling Nora and her friends that she'd be with them in a moment, Val began packing the men's plants in a small box.

Nora handed June some money. "Will you order for me? I want to check out that Language of Flowers display."

Scooting behind the two men, Nora examined the baskets of blooming flowers on a tiered display stand. Each basket came with a detailed label and a satin bow. The Sympathy basket was made of marigold for grief, mint for consolation, and chrysanthemum for condolences. The Friends Forever basket had crocus for cheerfulness, ivy for loyalty, and zinnia for friendship. Other baskets were called Love Me Tender, Happy Home, and Let's Celebrate. But Nora was most intrigued by the I Will Survive basket.

Leaning closer, she read the label to herself, " 'Carnation for heartache, yarrow to cure a broken heart, rue for regret, and lily of the valley for happiness in the future.' "

"Interesting?" June asked when Nora rejoined the group.

"Very. I never think about what flowers mean when I buy them at the grocery store—I just grab the colors I like and plop a bouquet in my cart. Who knows? All this time I might've been buying flowers for the shop that mean, 'I hope you drop dead,' instead of 'please spend lots of money here today.' "

June laughed. "I want a bouquet that says, 'Stop leaving your dirty dishes in the break room sink when the dishwasher is a foot away.' "

Having finished ringing in their tea and sandwich orders, Val gave Estella a number flag to put on their table.

While they waited for their food, Nora told her other friends about the basket of flowers. Like June, Hester was interested, but Estella was lost in her own thoughts. She stared at the number in the center of their table and didn't say a word.

"What's wrong?" Nora asked.

By way of reply, Estella opened her copy of *The Tea Girl of Hummingbird Lane* to a passage marked with a pink sticky tab. "Want to hear my favorite quote? It feels like it was written for us."

"Go on," Hester prompted.

" 'One mistake can change the course of your life. You can never return to your original path or go back to the person you were.' "

The women exchanged meaningful looks. They'd all made mistakes. Big ones. The kind of mistakes that turned family into strangers and made homes uninhabitable. Each woman had done something they deeply regretted. Their mistakes had left deep scars, and though the pain had lessened with time, it would never fully disappear. They couldn't think about the past without being pricked by cactus spines of regret.

Nora would forever feel shame over what she'd done. She'd gotten behind the wheel after drinking way too much and had crashed into another car. The victims of her reckless behavior had been a mother and child. Their car caught fire and Nora had been burned pulling the woman and her toddler to safety. They sustained minor injuries, but Nora sustained burns from her right hand to her hairline. She lost half a pinkie finger and gained lots of shiny, shell-smooth scars.

A few years ago, a plastic surgeon had worked wonders on her face. Unless one looked closely, her scars were nearly invisible. The surgeon had offered to repair all the evidence of Nora's burns, but she'd refused. The damaged skin on her neck, arm, and hand served as a constant reminder that she nearly killed two innocent people.

Before June began working at the hotel, she cared for seniors at an assisted living facility in New York. During her fifteen-year tenure, she'd treated each and every resident with compassion and respect. But when the facility was acquired by a national chain, things changed. The grade school kids who came once a week to play board games with the residents were no longer allowed to visit. There was no more animal therapy. The beautiful gardens were neglected, and outings became more and more infrequent. Seeing how depressed the residents had become, June sought to cheer them up by bringing them to a carnival.

Unfortunately, a gentleman in her care suffered a fatal heart attack that day. When his family sued June for damages, she lost her life savings and the money she and her husband had saved for their son's college tuition. In the aftermath, her husband filed for divorce and she and her son became estranged.

Hester, the youngest of the four women, had faced an unexpected pregnancy as a high schooler. After degrading her and imprisoning her in her room, Hester's parents sent her to a home for unwed mothers. The moment the baby was born, Hester's daughter was whisked away into the waiting arms of her new parents. Hester never had the chance to hold her. Traumatized by the experience, she never told the baby's father about the pregnancy or searched for her daughter. Twenty years later, her daughter tracked her down. What could have been a joyful occasion was marred by violence and grief, and now, weekly letters were Hester's only communication with her child.

Estella was the only Miracle Springs native of the Secret, Book, and Scone Society. Hers had been a hardscrabble childhood. Raised by a negligent mother, Estella had not only been physically and emotionally abused by her mother's boyfriends, but she'd also experienced the hunger and humiliation of poverty. And when her biological father, a man who'd been absent for most of Estella's childhood, returned home to find the new man in the house assaulting his daughter, he drew a gun and killed the man on the spot. Estella had always dreamed of escaping Miracle Springs, but with her father imprisoned nearby, she couldn't leave. She felt responsible for his incarceration, and that guilt had manifested in a series of flings with strangers. The dalliances, which left Estella feeling hollow and tarnished her reputation, ended when she fell in love with a local man named Jack Nakamura.

Right now, Estella didn't look like a woman in love. Nora saw tension in the fine lines around her mouth and brows.

"I liked that quote too," Nora said. "It reminded me of why we became the Secret, Book, and Scone Society. We've always trusted each other with our secrets. We tell each other things we'd never tell anyone else. So what's going on? Whatever it is, we've got you."

Estella touched the number card. "Fifteen. That's how many years my daddy's been in prison. He's being released next week."

"That's a good thing, right?" Hester asked.

"Yes. Of course, it is." Estella unfolded her napkin and spread it over her lap. She smoothed the white cloth over and over. "He and I have talked about this a hundred times. You know, which foods he'd want and how he couldn't wait to go to a barbershop, take a walk around town, or have the bathroom all to himself. But we've never talked about the nuts and bolts. What's he going to do for money? How is he going to adjust? This is a very different world from the one he used to live in."

June murmured in agreement. "Listen, honey, I know a bit of what you're going through. Tyson was in rehab for a long time, and you remember what it was like when he got out. He had to spend months in the halfway house before he was ready to live and work on his own. He's come a long way, but he's still uncomfortable around strangers. He still looks over his shoulder, half expecting to see the dealers he stole from when he was using. My boy is in his thirties, but he lost years to those damned drugs. In some ways, he's still a kid. In others, he's an old man. Time didn't stand still for your father, but it didn't move as fast as it did for you. The pace is going to be hard for him to handle at first."

"People weren't glued to their cell phones fifteen years ago. They didn't drive electric cars or fly to space just for kicks," said Nora. "He doesn't need to adjust to any of that, but I imagine it'll be a shock to see how different the town is now. And the people he knew before he went inside—they're going to look different too."

Estella said, "I've brought him the local paper for years, so he's not totally in the dark about our area. He's going to live with me until he finds his feet. I don't know what he'll do for work, but all the articles I've read say that a job is super important. It's the one thing all former prisoners need to feel like they're back in society. They need the routine and the responsibility. Earning money is important. Working gives them a sense of pride. It'll keep Daddy from getting depressed."

"Has he had any vocational training?" asked June.

"Just food service. He cooked for the inmates whenever he had the chance. He even developed special menus. Superbowl meals and things like that. I bought him a few cookbooks so he could have some fun in my kitchen. I figured it would be good for him to putter around at home for a few days and get used to his freedom before he goes looking for a job."

Nora cocked her head. "Would Jack hire him to work in the diner?"

"I don't think that's a good idea," Estella said. "He'll find something, but in the meantime, I'd like to read some books talk about reentering society after prison. I have a week to do whatever I can to help him transition."

June smiled at Estella. "You're a good woman."

"Don't tell anyone. I have my bad-girl reputation to protect."

Their conversation was curtailed when Val appeared with their orders. She distributed four small glass teapots and four plates of sandwiches. Finally, she put a plate of flower-shaped macarons in the center of the table.

"These are on the house," she said with a smile. "And since this is your first time, let me tell how your flowering tea works. Each teapot has a bulb made of tea leaves and flowers. In a few seconds, the bulbs will expand and slowly unfurl. Once it blooms, you'll see the flowers inside. Let your tea steep for a few minutes before you drink it."

Hester said, "Do you mind if I take a video?"

"Not at all. Enjoy."

Val started to turn away when her gaze caught on Nora's right arm.

Strangers were always fascinated by the burn scars that floated like jellyfish over the back of Nora's hand and up the length of her arm.

Most adults gave her a good once-over before eventually turning away in embarrassment. Children had no such compunction and would often ask why her skin was bubbly or why she was missing the top half of her finger. She always told them she'd been in an accident but her scars no longer hurt.

Though Nora felt the weight of Val's stare, she was too enraptured by her flowering tea to worry about it. The bulb of tea leaves slowly unfurled, and a centerpiece of dried flowers floated in her glass teapot.

"That's the coolest thing I've ever seen," she said to Val.

Finally tearing her eyes away from Nora, Val saw customers waiting at the counter and hurried off.

Nora and her friends resumed their discussion of *The Tea Girl of Hummingbird Lane*, bouncing back and forth between scenes from the book and anecdotes from their own lives. They also talked about the upcoming Honeybee Jubilee.

"For the next two weeks, my bakery will be stuffed to the gills with honey-flavored treats and flower-shaped cookies." Hester plucked a daisy macaron off the plate and examined it with a critical eye. "This is beautiful work. I'm glad it's the only dessert item on their menu. You know I like being the only baked goods game in town."

June bit into a sunflower macaron. "Oh, yum. Mine's lemon and strawberry."

Estella took a nibble out of her tulip-shaped cookie and grimaced. "Ick. Coconut."

"The rose is red velvet," said Nora. "You picked the winner, June."

Hester chewed her cookie thoughtfully. "They're pretty, but I think they were baked somewhere else and shipped frozen."

"I'm going to bring some back for Sheldon," Nora said. "That man needs a treat because even though he pretends he's not, he's still tired from yesterday's storytime. He read *Where the Wild Things Are* and made monster crowns with the kids. The whole children's section was covered in glitter and feathers—including Sheldon! His mustache was twinkling like a disco ball."

While her friends cackled with glee, Nora headed to the counter to order a sampler box of macarons. Val was taking a phone order and didn't see Nora, so she ambled over to a display of low maintenance houseplants. She was immediately drawn to a Chinese money plant in a hedgehog pot. The hedgehog wore glasses and was too cute to ignore.

"That plant will bring you luck," said a man holding a pricing gun.

"I could always use more of that."

The man moved closer. His name tag, which read Kirk, was pinned to the front pocket of his khaki work shirt. Of average height, he had a thick torso and hands as wide and square as slices of bread. His brown hair was graying at the temples, his brows were bushy, and he had the weather-beaten skin of an outdoorsman.

"The luck is specific to money," Kirk said. "See how the leaves look like coins?"

"I could *really* use that kind of luck. I'm trying to save up for a car." She sighed. "I'd like to put this on the checkout counter in my bookshop, but I have a brown thumb."

Kirk's brows twitched. "The bookstore on the corner? That's you?" At Nora's nod, he gave her the same overt assessment Val had given her. The only difference was, he was quicker to break eye contact.

Gesturing at the plant, he said, "Here's all you need to know to care for it. Don't overwater. Let the soil dry out between waterings. You'll know when it needs a drink because the leaves will look droopy. It doesn't like direct sunlight, but if it gets indirect light and you rotate it once in a while, you won't kill it. If you need a plant medic, you know where to find me."

"The man I work with keeps saying that we need a store mascot. What could beat a ceramic hedgehog with glasses?"

As Nora carried the potted plant to the checkout counter, she felt the tickle of Kirk's stare on her back.

Val rang her up, packed the macarons, and lowered the plant into a box, shooting glances at Nora's face the whole time.

Nora had had enough of the woman's ogling.

"Here's the deal," she said. "Ten years ago, I was in a fire. That's why my right arm looks the way it does. My face used to be much worse, but I had surgery. I only have half a pinkie, but that didn't stop me from eating that curried egg salad sandwich in record time. Do you make all of the food here?"

Pink splotches appeared on Val's cheeks. "Not the macarons. We order those from a bakery in Brooklyn. I do the tea and the sandwiches. Kirk, that's my husband, takes care of the plant side of things. We're new to town."

Val was talking a mile a minute and her movements were jerky. Nora couldn't understand why she was so flustered.

Get over it, lady. I have a few scars. I'm not the Phantom of the Opera.

Kirk appeared from the back room and began looking through some papers on the desk directly behind his wife. When he didn't find what he wanted, he touched Val's shoulder. She startled so violently that she swept the box with the potted plant right off the counter. It crashed to the floor in front of Nora, flinging soil and bits of broken pottery everywhere.

"Oh! I'm so sorry!" she cried.

Kirk pivoted his wife around until she faced the back room.

"I'll clean it up. There's another hedgehog pot on the third shelf in the storeroom. Get it and I'll fix the plant right up."

Clinging to his arm, Val whispered, "I'm sorry. I got nervous when I saw her."

"Go on, Val. I'll sweep up."

Nora was tempted to take her macarons and leave, but she'd already paid for the potted plant and didn't want to wait around for Val to refund her money. She didn't want to interact with Val at all. The woman was clearly fascinated and repulsed by Nora, and Nora wasn't interested in being studied like a specimen under glass.

Kirk came around the counter with a broom and dustpan. "The good news is the plant's fine. Give me just a minute while I add a little soil to a new pot."

Leaving him to clean up the mess and repot the plant, Nora returned to her friends.

"Are you causing trouble?" Estella teased.

Nora pulled a face. "Do I have lettuce in my teeth or something? I'm used to people giving me the once-over, but that woman is making me feel like a circus attraction."

"You think everyone's grossed out by your scars, but she's probably staring at you because you're beautiful," said June. "People do it all the time. You still see yourself as the woman with the scarred face, but no one else does. You need to say goodbye to her once and for all."

Though Nora knew Val hadn't been admiring her, she let the subject drop. Since it was a Monday and Hester was the only one who didn't need to get back to work, Nora told them to go ahead without her.

June slipped her crossbody bag over her head and wiggled a finger at Nora. "Tell Sheldon not to eat those macarons right before dinner. I'm making one of his favorites tonight—lemon chicken and butter beans. That man hit the jackpot when he became my housemate."

"I'm having a big salad. All these diner meals are catching up to me," said Estella.

Hester eyed Estella's trim waist. "You never gain weight."

"That's the power of an A-line dress," Estella said, glancing at her watch. "I need to run. The mayor is coming in at four. She's decided to go silver and is going to look amazing. She's ditching her French manicure too. She wants fuchsia on her hands and navy on her toes. Oh, how I love helping a woman transform!"

Estella bustled out of the shop to several admiring glances.

"She's a force of nature. I wish I was like that," Hester said with a sigh in her voice.

June waved her comment aside. "You have your own gifts. We all do. Estella can't conjure memories with her baked goods, I can't give people the perfect book recommendation, and none of you can knit worth a damn."

Hester laughed. "That's true. Maybe I don't want to be a force of nature either. Maybe I want a transformation like the mayor's getting."

"You want to go silver?" Nora joked.

Hester twirled a strand of honey-colored hair around her finger. "I want to get out of bed and not have to deal with these curls. I've worn my hair in a headband or ponytail since I was in high school, but when your workday starts at five a.m., being stylish is the last thing on your mind."

June ran a hand over her head. "You could shave it all off. It's incredibly liberating."

"That's a bit too liberating. How about a shag?"

"Is that a haircut or a proposal?"

Hester and June headed for the exit, laughing as they walked.

Nora returned to the counter, where Kirk had her potted plant ready to go.

"Hope to see you again soon," he said, pushing the box across the counter. His smile was perfunctory. He suddenly seemed eager for her to leave.

Nora bristled. Because she'd had her share of rude, impatient, and self-centered customers, she went out of her way to be polite to those in the service industry. If this is how Val and Kirk were going to react to her burn scars, how would they treat other customers with obvious physical differences?

Knowing she had no chance of getting through to them by being hostile, she took a deep breath and spoke in a casual but direct manner.

"I'd like to come back here again, but I'm not sure if I will. Your wife is clearly uncomfortable around me. I'm used to people staring at my scars, but they usually get over it after a few minutes."

Kirk flapped his hands like a pair of agitated birds. "No, no! She's just not herself right now. You see, we never planned on moving here. We came to be close to my sister and to help out with her son." His eyes clouded with sorrow. "My sister— she's sick. She's tried everything, including the hot springs, but now, she's just trying to manage her pain and live what little time she has in peace."

When Kirk turned away to compose himself, Nora said, "I'm sorry. That must be really hard."

Hundreds of years ago, the Cherokee traveled to the hot springs to experience the healing properties of mineral waters. Over time, the waters had attracted more and more people. As hotels, shops, and eateries were built to cater to these visitors, Miracle Springs became known as a retreat for those grappling with physical or emotional illness.

The hot springs weren't magical. The waters couldn't cure cancer, undo trauma, or fix a broken heart. They could offer rest and hope, and if these failed, the beautiful scenery, kind residents, and charming shops and eateries provided escapism and comfort.

Most visitors found their way to Miracle Books, lured in by colorful window displays and the promise of a good read.

Over the years, Nora had heard some sad stories. She knew how people could act when they were scared, and if Kirk's sister was gravely ill, it was no wonder he and Val were on edge.

Nora picked up her box and said, "This is a good place to find peace. I hope that's what your sister finds."

Another customer was approaching the counter. Kirk darted a glance his way as he murmured something in response.

Though it made no sense, Nora could have sworn he said, "That depends on you."

Chapter 2

She would disappear folded into origami like her own dreams.

—Lauren Beukes

Nora used the delivery door to enter Miracle Books. She dropped her handbag in the stockroom and wheeled a hand truck stacked with new releases up the hall. As she passed the restroom, she was greeted by familiar sounds. The blend of instrumental jazz, murmured voices, gurgling espresso machine, and rustling pages was the music of the bookstore.

Sheldon Vega, Nora's friend and only employee, called out, "I have a Jack London for Daphne, and a Louisa May Alcott for Zara. Heather, your Dante Alighieri is on deck."

For the next twenty seconds, the loud hiss of the milk frother obliterated all other sounds.

Nora parked the hand truck in the nook between Science Fiction and Fantasy and headed into the ticket agent's booth. Though it was now a kitchen and coffee station, the space had once been dedicated to the sale of train tickets. The building that housed Miracle Books was the town's original train station. When the modern station was built a mile down the line, the old one was put up for sale. It languished on the market for a long time, becoming more and more decrepit, until a patient in a burn unit saw the listing and decided to buy it.

It had taken every penny of Nora's savings to cover the down payment on the building and the stretch of land behind the store. She also bought a retired caboose, converted it into a tiny house, and parked it on the hill overlooking the train tracks. Every night, she heard the whistles of nighttime freight trains. The sweet, haunting sound evoked a desire for adventure or a sudden longing.

Passengers no longer rushed through the former station, because Miracle Books was a place of slow movements and lowered voices.

Upon entering the bookstore, people wandered through the rabbit warren of shelves, browsed the titles on the display tables, and spent hours in the reading chairs. They'd open books, scan blurbs, and sniff pages. They'd put away their phones and read. They'd meet friends for coffee or sit on the alphabet rug with their kids to read picture books. For an hour or so, they'd find peace in the oasis of colorful book spines.

Though Nora knew Miracle Books was a haven of quiet and calm in a chaotic world, she hadn't expected to see so many people in the store. A large after-lunch crowd was unusual, but a crowd of young adults occupied the area around the ticket agent's booth as well as the Readers' Circle.

"Where'd this group come from?" she whispered to Sheldon as he cleaned the milk-frother wand.

"They're on a five-day brewery tour of Western North Carolina. They started in Charlotte and continued to Asheville from there. After Miracle Springs, they'll head to Boone. See those two cuties by the Everything's Coming Up Romance endcap? They just got married, and instead of having a wedding reception, they rounded up the people they love most and did this trip. Isn't that cool? *So* much more fun than a dinner of rubber chicken and dancing to Sister Sledge on a parquet dance floor."

Pointing at the coffee mug in Sheldon's hand, Nora said, "Are you sobering them up before they get back on the road?"

"You know what they say about *ass*umptions?" Sheldon scolded. "These fine folks don't drink during the day. They hike, sample local cuisine, and visit art galleries or shops. One of the reasons they came to Miracle Springs was to hike part of the Appalachian Trail. The *other* reason was to visit our store. They've already put aside a stack of books to buy. I'm telling you; these are our people."

"I'll go say hello in a sec, but I wanted to give you your treat first. They're macarons from Tea Flowers."

Nora opened the box to show Sheldon the flower-shaped cookies.

"Oh! Pretty. How was the tea?"

"Also pretty. The owners seem out of their depth. They moved here with a sick family member and are running the business and helping out with the family member and her kid. I was relaxed when I got there. By the time I left? Not so much. But I *did* buy a magical plant that will make us rich."

Sheldon smoothed the silver tails of his glorious mustache with one hand while shooing her away with the other. "I want all the details, especially the rich part, but not now. Right now, I have lattes to make and cookies to eat."

Nora glanced at the tower of dirty mugs in the sink. "As soon as I put the new releases out, I'll be back to wash those mugs."

After greeting the twentysomethings, all of whom were contentedly amassing small piles of books while they socialized, Nora replenished missing titles from the New Fiction table and then wheeled the empty hand truck to the stockroom.

She returned to the front to find a customer waiting for her at the checkout counter. The woman's attention was focused on the boy spinning the bookmark tower around and around.

Nora could tell just by looking at her that the woman wasn't well.

Because she ran a business in a town known for its healing waters, Nora's customers had a wide range of medical conditions. Some were obvious. Others were less visible.

The woman at the counter looked extremely fragile. Her skin was stretched tight over her bones and was so pale that it was almost colorless. She wore a chemo cap covered in tiny Princess Leia figures. The royal-purple hue emphasized both her pallor and the brilliance of her blue-green eyes. Her brows were pencil lines drawn by an unsteady hand and her lips were chapped. She watched the boy so intently that she was unaware of Nora's presence.

A donkey-bray of a laugh echoed from deeper in the store, and the woman turned. Smiling at Nora, she said, "He'll do that all day if I let him. He likes how the glittery ones sparkle in the sunlight."

Unlike the children who spun the rack around fast enough to dislodge a handful of bookmarks, the woman's son was being very careful.

"They're my favorite too. Especially the peacock."

The woman seemed relieved that Nora wasn't going to ask her son to leave the bookmarks alone. "I came to find something for him—for Tucker. He's gotten really into origami lately and he's really good at it. Do you carry any origami books?"

"Let me check."

As Nora opened her laptop, she pictured the Puzzles and Games section. The shelves held such a hodgepodge of activity books that she wasn't sure exactly what she had in stock.

"It looks like we have one kit and two books. One of the books is called *Easy Origami*. It has over thirty projects but doesn't come with any paper. The kit comes with an instruction booklet of seventy-five patterns and a hundred sheets of paper. The projects range from easy to challenging. We also have *The Strange Case of Origami Yoda*. It's a middle grade fiction book about a sixth-grade boy who makes origami."

The woman's eyes lit up. "Tucker's in fifth grade. I bet he'd love that book. Can you show me that one and the kit with the different levels? He's done a bunch of beginner patterns already."

"Sure. Come on back."

The woman walked over to the bookmark spinner and, without touching her son or the spinner, held out her hand like a traffic cop. "Tucker, please stop. We're going to a different part of the store to look for your books. Do you want to stay here or come with us?"

Tucker continued to turn the spinner. His mother repeated her question and then told Tucker that she was going to walk away at the count of three. She finished the count and approached Nora. A second later, Tucker released the spinner and turned to follow her.

He took one step before directing a lightning-quick glance at Nora. Then he fixed his gaze on the ground. As they rounded the Fiction section and passed by the group occupying the chairs in the Readers' Circle, Tucker hunched his shoulders and lowered his head like a turtle pulling into its shell. He only relaxed when Nora took the origami kit off the shelf and held it out to him.

"What do you think, Tuck?" his mother said.

The boy's face glowed with excitement. "I like it! It has the cat and the butterfly. And the blinking eye. I can make a bunch of Pokémon, and a panda, and a box with a lid."

His speech was a rapid-fire mumble that Nora found difficult to follow. It was as if his mouth couldn't keep up with the avalanche of words tumbling through his brain.

"Hold on to that while we see what else this nice lady has to show us," his mother said.

On the way to the Children's Corner, Nora introduced herself.

"I've met you before, actually," the woman said. "I'm Kelly. Tucker and I just moved here, but I was in your shop the first time I came to this town."

"I'm happy to have a repeat customer as a new neighbor," Nora said.

When they reached the Children's Corner, Tucker walked over to the letter *T* on the alphabet rug and sat down to read the fine print on the back of the origami kit.

The Strange Case of Origami Yoda was sandwiched between Lloyd Alexander's *The Chronicles of Prydain* and *Darth Paper Strikes Back*. When Nora handed the book to Kelly, her eyes sparkled with delight.

"I've heard about this series. The author's neurodivergent! I read somewhere that he calls his Aspie behavior his superpower." She gazed at her son. "Tuck has superpowers too. I just hope people will be able to see them like I do."

Sorrow stole the light from Kelly's eyes. In that instant, she looked as small and fragile as a hummingbird egg.

Nora recognized the expression on Kelly's face. It was grief. And it was so all-encompassing that it took every ounce of her strength to keep from surrendering to it.

In that moment, Nora realized that Kelly didn't expect to live long enough to see her son become a man. She'd probably moved to Miracle Springs in hopes of gaining a little extra time. She'd bathe in the mineral waters. She'd get healing massages and acupuncture. She'd meditate and drink superfood smoothies. She'd do anything in her power to remain here, in this world, with her boy.

Nora wished she could wave a magic wand and change Kelly's fate, but all she could offer were books and kindness. Touching Kelly lightly on the shoulder, she said, "I bet his superpowers come from you. It's like The Force in *Star Wars*. It gets passed down."

Kelly grinned. "Did you hear that, Tucker? I'm like Princess Leia. Without all the hair."

She bought both Tom Angleberger books as well as the origami kit. She also asked Nora to order *The Secret of the Fortune Wookiee*.

After bagging the books, Nora came around the counter and offered the bag to Tucker. "I'd love to see your origami. If you want to show me any of your projects, you can bring them in. Your mom could have an iced coffee and *you* could have a not-so-hot hot chocolate with lots of rainbow marshmallows."

Though Tucker didn't make eye contact, he said, "Okay."

Kelly flashed Nora a grateful smile and opened the front door, causing the sleigh bells hanging from a hook on the back to jangle noisily. Tucker covered his ears and hurried outside.

Materializing at Nora's side, Sheldon pointed at the door. "See that? You're torturing children with hearing sensitivities with that jingle-jangling beast. A caring, thoughtful person would throw them in the trash and install a motion-automated chime instead."

"For the millionth time, the sleigh bells aren't going anywhere. I don't want more automation in my life." She gave Sheldon a playful poke. "Unless someone invented a robotic barista. If that's a thing, here's my credit card."

Sheldon pretended to pull a knife out of his chest. "Come on, Brutus, I'm going to have a snack while you wash dishes and tell me about the tea shop."

After making sure the brewery-tour folks were still happily sipping coffee and chatting, Nora started washing mugs. Sheldon followed her into the ticket agent's booth and popped a piece of bread into the toaster.

Not only was Sheldon the best barista within a hundred miles, but he also baked his own Cuban bread. He'd inherited his love of food and music from his Cuban father and his love of reading and fussing over people from his Jewish mother. Sheldon was a gregarious, kindhearted man with waves of silver hair and a glorious mustache of the same hue, a Santa Claus belly, and a loud laugh. His favorite snack was Nutella on toast, and it had become so popular with the customers that Nora added it to the menu, calling it the Shel Silverstein.

While he waited on the toaster, he wiped the display case where the book pockets were kept. These lighter-than-air pastries were shaped like books and had either a chocolate or raspberry filling. Hester made the pastries every morning and Sheldon picked them up on his way to work.

"We're running out of book pockets earlier and earlier these days. Maybe we should increase our order by half a dozen and see how it goes."

"Hester mentioned that at lunch today. She also thinks we should add a new food item to our menu. The *James and the Giant Peach* muffin."

Sheldon barked out a laugh. "I like it. She'll have to go easy on the streusel topping or we'll have crumbs everywhere. I don't mind vacuuming, but I've read *If You Give a Mouse a Cookie*, and I don't want an army of mice running over my shoes during storytime."

"But what *If You Give a Moose a Muffin* . . . ?"

"No mice, moose, meese, or mooses. The only wild animals allowed in this shop are the children. How's Hester?"

Nora turned the water off. "She gave her engagement ring back to Jasper."

The toaster popped but Sheldon didn't move. "*Pobrecita.*"

"It might not be a bad thing. They're trying to start over without the added pressure of a wedding."

"Taking a step back is okay *if* it's a two-step-forward-one-step-back situation. I hope they work it all out."

Sheldon opened the Nutella jar and spooned a generous glob

onto his toast. When Nora told him that Estella's father was finally being released from prison, he went very still.

Nora saw a range of emotions flit across his face. "Hey. Are
you okay?"

After another moment of silence, Sheldon said, "When I was
a kid, my papa's brother lived up the street. My cousin, Alvaro,
was older than me and was the coolest cat around. He'd cruise
through the neighborhood in this big, white Lincoln convert-
ible with red leather seats—always with a beautiful woman. Always blaring music. He wore leather jackets—in Miami!—and
slicked his hair back like a greaser from *The Outsiders*. He was
our *cubano* Matt Dillon."

"No wonder you idolized him."

Looking wistful, Sheldon went on. "Alvaro was a smart kid.
He got a full ride to college, but he didn't go. All he cared about
was cars. Fixing them. Driving them. Stealing them. He'd get
caught, go to jail, get out, and start the cycle all over again. But
the last time, there was a kid sleeping in the back seat of the car
he stole. Alvaro never noticed."

"Oh no."

"By the time he got out from that stint, he wasn't the Alvaro
I knew. He used to be a fun-loving kid. He had style and swag-
ger. But prison turned him into something else. Something lean
and mean. And damaged. He couldn't handle life on the outside, but he couldn't handle going back either. So, one day, he
tied a cinderblock to his ankle and jumped off a bridge."

Nora waited for Sheldon to go on, but his gaze was distant.
He was lost in the past.

Then he blinked and, pinching his toast between his thumb
and forefinger, dropped it on a plate. "There's a big difference
between Alvaro and—I don't know Estella's father's name."

"Gus."

"The difference between Alvaro and Gus is that Alvaro's family never forgave him. They didn't visit him in prison. They

didn't write. He was dead to them. Estella has been there for Gus. She visits, she writes, she makes sure he has enough money. She's a good egg."

Nora gave Sheldon a fond pat on the back. "So are you. You should eat and get out of here before the after-school crowd shows up."

"I'm not going anywhere until we duke it out over the window display. I want 'Jack and the Beanstalk.' You want *Alice in Wonderland*. Should we flip a coin or let our customers vote?"

"I thought this was a dictatorship," Nora grumbled.

Sheldon grabbed a coffee stirrer and waved it like a flag. "*Viva la revolución!*"

As soon as Sheldon finished his snack, he affixed a sign to the comment box, asking for customers to weigh in on the next theme.

"Let the battle begin," he said on his way out the door.

For the rest of the afternoon, Nora was too busy making espresso drinks and selling books, to notice who had voted for what. In truth, she'd be fine with either theme. What she most wanted was a glitter-free window display. Glitter stuck to everything, and no amount of vacuuming got rid of it completely, but if Sheldon had his way, every display would include glitter, tinsel, and disco balls. If Sheldon wanted "Jack and the Beanstalk," it was because he had visions of bejeweled silver harps and glittery golden goose eggs.

Nora wanted an *Alice in Wonderland* window with less glitter and more nonfiction titles. They could feature books on vegetable gardening, insects, croquet and card games, cake baking, and hosting tea parties.

My theme might help the town's new business too. The Mad Hatter could hold a little sign telling people to find their next adventure at Tea Flowers.

As Nora locked up that evening, she was already conjuring images of oversized mushrooms and books blooming in the center of tissue-paper roses.

She and Sheldon were proud of their current Read the Rainbow display, which featured a book rainbow and a silver pot filled with yellow books. The books had been written by BIPOC authors of every genre and Nora had printed a shopping list of all the titles to make it easier for her customers to shop for the books in the window.

With April coming to an end, Miracle Springs had shrugged off all vestiges of wintertime. The hillsides were a lush green, the trees were flowering, and pollen dusted every surface. A few more rains would wash away the rest of the yellow-green sneezing powder, and the residents of Miracle Springs would spend the month of May working on their gardens. Between the Honeybee Jubilee and the annual garden tour, locals would spend less time reading and more time outdoors. And since Nora was saving up to buy a car, she wanted every customer to leave her shop carrying a bag full of books.

She was thinking about her car budget as she walked along the edge of the parking lot behind the bookshop. When an SUV with a sheriff's department seal pulled into a spot right in front of her, she stopped and waited for the driver to hop out.

"Parking in the loading zone, eh?" Nora said as she moved toward the man in uniform. "I'll have to report you to your superior officer."

Sheriff Grant McCabe hooked his thumbs through his utility belt. "I only answer to one person in this town. Maybe you know her? She sells books. She's beautiful and smart. She can be a little bossy, but she has great taste in men."

Laughing, Nora gave McCabe a hello kiss. "I didn't expect to see you until later."

"I know it's my turn to make dinner, but my afternoon meeting ran way late so—"

"We're eating out?" Nora guessed.

McCabe nodded. "We haven't been to Pearl's in a while. Do you feel like soul food?"

"Always. You can tell me about your day while I get changed."

Grabbing her hand, McCabe raised his brows in suggestion. "How hungry are you?"

Nora studied the man she'd been friends with for years but had only begun to date a few months ago. McCabe was in his midfifties and bore a slight resemblance to Sam Elliot. Though he didn't sport a mustache, McCabe had a perpetual five o'clock shadow. His salt-and-pepper hair was close-trimmed, he carried a little extra weight around his middle, and he had a low, rumbling laugh. Nora loved his dedication to his community, his sharp mind, and the way he listened with his whole being. Most of all, she liked sitting across a table from him, sharing food and talking.

"Lunch *was* a long time ago," she said, her eyes dancing.

"I can get us there real fast. I have a siren."

Nora shook her head in mock disappointment. "That'd be an abuse of power."

As they walked toward her house, Nora told McCabe about Tea Flowers. She was about to describe how the tea bloomed in the pot when she saw a woven basket filled with flowering plants on the café table next to her front door.

"Do I have a rival?" asked McCabe.

"No idea. I saw a bunch of baskets just like this at Tea Flowers. All the flowers have different meanings and there's a label explaining—oh!"

Nora leaped backward, ramming into McCabe's chest. He grabbed hold of her upper arms, steadying her, and peered down at the basket.

In the center of the flowering plants was a dead blackbird.

McCabe took a tissue from his pocket and picked up the bird's body. From the way its head bobbed limply to one side, it was obvious that the poor thing had a broken neck.

"Would you put it out there, in the grass?" Nora pointed at

the verdant slope leading down to the train tracks. She often heard foxes barking in the night and knew there was a good chance they'd eat the bird carcass. That felt more in keeping with the natural order than tossing it in the trash. Besides, she didn't want it in her house. Seeing it in the flower basket had already unsettled her.

While McCabe disposed of the bird, Nora carried the flower basket into her kitchen. She turned on the overhead lights and took a close look at her surprise gift.

The arrangement was made up of hyacinth, bluebell, and what Nora thought might be a pair of giant red dahlia blossoms. In North Carolina, dahlias were a summer plant, but this one could've come from a greenhouse. She'd never seen a dahlia with blooms as big as dinner plates, but when she gently pushed a bluebell stem aside, she saw that the dahlia stems had been pressed into a square of floral foam.

Nora couldn't identify the little green plant that had been partially crushed by the bird.

"They got two of your favorite flower colors right," McCabe said as he entered the kitchen. "Blue and yellow."

"Where's the yellow?"

McCabe showed her the tissue he'd used to pick up the dead bird. The carcass was gone, but in its place was a cluster of bright yellow flowers attached to a thin green stem.

Nora brought the stem to her nose and inhaled. The scent was somewhat bitter. Almost astringent. Glancing at the arrangement again, she could see where the stem had broken off the plant.

"Must be some kind of herb," she said. "There's no label. No note. Nothing."

"If this came from Tea Flowers, why not call over there and ask who sent this to you?"

Nora was about to reach for her phone when she remembered the time. "They're closed now. Maybe I can guess who the sender is if I know what the flowers mean. The other arrangements had themes."

"Did they also come with dead birds?"

Nora shot him a look and told him that there was beer in the fridge. As she moved to the table with her laptop, she heard McCabe pop the cap off his beer. She ran a search on the Victorian language of flowers and scanned over the results. McCabe joined her at the table with his beer and a glass of prosecco for her.

"I don't know if there's a universal translation for these flowers, but according to this site, hyacinth means someone is asking for forgiveness and bluebells mean humility."

"Sounds like an apology. Anyone ding your moped or break something in the shop?"

Nora shook her head. "No, nothing like that. I haven't argued with anyone either. If a customer had complained to Sheldon, he would've told me. I just had lunch with my three closest friends, and we're all good. Let's see if this is a dahlia and if so, what it means."

It was easier to identify the flower than to deduce its symbolism. After scrolling through several websites, it became obvious that the meaning was often tied to the flower's color.

"This site says a dahlia is a warning, but another one says it's a symbol of lasting commitment between two people—a flower celebrating love and marriage. So, if I put all of them together, I get a warning about commitment?"

McCabe looked past Nora to the arrangement. "Is there anything special about a red dahlia?"

Nora started a new search. When the results appeared onscreen, she absently reached for her wineglass. She took two big sips before saying, "Betrayal. Red dahlias symbolize betrayal."

"Forgiveness, humility, betrayal—possibly having to do with a marriage. What's next?"

His question went unanswered because Nora was too absorbed by a chart showing red dahlia varieties. She carried the laptop into the kitchen and quickly found a match for her dahlia.

"This variety is called *crève coeur.* That's French for heartbreak."

McCabe frowned. "What about the funny-smelling plant?"

Nora found a graphic to help new gardeners identify herbs. "Here it is. Rue." She looked at McCabe. "I saw this in another basket at Tea Flowers. It means regret."

McCabe had his pocket notebook out. He jotted something down and sat back in his chair. "Forgiveness, humility, betrayal, regret. Someone's definitely sorry, but for what?"

Nora's fingers moved over the keyboard. "And then there's the blackbird."

McCabe grimaced. "I don't think a dead bird is a good way to smooth things over. Do birds have meanings too?"

"According to the almighty Internet, a blackbird is a bad omen."

Nora thought about how Val had stared at her, and she remembered what Val had said to Kirk. "I just got nervous when I saw her."

I assumed my burn scars made her nervous, but what if that's not what she meant?

After gulping down the rest of her wine, Nora said, "I'll figure it out in the morning. Let's forget about this and go to Pearl's. Hush puppies make everything better."

McCabe finished his beer and put their empty glasses in the kitchen sink. He then followed Nora back outside and waited for her to lock up before pulling her into his arms. As he pressed his lips to her forehead, the stubble on his chin gave her nose a sandpaper kiss.

I'm not going to let some stupid flower arrangement ruin my night, she thought.

On the way to McCabe's car, they paused to take in the brilliant sunset. Flamingo-pink, orange-mango, and purple-orchid hues bled over the horizon. It looked like a pitcher of tropical punch had spilled across the lower half of the sky.

Suddenly an explosion of movement erupted from the beech trees across the parking lot.

Hundreds of birds burst into the air to form an undulating cloud of black. A mass of black bodies moved in perfect unison—dipping and swirling and knifing through the flaming clouds.

Nora should have been spellbound by the poetry of their flight, but she remembered the dead bird in the flower basket and saw something more ominous.

She saw a skyful of bad omens.

Chapter 3

My weapon has always been language, and I've always used it, but it has changed. Instead of shaping the words like knives now, I think they're flowers, or bridges.

—Sandra Cisneros

As usual, Pearl's was packed. People were willing to cross several county lines to dine on her famed southern fried catfish, gumbo, or chicken pot pie.

Because Nora and McCabe were regulars, Pearl treated them like family. Their glasses of sweet tea were never empty. Their basket of cornbread was always full. Before taking their order, Pearl would ask after Nora's friends and McCabe's colleagues, share stories about her husband and kids, and describe the daily specials like an actor performing a Shakespearean monologue.

When Pearl put a hand on her hip, it meant she was settling in for a good long chat. Her hand was on her hip now.

"Everybody's talking about the Cherokee casino. Is it gonna happen or not? Folks are tired of not knowing. The longer they wait, the more fractious they get. You can't keep dangling a bone in front of a dog and expect him to just sit there. Eventually, he's gonna jump up and grab it with his teeth. Sheriff, did you know that we had to break up a fight in here the other night between the folks who support the Cherokee and the folks who don't?"

"I'm sorry to hear that," McCabe said. "But I can tell you that a casino's coming. It'll either be a Cherokee casino on Cherokee land, or it'll be another casino chain built on farm-land."

"The Cherokee get my vote," Pearl declared. "It's about time this country *gave* them something after so much taking. That big Vegas casino chain won't give a damn about the peo-ple of this county. They won't build libraries or schools with the money they make. They'll buy more private jets and build more McMansions. The Cherokee will put that money to good use. They're our neighbors and we should support our neigh-bors."

"I had a meeting with Quentin Atkins today," McCabe said, referring to the sheriff of Haywood County. "His department is definitely feeling the tension. He's had to call in all shifts for every town council meeting. I know he'll be glad when the final votes are cast."

"He's a fine man, and I'm glad he's got someone to talk to." Pearl gave McCabe a wink and headed off to the kitchen.

Nora watched her go and then turned to McCabe. "Your meeting that ran late? Was it with Sheriff Atkins?"

"It was. Quentin needed a safe place to vent. I've never seen him this rattled before. He's on his sixth term and has taken over two hundred law enforcement training courses. The man's a rock, but this casino business is wearing him down."

Their hush puppies arrived and McCabe eyed them with such yearning that Nora had to laugh. "Dig in. I'll tell you about the window-display war."

"Sheldon will still find a way to use glitter," McCabe said when Nora was done. "I can see it now. The caterpillar on the mushroom? Head-to-toe glitter." Having eaten half of the hush puppies, he pushed the basket closer to Nora.

"Don't the Cherokee already have a casino?" she asked as she reached for a hush puppy.

McCabe nodded. "Harrah's Cherokee Casino Resort. It's been very successful, which is why the Eastern Band of Cherokee would like to open another one in Haywood County. Their proposal was approved by the powers-that-be, but the amount of tribal land in the county is small, which means they can't build a Harrah's-style resort. They'd like to focus on the casino and partner with a hospitality company who'd build a hotel and other amenities."

"If a casino means a new library, more schools, and employment for the locals, it sounds like a good thing all around."

"I agree, but there are two problems. For starters, the area surrounding the tribal land is sparsely populated. It's hilly with very few homesteads. Yes, it's right off the Blue Ridge Parkway, but there isn't even a gas station nearby. The closest town is Maddie Valley. And even though it has Sally's Pancakes and the Hillbilly Hideway, those might not be enough to entice Marriot or Hilton into a partnership."

Nora dunked her hush puppy in Pearl's secret Cajun sauce. "The Hillbilly Hideaway? Is that a bar?"

McCabe grinned. "It's a campground. One with a spectacular view. Most folks stop at Maddie Valley on their way to other places, but a casino would make the town a destination. The other hurdle for the Cherokee is competition. Right after the tribe announced its plans to build another casino, one of the big gaming companies swooped in and said that *they* wanted to build a world-class resort in Haywood County. *Their* casino would include fine dining, a spa, two pools, tennis courts, and a meeting space. It would mean even more revenue for the county in terms of jobs, but most of the actual profits would end up in the pockets of the gaming company."

"Sounds like a David and Goliath situation."

"And Goliath is fighting dirty. The gaming company, Blue

Leviathan, is already running a nasty ad campaign. Without saying it outright, the ads imply that an 'Indian' casino will lead to an increase in crime."

Nora gaped at him. "That's totally racist."

"It's also untrue. Casinos provide jobs and money for education, community buildings, and services. The idea that a casino will lead to increased alcohol consumption which will then lead to more crime is a negative stereotype. The biggest risk a casino poses is gambling addiction, and according to the article Quentin showed me, it affects indigenous people more than anyone else."

Pearl arrived with their dinner. Nora's spicy baked chicken platter came with black-eyed peas and mashed potatoes. Mc-Cabe's catfish was usually served with collards and grits, but Pearl knew that he preferred red beans and rice.

"Did you bring Nora up to speed, Sheriff?" Pearl waited for his nod before continuing. "The Cherokee deserve this casino and a whole lot more besides. I saw a commercial the other night that made me madder than a puffed toad. It showed a man who was supposed to be a Native American coming out of a casino with a handful of cash. He goes straight to the liquor store, buys a bottle of hard stuff, and then harasses a bunch of high school girls at the ice cream shop. It's awful. There's a petition going around to have it taken off the air, but it's already brainwashed way too many people."

"I'd like to sign that petition," Nora said.

Pearl smiled at her. "I'll stop running my mouth and leave you to your supper. I believe it was Julia Child who said, 'Dinner hour is a sacred, happy time.'"

"Amen," said a woman passing by their table.

"Myrtle Green, as I live and breathe!" Pearl cried, putting an arm around the woman.

McCabe plunged his fork into a mound of rice. "Quentin thinks Blue Leviathan has been greasing the palms of too many county officials. It's hard for one honest man to uphold the law, but if anyone can keep the peace, it's Quentin. Enough about my workday. How's your chicken?"

Their conversation wandered from topic to topic. When they were too full to eat another bite, Nora wiped her hands with her paper napkin and folded it in half. The action reminded her of Tucker, the boy who loved origami. She told McCabe about him.

A few minutes later, Pearl stopped by with the check and a takeout container. "Some brown buttermilk pie for later tonight. My daughter made it fresh this morning. She says it's better than her daddy's." She lowered her voice. "It is too, but don't tell my husband I said that."

On the way home, Nora's thoughts returned to lunch with her friends, and to how Estella said that her father knew his way around a kitchen. She wondered which area restaurants would hire ex-offenders.

"Your gears are turning," McCabe said as they crossed the county line.

Nora told him about Gus.

"He might want to apply for a government job," McCabe said. "The state passed the 'ban the box' bill three years ago, which means Mr. Sadler doesn't have to mention his criminal record on an application. That'll help him get an interview and give him a chance to talk about his past in person. There's no hiding a criminal record, but former felons deserve a shot at an interview. I know you believe in second chances, so let's hope the right employer does too. Gus will do better on the outside if he has structure. Finding a job is key."

"But where? The Lodge always needs food service staff, but since June didn't suggest it, she probably knew he wouldn't be hired."

McCabe slowed as he turned onto Main Street, his eyes moving over the storefronts of downtown Miracle Springs.

"I love that our town doesn't have fast food chains or big box stores, but those are exactly the places Gus should apply. McDonald's, Starbucks, Walmart, Coca-Cola—they all hire ex-offenders."

"But he'd have to commute to another town," Nora said. "He hasn't driven a car in fifteen years. Think about how cars have changed since then. How much the whole world has changed. I can't imagine how scary that would be. Nothing will look familiar. Neither will any of the people Gus knew from before."

McCabe reached for her hand. "If a few people make him feel welcome, that'll help. The sooner he feels like he's part of a community, the better."

On Sunday, Nora would head to the flea market to look for vintage items to sell at the bookstore, and she'd ask Bea, her favorite vendor, for ideas on how to support Estella and her father. Bea's cousin had been to prison, and she was always willing to offer up advice.

At home, Nora put the pie in the fridge and slipped her arms around McCabe's waist. "Are you sleeping over?"

"I fed the cats before I got here, so yes."

Over his shoulder, Nora saw the flower arrangement on the kitchen counter. The giant red dahlias were like two big eyes, staring at her.

"One sec," she said, pulling away from McCabe. She took the basket outside and left it on the café table.

She walked back through the house and found McCabe in the bedroom, unbuttoning his shirt.

"Better?" he asked.

Nora pushed his hands away so she could undo the final two buttons and smiled.

"Better."

Tea Flowers didn't open until ten thirty, which meant Nora couldn't ask Val about the mystery arrangement in person. She planned to give them a call, but from the moment she opened the bookstore, she'd been busy helping customers.

It was a perfect spring Saturday, and the town was bursting with visitors, all of whom seemed keen to shop at Miracle Books. Their alluring window display wasn't the only draw. The bookstore was the only game in town when it came to coffee. Even though the hotels had coffee, none of them served espresso drinks or brewed Sheldon's special Cuban coffee blend.

Nora was too busy selling books, candles, and shelf enhancers—the term she used to describe the vintage knickknacks decorating her shelves—to use the restroom, let alone make a phone call. It was well after two when she finally had the chance to contact Tea Flowers.

Val answered the phone. After the two women exchanged pleasantries, Nora explained that she'd received a basket from their shop that had no label.

"Are you sure it was one of ours?" asked Val.

"Yes. I saw similar arrangements yesterday when I had tea with my friends. My basket had a rue plant, as well as hyacinth, bluebells, and two red dahlias. Does that sound familiar?"

"I really couldn't say." Val's tone was curt. "I was way too focused on my tea shop customers to pay attention to what Kirk was doing."

Nora was taken aback by Val's reaction. She just wanted to know who'd sent the arrangement. She wasn't accusing the woman of a crime.

Determined to take the high road, she politely asked, "May I speak to Kirk, please?"

"He's with a customer. Give me your number and I'll have him get back to you when he's free."

Though Nora doubted she'd hear from Kirk, she recited her number, thanked Val, and hung up.

By midafternoon, Sheldon was worn out. Because he suffered from osteoporosis and fibromyalgia, his health was in a state of constant flux. On a good day, his pain and inflammation hibernated. On a bad day, they crippled his mobility. He might spend twelve to twenty hours in bed, too miserable to sleep yet too sore to move.

Though he was an unreliable employee, often showing up late or not at all, Nora wouldn't change a thing about him. His chronic illness had made him one of the most empathic people Nora had ever met. Customers of all ages and backgrounds felt comfortable confiding in him. As did the members of the Secret, Book, and Scone Society. Sheldon wanted Miracle Books to thrive as much as Nora did, which is why she often had to force him to leave when he wasn't feeling well.

"You need to call it quits for today," she told him over the hum of the espresso machine. When he shook his head, she lightly touched his hand. "Your knuckles are swollen. Hang up your apron and ice those joints."

Sheldon rolled his eyes. "I'm fine, *mamita*."

Nora waited for him to finish with the cappuccino before untying his apron and easing it over his head. "Go sit down. I'll bring you hand wraps and Tylenol."

Five minutes later, Sheldon was resting in June's favorite purple velvet chair in the Readers' Circle. It wasn't long before a customer noticed his hand wraps and told him about her rheumatoid arthritis. Even when he was bone weary and aching all over, Sheldon was willing to listen to the complaints of a fellow "spoonie."

Because he'd read dozens of sick-lit novels, his conversations with other sufferers often led to sales. Nora had just finished tidying the ticket agent's booth when the woman thanked Sheldon and appeared at the pass-through window. She glanced at the chalkboard menu and said, "May I have an Ernest Hemingway? And the gentleman in the purple chair said that you could find a few novels for me. I'm looking for characters with chronic illness."

"Absolutely. After I get your drink, I'll put a pile of books on the coffee table. Take all the time you want with them."

Nora poured dark roast coffee into a mug labeled IS YOUR NAME JUDY? DON'T JUDGE ME. The woman read the text and chuckled on her way back to the Readers' Circle.

Moving through the stacks, Nora pulled titles from Fiction, Romance, and Young Adult and then piled eight books on the coffee table. It took the woman twenty minutes to finish her coffee and choose five books. Nora rang up Talia Hibbert's *Get a Life, Chloe Brown*; Karol Ruth Silverstein's *Cursed*; *The State of Me* by Nasim Marie Jafry; *All's Well* by Mona Awad, and *Seduce Me at Sunrise* by Lisa Kleypas.

By the time Sheldon left, coffee orders had slowed to a manageable rate and Nora was able to focus her energy on selling books. Her passion for certain titles was so infectious that those within earshot often bought the books she'd been recommending to another customer.

Every sale brought her a little closer to car ownership, which was a cause for elation and fear. Nora hadn't owned a car since her accident. She'd almost killed two people the last time she'd gotten behind the wheel and knew there'd be demons waiting when she decided to drive again.

Ten years ago, Nora had discovered that her husband was having an affair. Enraged, she'd glugged down a bottle of liquor, hoping the booze would numb the pain. No amount of alcohol could dislodge the knife blade in her heart, but it did fill her head with irrational ideas. Spurred on by anger and whiskey, Nora tracked her husband to his lover's house.

He answered the door and explained that he was in love. His voice had been calm. It had also been condescending. When he put out a protective hand to shield the woman behind him, Nora saw the swell of her belly. At that moment, something inside of her cracked. *She'd* wanted a baby. *She'd* wanted a family.

As she stood on the stoop, her dreams died. All that remained was despair.

Nora shouldn't have gotten back in the car. She shouldn't

have merged onto the highway, flattening the gas pedal as she keened with grief.

Suddenly she was spinning. There was a deafening scream of tires and the crash of metal slamming into metal. This was followed by fire, months in the burn unit, and Nora's decision to shed her old life like a pair of pants that no longer fit.

She changed her name, severed all ties with the people she knew from before the accident, and moved to Miracle Springs. She acquired a used moped from one of her customers, which was how she got from point A to point B. It was an impractical mode of transportation for someone who spent every Sunday at the flea market and yard sales. She couldn't use it in the snow, and it wasn't ideal for rainy weather either.

After more than a decade, Nora was ready for a car. A reliable, no-frills vehicle that could hold plenty of books. She'd seen a used Ford Escape in the classified section two weeks ago that fit the bill perfectly, and while she waited for her last customers of the day to finish browsing, she opened the newspaper to search for the listing. Not only was it still there, but the seller had reduced the price.

Nora grinned. "That's my car."

Her phone pinged. Estella had sent a text, asking Nora if she wanted to meet for dinner at the diner.

Since McCabe was working the late shift, she'd planned a quiet evening at home. She was going to plop down on her couch and eat a bowl of ice cream while watching a period drama on PBS. After that, she'd read until bedtime. It wasn't an exciting Saturday night, but Nora wasn't looking for excitement. But she didn't want to cook either.

She wrote back: **Save me a seat. I'll be there in fifteen minutes.**

Nora walked into the Pink Lady to find the usual crowd milling about the hostess stand. The hostess caught sight of Nora and waved her through.

Estella was seated at the counter, watching her man work. Jack served a platter of chicken fried steak to the customer sitting next to Estella and topped off another person's drink. After making sure everyone had what they needed, he glanced around his restaurant. Seeing Nora, he waved.

Jack was a handsome man with dark, wavy hair and lively eyes. He had a steady voice and a calm disposition. All the locals liked and admired him. Despite his lean frame, he was strong enough to toss a drunk or an abrasive customer out on the curb without breaking a sweat.

"I'm glad you came." Estella patted the empty stool beside her. "Do you feel like breakfast for dinner?"

"Always," Nora said.

Jack saluted them and returned to the kitchen. When he was gone, Estella said, "Daddy's getting out early. I pick him up first thing Monday morning."

"Are you nervous?"

Estella spread her napkin on her lap. "Definitely. He's so different from the man he used to be. His parents never had any money, so he dropped out of school and got a job at the paper mill. It's been closed for two decades now, but so many people from Miracle Springs used to work there that the mill bussed them in every morning and brought them back every afternoon. One day, my daddy missed the bus and had to thumb a ride home. My mama was in a car with some of her friends and they pulled over and picked him up."

A server placed water glasses in front of them and asked if they'd like to order anything to drink. Nora politely declined. A moment later, Estella followed suit.

"I'm skipping wine with supper for the time being. Sobriety's been good for Daddy, so mine will be an alcohol-free house for now. I'm not giving up my book club cocktails, though. There's a limit to my saintliness." Estella mimed a halo over her head. "Anyway, back to my parents. Their story is a total cliché. They got married too young and had a baby exactly nine months later. Mama regretted both decisions and started sleeping around. Then Daddy got drafted."

Nora said, "Vietnam?"

"Yeah. People said that Gus Sadler was a different man before that war, but the only version I ever knew was a man who yelled too loud, drank too much, and broke stuff. After the war, he took a job that kept him on the road for weeks at a time. One day, he just didn't come home. I didn't see him again until I was a teenager and Mama was dating a piece of trash named Sherman Barnes. Sherman was giving me a beating when Daddy walked in. He was winding up to kick me in the ribs when Daddy shot him. Sherman was dead before he hit the floor."

In the silence that followed, their food arrived. When the server asked if they needed ketchup for their potatoes, they both shook their heads.

Nora poked holes in her omelet to let the steam escape. "That was the Gus Sadler from before. So, who is he now?"

Estella brightened. "A college graduate, for starters. After he got his GED, he became addicted to learning. He's a skilled cook and big-time reader. You know how I like talking books with him. We have our own father/daughter book club. Daddy also found Jesus in prison. I'm hoping that faith, books, and a job will help him transition to his next phase in life."

"He also has you, which means he's going to be okay," Nora said.

The two friends chatted about their workdays. Estella had done a Brazilian blowout for one of her pickiest clients. The service had taken two hours and Estella's arms felt like rubber by the time she was done. Her client was delighted by the results but complained about the cost until Estella gave her a free bottle of shampoo just to shut her up.

"What about you? Any troublemakers in the bookstore?"

"Nope. I had a great day. So great that I now have enough

money to buy a car. But I *do* have a story to tell you. It's about something I found on my deck yesterday."

Nora described the flower arrangement and explained what each flower meant according to Victorian lore. Their server cleared their plates and, after failing to convince them to try a slice of peanut butter pie, left them alone to talk.

"Did you call Tea Flowers?"

"Yep. Val—the woman working behind the counter on Friday—said her husband makes all the arrangements. Since he was with a customer, she said she'd have him call me back. I never heard from him, which didn't surprise me. Val just wanted to get me off the phone."

A smug look came over Estella's face. "Well, well. Guess who's sitting in a booth near the restrooms?"

Nora craned her neck to see over the other customers. Sure enough, Val and Kirk were at a booth facing the parking lot. And they weren't alone. Nora recognized their dinner companions. The woman with the purple Princess Leia chemo cap was Kelly and the boy sitting next to her was Tucker.

"They're getting ready to leave," said Estella. When Nora jumped to her feet, Estella whispered, "What are you going to do?"

"I'm going to bump into them on the sidewalk. Be right back."

Nora hurried outside and stood by her moped. When Kirk exited the diner and held the door for the ladies, Nora started walking toward their party.

Tucker noticed her first and plucked his mother's shirt to get her attention. When she leaned closer to him, he pointed at Nora. Kelly put her arm around her son and smiled.

"I'm glad we ran into you!" Kelly said, moving forward to greet Nora. "Tucker wanted to give you something the next time he saw you, and here you are! He just finished working on it during dinner. Go on, Tuck."

Nora darted a quick glance at Val and Kirk. They were both wearing furtive expressions.

What is with these people?

Keeping his eyes lowered, Tucker approached Nora with his arm outstretched. In his hand, he held a lily pad made of marbled green paper. In the center of the lily pad sat a pink origami flower.

"You can open the flower," he said.

The lily pad fit neatly in the bowl of Nora's hand and weighed only a few ounces. It was a delicate, beautiful thing. Every fold was sharp and precise.

She said, "This is so lovely, Tucker. Can you show me how to open the flower?"

Tucker peeled back two of the petals, revealing a tiny origami bee.

Nora let out a little gasp of delight. "Tucker, this is paper magic! I'm super impressed. Are you sure you want me to have this? It must've taken you a long time to make it."

"I've made bees before. They're easy. The flower was the hardest. I wanted to put a dragonfly in there, but it wouldn't fit."

"Oh, I love the bee. Plus, we're having a honeybee festival next week. I'm going to put this work of art on my checkout counter because I want every customer to see what you made. Is that okay with you?"

Though Tucker didn't meet her eyes, he nodded, his face flushing with pleasure.

Nora took a few steps forward. Once she was close enough to be heard by Val and Kirk, she said, "I'm happy to see you both. Now you can tell who sent me that arrangement. So? Who was it?"

Val turned to her husband while Kirk looked a question at Kelly.

Kelly said, "Tucker, I need you to go to the car with Aunt Val and Uncle Kirk. Show them the design you're going to make next. I'll be there in a minute."

Kirk put an arm around Tucker's shoulders, and they began to walk away with Val following a few steps behind.

With their departure, something in the air shifted. Nora didn't understand what was happening. One minute, she was sharing a sweet moment with Tucker. Now, the air between her and Kelly sizzled with tension. Nora couldn't understand the reason for it. Until Kelly spoke.

She said, "The flowers are from me."

Nora let her confusion show. "*You?* But why?"

"Because I wanted to express regret, admit betrayal, and hope for forgiveness. I didn't write a note because I needed to look you in the eye. I wanted you to see how very sorry I am."

"I don't understand."

Kelly took a step forward. "I told you that we've met before. A few years ago, my husband had business in this area. While he was in a meeting, I took the rental car and drove to your bookstore. As soon as I walked in, I recognized you. I knew you from before—when you went by a different name."

Nora flinched as if she'd been struck. She tried to yell, "Stop!" but the words congealed in her throat.

Kelly's bony hands fluttered to her mouth. Her eyes were dewy with tears. "I met you years ago, at my house. The night you came to find your husband."

Chapter 4

*There is a shock that comes so quickly and strikes so
deep that the blow is internalized even before the
skin feels it.*

—Maya Angelou

A memory struck Nora like a thunderbolt.

Ten years ago, she'd caught a fleeting glimpse of the other
woman. It all came rushing back to her now.

She remembered pounding on a stranger's door. She remembered screaming her husband's name.

No matter how hard she tried, she'd never be able to forget
the sight of her husband in the doorway, glaring at Nora as he
hissed at her to lower her voice.

Nora remembered her fingers curling into fists. How she'd
wanted to smack the patronizing look off his face. How she'd
wanted to strike him again and again. Every time she thought
back on that moment, she wished she'd found a way to make
him crumple in pain.

But she hadn't hit him. She'd just stood there, quivering with
rage, as her husband held his arm out to protect the woman behind him. He'd shielded his pregnant lover from his wife.

Nora had never known the woman's name.

Until now.

Kelly.

She stared at this version of Kelly Walsh. Her hands were clasped, and her lips were moving. Nora heard her voice, but she couldn't make out the words. She felt like she was under-water, but Nora her head that full of water.

Sounds began penetrating the membrane of shock, but Nora didn't want to hear anything Kelly had to say. She was desperate for quiet. The motion of passing cars was dizzying. The streetlamps and traffic lights were too bright. They hurt her eyes.

I have to get out of here.

Nora ran to her moped.

"I'm sorry for hurting you!" Kelly called after her.

The words pummeled Nora in the back.

"I'm not asking for forgiveness. I just wanted to tell you that I'm sorry!"

Nora shoved the origami flower into the storage compartment under her seat and fumbled with the lock securing her helmet. All she had to do was rotate four letters until they spelled the word *book*, but her fingers felt thick and useless. She got the B and the first O, but the second O refused to line up.

Seeing Kelly approach, Nora began to spin the letter dial with the feverish intensity of someone trying to escape a serial killer.

"Please wait!" Kelly raised her hands in a placating gesture.

The lock released and Nora grabbed the helmet. As she fired the engine, she jabbed her helmet in Kelly's direction.

"Stay back!"

Kelly kept moving closer.

"I'm warning you. *Stay away from me!*"

Nora jerked her helmet on, took a cursory glance in her mirror, and backed out of her parking spot. Before she could change gears, Kelly had grabbed hold of her shirt.

"If I could only tell you my side of the story, you might understand! Tomorrow, I'll come to the bookstore—"

"*No!*" Nora pushed Kelly in the chest, hard.

Kelly pinwheeled her arms, fighting to keep her balance, but Nora didn't wait around to see if she succeeded. The second Kelly let go of her shirt, she drove away.

Behind her, she heard shouts. A woman shrieked. A man hurled a curse in Nora's direction, but she kept her eyes on the road.

There was a roaring in her head.

The dam she'd built to hold back the past was leaking, and she had to get home before it broke. Names trickled through holes in the mortar. City names. Street names. The names of buildings and neighborhoods. Businesses, monuments, and libraries. People. Friends. Family. Her ex-husband.

Lawrence.

She hadn't spoken his name out loud since the night he'd answered Kelly's door. After the accident, she'd trained herself to forget it. As soon as their divorce was finalized, she'd destroyed every document mentioning his name. She'd burned or shredded any evidence of his existence. She'd gathered up their shared history and dropped it in the ocean of her memory.

But Kelly had brought it all to the surface.

Nora had never felt so naked. So exposed.

She pushed her moped to its top speed, but it wasn't fast enough. She wove around stopped cars and even drove on the sidewalk because she couldn't stop. She had to keep moving.

Finally, she made it home.

She slid off the moped without removing her helmet. She found comfort in its weight and the anonymity of its visor. She didn't take it off until she was inside her house and had closed and locked the door.

She didn't switch on any lights. Dropping her helmet on the kitchen table, she lurched toward the sink. She turned on the tap and splashed water on her face over and over. The water cooled her skin and washed her hot tears away.

As the minutes passed, she grew calmer. She turned off the tap and dried her face with a tea towel.

As she stood in her dark kitchen, her gaze landed on the wine bottle on the opposite counter. She and McCabe had tried the wine last night, and though neither of them had liked it much, Nora desperately wanted some now.

She poured the wine into the coffee mug and chugged it. Then she carried the mug and bottle to the living room and sank down on the sofa.

It was too much effort to refill the mug, so she curled into a fetal position and pulled her chunky knit throw blanket up to her chin.

One thought echoed in her head.

Is Lawrence in Miracle Springs?

The possibility of seeing him again was Nora's worst nightmare. The idea of him walking around her town, shopping at her grocery store, eating at her diner, and interacting with her neighbors made her feel sick.

He was here.

Of course, he was. Kelly was here. And so was Tucker.

"His son," Nora whispered.

Her phone chirped from inside her crossbody bag, which she was still wearing. Nora reached into the bag and flicked the button on the side of the phone to mute. She then pulled the bag over her head and tossed it on the coffee table. The wine bottle teetered dangerously but didn't fall.

Nora resumed her fetal position and closed her eyes.

Of all the towns in the world, why did he have to come to mine?

The anger she thought she'd doused years ago reignited. It burned in her chest, as if her scarred heart had caught fire.

But then she remembered the look of pleasure on Tucker's

face as he'd held out the origami flower in his cupped hand, and the anger drained away.

Tucker was his mother's child. He'd inherited Kelly's freckles and delicate features. His tousled hair, long fingers, and gentle manner were hers too. Lawrence was direct to the point of rudeness, and he always looked people in the eye. Tucker might have inherited his father's height and strong chin, but that was about it.

Nora couldn't picture her ex as a father. He'd never been a patient man and he disdained weakness.

On the other hand, Tucker was his son. His own flesh and blood. Surely, Lawrence loved him more than anything in the world

I hope so because Tucker is going to lose his mother soon.

Nora didn't want to think about Kelly's too-thin frame. It was impossible to feel any animosity toward the woman in the purple Princess Leia head wrap. She felt only pity. Whatever mistakes Kelly had made, she didn't deserve this cruel ending. She didn't deserve to be separated from her son.

In the darkness, Nora's thoughts went around in circles until she became too tired to think cohesively anymore. She fell asleep on the sofa, while inside her bag, her phone rang and rang.

Nora woke to the sound of church bells.

For a moment, she was confused. Why was she on the sofa? Why was her neck so sore? Why was there an open bottle of wine on the coffee table?

Then she remembered.

"Oh, God."

After wiping the sleep from her eyes, she got up, shuffled to the kitchen, and looked at the clock on her microwave. It was ten, which meant the flea market had just opened.

Nora cursed under her breath and started the coffeemaker. Then she showered and dressed in clean jeans and a T-shirt.

After filling a travel mug with coffee, she slung her crossbody bag over her head, and left the house.

The air smelled of fresh grass. The warm April sunshine caressed her skin. She hadn't applied sunscreen to her burn scars but decided not to bother. She was eager to lose herself in the crowd of shoppers and to focus on anything that helped her forget about last night, if only for a few minutes.

Since the parking lot in front of the big red barn was already full when Nora arrived, she left her moped next to the bike rack and hurried inside.

The booths near the entrance held nothing of interest, but the local candlemaker had an array of new scents for sale.

"I thought I'd see you today," she said, gesturing at a cardboard box poking out from under the table. "You were so disappointed when I sold out of Spring Fling that I set four aside for you. I also added a few of the new scents. Give the samples a sniff and see which ones you like."

Nora thanked the woman for her thoughtfulness and reached for a mason jar with a label reading DAYLIGHT SAVINGS. It smelled like sunshine and daffodils.

"That's lovely," she said.

Moving down the row of scents, Nora sniffed SUGARED CHERRY, DAISY CHAIN, BLESS THIS NEST, and BEE KIND.

With the Honeybee Jubilee coming up, Nora asked if she could pass on the daisy candles and get twice as many honey-scented candles. After paying the vendor, she promised to collect her purchases on her way out.

She moved deeper into the barn, admiring antique quilts, framed needlework, and delicate porcelain. Most of the items she liked were too large or too expensive for her needs, but she brightened when she saw a pair of vintage watering cans for sale. Both cans were child-sized and had been painted a robin's-egg blue. Because the vendor was too busy to haggle, he accepted Nora's offer right away.

More treasures awaited her at the end of the next row. The

antique-postcard vendor had a lovely set of miniature vintage botanicals on display. Each print was framed and would look amazing on a bookshelf.

The vendor smiled when he saw Nora examining the shepherd's purse print. "Do you know this plant? It's in the mustard family."

"Interesting. And this one?" Nora showed him the poppy print.

He laughed. "The opium family?"

This made Nora chuckle. "I want the whole set, but I can't resell them if I pay your asking price. Can you do any better?"

"Ten percent's as low as I can go. There isn't much profit there to begin with."

Nora had dealt with this vendor before and knew him to be an honest man. The price was a little high, but she decided to take a chance. If she sold each print separately, she could still make a little money.

The vendor wrapped the prints and put them in a bag. Nora thanked him and made her way to her favorite booth, Bea's Bounty.

The owner, a middle-aged woman with stringy blond hair and translucent blue eyes, carried the best vintage items around. She came from a large family and had a network of cousins spread across North Carolina and Virginia. If Bea couldn't find something, one of her family members could.

Bea loved three things in life: smoking Parliament cigarettes, taking tourists' money, and accumulating information. Because she was interested in facts and gossip on an equal level, Nora saved up anecdotes from the shop to share with her every week. In turn, Bea always put a few items under the table for Nora to peruse before offering them to the general public.

"Guuuurl! You're a wreck. What happened to you?" Bea hollered as soon as she laid eyes on Nora.

"Cheap wine."

Bea's brows shot up. "How much did you drink? Enough to fill a bathtub?"

Nora didn't want to tell Bea the truth, so she said, "Too much." Her gaze wandered over Bea's wares. "Your booth looks great. I love this pink glassware."

"It's Depression glass. Got the whole lot from an estate sale outside of Boone back in February. Thanks to an ice storm, I got a ton of fine things dirt cheap. Speaking of fine things, there's a box under the table that'll make you mighty happy."

Could anything make me happy right now?

Mustering a smile, Nora said, "Sounds expensive."

"There's a whole window's worth of goodies in that box. See for yourself." Bea jerked a thumb at the table and then moved to the far side of the booth to help another customer.

Nora squeezed through the narrow gap between two tables and opened the box flaps. Inside, she found a stack of tin farm-stand signs. Each one featured a different fruit or vegetable in the foreground with a barn, tractor, or cornfields in the background. They weren't especially old—probably twenty years or less—but Bea was right. The signs would look terrific in the window and were likely to sell quickly after the display came down.

The signs weren't the only treasures in the box. There was also a collection of crocheted insects including bees, ladybugs, butterflies, and grasshoppers. The bugs were as big as Nora's shoe and would look wonderful flying around a selection of gardening books.

"Pretty cool, eh?"

Glancing up at Bea, Nora nodded. "Sheldon and I haven't been able to decide on our next window theme, but you just settled it for us. We're going to create a garden. Instead of plants, we'll grow books. There's no point in pretending that I don't want everything in this box, so let's talk price."

Bea scrunched her lips to one side and pretended to think. She knew exactly what she wanted Nora to pay, but this posturing was all part of the act. Bea loved a good haggling session.

They went back and forth a few times and were getting close to an agreement when Bea had to pause their bartering session to wrap two pieces of Depression glass for another customer. When she was done, she gave Nora an appraising look.

"Folks are talking about you."

Nora glanced around as if she might be able to identify the culprits. Then she shrugged and said, "Nothing new about that."

"They say you hit a woman with cancer." Bea cocked her head. "Where did they get such a crazy idea?"

Nora lowered her head in shame. "I didn't hit her, but I did push her." She let out a heavy sigh and continued. "I was on my moped and I just wanted to go home, but Kelly—that's her name—wouldn't get out of my way. I was upset, so I pushed her. I was rougher than I should've been."

"Did she upset you or did somebody else?"

Nora watched people mill around the booths and stroll between aisles. She saw couples holding hands and parents pushing strollers. Friends and neighbors paused in the middle of shopping to chat. The air, which smelled of candied nuts, hummed with energy.

Though she loved this place and its people, Nora felt like bolting.

Bea touched her arm. "You okay?"

Nora shook her head and said, "Kelly married my ex-husband."

"Well, swat my behind with a melon rind. What's she doing in Miracle Springs?"

"Dying."

Bea closed her eyes and whispered, "Show mercy on Kelly, Jesus." To Nora, she said, "Were they together?"

"No."

Bea held up a finger. "I know your story, so I see why you're shook. But don't give that jackass any power. He can only bother you if you let him." She tapped the box with the toe of her sneaker. "As for this, I can drop it off tomorrow. I need to go to the post office anyhow, and I'm gonna want to check in on you."

"Thank you, Bea."

"It'll cost you a cup of coffee. Now, where were we on the price?"

Nora gave Bea her preferred method of payment—cash—and swung back to the candle booth to collect her purchases. With the candles, botanical prints, and watering cans, she was pretty weighed down. She did her best to pack things in the storage box on the back of her moped, but it was going to be an awkward ride home.

Inside her bag, her phone vibrated, and for the first time that day, Nora looked at the screen. She saw a long list of missed calls and texts.

"Nope," she said, shoving the phone into her bag.

As she strapped on her helmet, she noticed one of the teachers at the local elementary school point her way and whisper to the man beside her.

Nora's cheeks burned.

Hiding her face behind her visor, she drove to Miracle Books. After depositing her flea market finds in the stockroom, she sat down in the Readers' Circle.

The orderliness of the books, lined up on their shelves like good little soldiers, allowed her to relax. She hugged the quiet to her, breathing in the familiar scents of coffee, old paper, and beeswax polish.

No one could touch her here, in her fortress of books. They were her armor against life's jagged edges. Her safe harbor in the raging storm. A soft landing when she fell onto hard, un-yielding ground.

Nora's sanctuary was open to everyone. She wanted to share

the joy and fulfilment of books with her customers. With one exception, she'd welcome the whole world into Miracle Books. And that one exception was her ex-husband. He'd never be allowed in. Never.

A gurgle came from Nora's stomach. She wasn't hungry but knew she should eat. And since there was no point in hitting the yard sales because anything worth buying would already be gone, she decided to have lunch.

Annoyed with herself, Nora plodded home. She made a cheese and tomato sandwich and ate it while reading the latest in Alexander McCall Smith's No. 1 Ladies' Detective Agency series.

For the next hour, she was completely absorbed by Precious Ramotswe's latest case. It was a pleasant respite to travel to Botswana and sit under an acacia tree with McCall's kind and humble characters.

Eventually, she closed her book and cleaned up her lunch things. After starting a load of laundry, she filled up her water bottle and grabbed her walking stick. The stick, which had a playful fox, a flowery meadow, and a stream carved into its shaft, was a necessity when hiking less traveled trails in the Blue Ridge Mountains. Not only did Nora use it to bat down spider webs, but she also thumped the ground to scare the snakes. Having seen rattlers and copperheads in these hills, she never hiked without her trusty stick.

Nora descended the slope behind her house and crossed the train tracks. A narrow path used by the locals wound through the woods until it merged with the Appalachian Trail.

April was a busy month on the AT. Day hikers came from all over to reach the famous lookout. On a clear day, it was possible to see four states from this place. The day hikers were joined by through hikers—a term used to describe those who traveled the trail from Georgia to Maine.

Nora was also bound for the lookout. She liked to sit on a

sun-warmed boulder and gaze at the humpbacked mountains. Humbled by their timeless majesty, the mountains helped her gain perspective.

On some days, their peaks were veiled in mist or wreathed in clouds. Today, there was only a vast canopy of blue.

Perching on a boulder, Nora drew her knees into her chest and replayed the scene from last night. She'd been angry, but her anger was born from fear. As soon as she learned who Kelly was, Nora realized that her past and present were about to collide. It was her worst nightmare.

But it's a survivable nightmare.

Lawrence meant nothing to her. If she saw him, she'd look the other way. If he spoke to her, she'd ignore him. If he tried to enter the bookstore, she'd stop him. Bea was right. She wouldn't give him the power to spoil the life she'd built in Miracle Springs.

And Kelly?

Kelly had been trying to apologize. She'd been honest and brave, and Nora had run away.

Now it's my turn to make amends.

She'd go to Tea Flowers during her lunch break tomorrow. She'd sit down with Kelly and talk things through. Once everything was out in the open, they would both feel better.

With this plan in mind, Nora could focus on the beauty of her surroundings. She gazed at the mountaintops and endless sky for a long time before climbing off her boulder and turning toward home.

Passing under an outcropping of rocks, she saw that her left bootlace had come untied and knelt down to fix it. As she did, she heard voices coming from the rocks above.

"You've only been out of the pen for six months, Colt," a man said. "What does this chick want you to do? Somethin' that could send you right back to Club Fed?"

A woman with a thin, high voice piped up. "We're not tellin' you a damn thing. All you need to know is that Colt'll make ten times what he'd make sellin' chicken grease."

Nora smelled cigarette smoke and heard someone belch.

"That's right, babe," said a man with a gravelly voice. "I'm a free man. I can do whatever the hell I want. If I wanna smoke, I'll smoke. If I wanna smash this bottle, I'll smash it." Nora cringed at the sound of glass shattering. "If I want this chick's money, I'll take it."

"What do you have to do for it?" pressed the first man.

"Not much. Scare some chick into telling me a secret. Soon as I know where she'd hiding a certain something, I'll hand it over and get paid. It's a conversation. Nothin' more. Why *wouldn't* I take the job?"

"Why wouldn't *we* take the job," the woman corrected.

"Well, my old lady is dragging me to the beach next week, so you'll have to tell me how it all went down when I get back," the first man said. "I just pounded the last beer, so let's get out of here before one of those crunchy nature freaks asks me to share my weed."

Having tied her bootlace, Nora stood up and continued walking. Behind her, she heard sniggering followed by the sound of more breaking glass.

As she descended the trail, she passed a park ranger installing a new trail sign and told him about the broken bottles.

"Littering makes me madder than a wet panther," he grumbled.

At home, Nora switched her laundry over and brewed half a pot of decaf. She carried her mug and phone out to the deck and prepared to sort through her missed calls and texts.

Estella's **Where are you?** text from last night was no surprise. Nora had left the diner with no explanation, and knowing Miracle Springs, the rumor that she'd hit a sick woman had probably spread through the diner like a virus.

Nora was about to reply to Estella when someone said, "Nora Pennington, where have you been? You had us worried."

June climbed the stairs to the deck. Hester was right behind her.

"Estella said you ran off in the middle of dinner without saying goodbye. Are you okay?" Hester held out a plate covered with a piece of foil. "I brought cookies."

Nora stood up. "I have coffee. Let's go inside."

The three friends sat around the kitchen table. Hester peeled the foil off the plate, revealing one of Nora's favorite treats.

"Thumbprint cookies." She smiled at Hester. "You know how to cheer a girl up."

While June and Hester sipped their coffee, Nora told them about Kelly. When she was done, June shook her head and muttered, "Lordy, Lordy."

"Which part are you reacting to? That Kelly's the woman my husband left me for or that I shoved a terminally ill woman in the chest?"

June said, "Both."

Hester grabbed Nora's hand. "No wonder you went radio silent today. You poor thing. What can we do to help?"

Nora smiled at her. "I feel better now that I've told you. As soon as I make peace with Kelly, I think I'll be okay."

"But your ex . . ." Hester began.

"Seeing him will be hell. I'm going to hate every second of it, but I might be able to avoid him until he leaves. After that, I'll forget about him again."

"You mean, after Kelly passes? Is she really that sick?"

Nora was about to describe Kelly's fragility when someone knocked on her door.

"That's probably Grant wondering why I've ignored all of his calls."

She was right. McCabe stood on her welcome mat, wearing a dour expression. He wasn't alone either. Deputy Fuentes was with him.

Nora knew something was wrong when he refused to look

her in the eye. His gaze skimmed over her face and came to rest somewhere over her shoulder.

"Sorry that I haven't gotten back to you. I was going to call in a bit to explain." She waved McCabe and Fuentes inside. "Come on in. June and Hester brought cookies."

McCabe didn't move. "Nora, I'm here in an official capacity. I need you to come to the station with me."

June and Hester shot to their feet. Seeing the fear on their faces, Nora felt a chill dance up her spine.

Turning to McCabe again, she said, "What's going on, Grant?"

McCabe stared at Nora for a long moment. Then he took hold of her elbow as if to steady her and whispered, "Kelly Walsh is dead."

Chapter 5

If I have left a wound inside you, it is not just your
wound, but mine as well.

—Haruki Murakami

McCabe refused to say more in front of June and Hester.
When they insisted on accompanying Nora to the station, he
shook his head.

"She's going to be a while. Just go home."

His rudeness made June bristle. She put her hands on her
hips and glared at McCabe. "Last time I checked, the station
was a public building. We're members of the public, which
means we can sit in the lobby and darn socks if we want to. It
just so happens that my knitting bag is in the car. Busy hands
make a happy heart. Isn't that right, Hester?"

"It sure is. I need to work on my May menu, and the lobby
seems as good a place as any."

Their small procession left Nora's house, bound for the
sheriff's department. June and Hester rode together while Nora
sat in the back of McCabe's SUV. It felt strange to watch him in
the rearview mirror—to see his gaze flick from the road to her
face and back to the road again.

The awkward silence in the car was enhanced by Deputy
Fuentes's presence. Normally, he was a talker. He loved to

share stories about the various members of his large family and could never resist telling Nora about the book his favorite sister was reading. He was an amiable man with an infectious, throaty laugh, so it was strange not to hear him speak.

Nora knew she should be frightened, but she was too busy processing what McCabe had said to feel much of anything.

What had happened to Kelly since yesterday? How could she be dead when less than twenty-four hours ago, she and her family were having dinner at the Pink Lady?

Kelly had been sick. Anyone could see that a disease had been whittling her away. Kirk said that his sister had moved to Miracle Springs to bathe in the mineral springs and take advantage of other holistic treatments. He hadn't said how much time she had left, but based on the grief in his eyes and the weight of his words, it wasn't very long.

And yet Kelly's death felt too sudden. She hadn't acted like someone on the verge of collapse, so why had the end come so quickly?

Because cancer didn't kill her.

Nora wanted to slam the lid closed on this Pandora's box, but the thought had already escaped.

An unnatural death would explain McCabe's stony demeanor and Fuentes's silence. It would explain why Nora was in the back of this car, bound for the station.

It seemed impossible to believe that something even more terrible than incurable disease had ended Kelly Walsh's life, but deep down Nora knew that it had.

And somehow, I'm connected.

She guessed that it had something to do with last night. She'd had a heated exchange with Kelly—right in front of the diner—and McCabe wanted to know what it had been about. He'd also want to know why she'd shoved a sick woman. Was that an act of assault?

Nora remembered putting her palm on Kelly's chest. She'd

felt the soft cotton of Kelly's shirt and the unyielding sternum beneath that shirt. Had the push knocked the air from Kelly's lungs? Had it somehow injured Kelly's heart? Did she lose her balance and fall? Had her head hit the asphalt?

The SUV swayed a little as McCabe drove over a speed bump and Nora felt her gorge rise.

"Pull over," she croaked before clamping her hand over her mouth.

After shooting a glance in the rearview mirror, McCabe did as she asked. He hit the brakes in the middle of the municipal complex parking lot and released the door locks.

Nora lurched from the car and made it three steps before vomiting on a patch of scraggly grass. Crumpling to her knees, she emptied the contents of her stomach, retching over and over until there was nothing left.

By the time the convulsions ceased, her eyes were watering, and her throat felt scorched. As she sat back on her heels and took shallow breaths, she heard McCabe approach from behind. He reached over her shoulder, offering her a wad of tissues.

"You okay?" he asked.

The gentle tone belonged to the man she loved. Even if Sheriff McCabe couldn't show it, Grant McCabe was worried about her.

She was too queasy to look at him, let alone speak, so he cradled the back of her head in his hand and said, "Breathe in slowly through your nose. Ready? Now hold it for three, two, one. Now let it out, nice and slow. Good. Do it again. In through your nose."

McCabe led her through a few rounds of deep breathing until she was able to whisper, "I'm okay."

He squatted down next to her and handed her a water bottle. He'd already unscrewed the cap. It sat in the center of his palm until McCabe's fingers curled around it, the veins on the back of his hand pulsating as he squeezed the coin-sized plastic.

Nora was suddenly swept up by the memory of another scene. Years ago, she'd been kneeling in a patch of rough grass by the side of the road when another officer had given her water. Like McCabe, the highway patrolman had worn black boots. Nora remembered turning away from smoke and flames to focus on those boots. Her skin was blackened and blistered. Her throat was raw and full of grit. But the boots meant that help had arrived. The fire would be extinguished, and the ambulances would come. The boots meant rescue.

That night, she'd been numb with shock. Now, Nora was hyperaware of every little thing. The pebbles digging into her knees, the brittle grass under her palms, the smell of sick. She felt the sun warming her hair, and the beads of sweat on her brow. She could hear McCabe's breathing. The purr of car engines. Conversations between birds.

"Nora?"

She took a few sips of tepid water and said, "I'm better now."

After helping her to stand, McCabe opened the car door for her. Before he shut it, she saw worry flash in his eyes.

He's scared for me, she thought, her heart constricting with fear.

Inside the station, McCabe led Nora to an interview room. She sat down while he lingered in the doorway. Gesturing at Fuentes, McCabe said, "I won't be the one talking to you. Because of our relationship, I can't. But I'll be close by."

Nora didn't want McCabe to leave, so when he turned to go, she said his name. When he paused in the doorway, she whispered, "Am I under arrest?"

"We have some questions to ask you," he replied before walking away.

Fuentes closed the door and sat down across the small table from Nora. He placed a recorder on the table and withdrew a notebook from his shirt pocket.

After explaining that he'd be recording the interview, he pressed a button on the device and stated the date, time, and their names. It didn't escape Nora's notice that he'd used the word *interview*. She might not be under arrest, but this was no informal chat.

What did you expect? A woman is dead.

The truth hit her anew. Kelly was dead. Nora couldn't apologize to her. She couldn't invite her to the bookstore to talk things over. She'd never hear Kelly's side of the story.

Is it my fault?

Nora willed Fuentes to begin. The sooner she knew what had happened, the sooner she could own up to her mistakes and face the consequences.

"When did you and Ms. Walsh first meet?" Fuentes asked.

"She and her son came into the bookstore on Friday. She introduced herself as Kelly. Her son was Tucker. While Tucker looked at bookmarks, Kelly said that she was shopping for books on origami. I showed her some books and we chatted, mostly about Tucker's origami skills, and then she said that she'd seen me before."

Fuentes said, "When did she see you?"

"A few years ago. On a trip with her husband. She came to the shop while he was tied up with a business deal. She remembers seeing me, but I don't remember her. She probably looked different then."

"What else did you talk about?"

After describing the visit in its entirety, Nora went on to tell Fuentes about the flower arrangement on her deck. When she got to the part about the dead bird, he frowned and said, "Do you think someone put it there on purpose?"

"I don't know. When I called Tea Flowers the next day to ask who'd sent the arrangement, Val answered. I didn't mention the bird to her."

"Is there a window over that table?"

Nora nodded. "There is. It faces west, so the sun hits it in the afternoon. Birds have bumped into it before. Not hard enough to kill, but hard enough to stun."

Fuentes wrote this down. "Did Valerie Walsh identify the person who sent the arrangement?"

"No." Nora explained that it was Kirk, not Val, who handled the arrangements. "Val promised to have Kirk call me back. He never did, but now I know why. The flowers were from Kelly. They were supposed to kickstart a conversation."

"How?"

"At the time, I had no idea. I'd never met Kelly until she came into the store, and she certainly didn't do anything worth apologizing for when she was there. Neither did her son. We had a pleasant interaction, and she was satisfied with her purchases. It was a friendly, positive experience." After a brief pause, Nora added, "Though I treated her like I would any other customer, I felt sorry for her. She looked incredibly fragile. I got the sense that she didn't have much time left, which made me sad for her and for her son. She and Tucker were obviously close. She clearly loved him very much."

Fuentes laced his fingers together and leaned forward a little. "Could she have sent the flowers as a thank-you for being nice?"

"I don't think so. The arrangements from Tea Flowers have themes based on which plants or flowers are grouped together in one basket. They're based on the Victorian language of flowers. Every flower has a meaning. I looked up my flowers online. They symbolized apology, regret, and betrayal."

Fuentes asked her to recite the contents of the basket and provide him with the name of the site she'd used.

"Did you see Kelly Walsh after you received the flower arrangement?"

They'd reached the crucial part of the interview. Nora knew she needed to stay calm and speak slowly. If they could just get through this part, she might learn why she was in this room.

"Last night, I met Estella Sadler for dinner at the Pink Lady. We sat at the counter. I told Estella about the mystery flowers. When I was done, she pointed out that Kelly, Tucker, Val, and Kirk were sitting in a booth at the back. The diner was crowded, and I hadn't noticed them before, but when I looked over at their booth, I could see that they were getting ready to leave."

Fuentes went very still. Only his mouth moved when he said, "What happened next?"

"I decided to intercept them as soon as they left the diner because I wanted to find out who'd sent the flower arrangement. My plan was to walk from the parking lot to the diner and act like I'd just bumped into them by chance. Then I'd ask Kirk about the flowers."

Fuentes held up a finger. "What time was this?"

Nora took a moment to consider this. "Around eight? Anyway, I followed through with my plan but didn't get an answer about who sent the flowers. Val and Kirk kept looking at Kelly like they expected her to say something. They hung back while she came closer to me. Then she said that the flowers were from her. As an apology. I was totally confused."

"You had no idea why she was sorry?" pressed Fuentes.

"No. Not until she explained everything to me."

Nora had no trouble remembering Kelly's exact words. She repeated them verbatim, describing how each one had been a sucker-punch to the gut. She told Fuentes how she yelled at Kelly to stop talking—to leave her alone. She told him that all she could think about was getting away, and how she backed her moped out of her parking space, intent on escaping.

"I just wanted to go home. I couldn't listen to her anymore. Every sentence was a bullet, punching holes in me." Nora gave Fuentes a pleading look, silently begging him to understand. But he was a veteran officer who'd seen and heard it all, and his gaze remained impassive.

"Go on."

Nora didn't try to paint herself in a better light. She told Fuentes how Kelly had grabbed hold of her shirt. She told him about pushing Kelly hard enough to make her backpedal.

"I didn't even look in my mirror to see if she fell. The second she let go of my shirt, I focused on driving away. The ride home is a blur. I know I drove erratically. I went through red lights and rode on the sidewalk. When I got to my house, I poured a glass of wine and chugged it. Then I curled up on the sofa and cried. Eventually, I fell asleep."

Fuentes held his pen over his notepad. "When did you wake up?"

"The next morning. Much later than usual. When I checked the time on my microwave clock, it was just after ten. I'm usually at the flea market when the doors open, but—" Nora's composure finally broke, and she stretched her hands out toward Fuentes. "I know you can't give me details, but can you at least tell me if I hurt her. *Please.* When I pushed her, did she fall? Did she hit her head? Did I . . . did I kill her?"

Ignoring the question, Fuentes said, "Several people witnessed the scene between you and Kelly Walsh. They heard you yelling at her. Some say that you pushed her. Others say that you hit her."

Nora shook her head vigorously. "I did *not* hit her. It was a shove. My hand was flat. I pushed right here." She put her palm to the center of her chest. "Yes, I yelled at her. I shouted for her to back off. I was on my moped. The engine was running. I was loud and shrill because I wanted her to let go of my shirt. I wanted her to leave me alone."

"You had a pretty good reason to be angry at Kelly Walsh. I mean, your husband left you for her. Did you want to hurt her because of that?"

"No, I didn't," Nora said firmly. "My husband left me a long time ago, and when I moved here, I vowed to forget about that part of my life. Of course, I could never really forget it, but I *did* pack it away. I didn't think about it. I didn't think about *him*. I never looked him up online. We never spoke. I didn't care what he was doing or who he was with. I didn't want revenge against Kelly. I was upset because the past I've worked so hard to escape had slammed into my present like a wrecking ball. It shocked the hell out of me. I was scared and confused. I just wanted to get away and hide."

Fuentes opened his mouth, but Nora didn't give him a chance to speak.

"Listen to me. *Please*. I needed to be alone to process the fact that my ex was in Miracle Springs. With his wife and son. I liked Kelly as soon as I met her. Tucker too. And I'm sorry for yelling at Kelly. I'm sorry that I pushed her. I was going to apologize to her tomorrow. Ask June and Hester. I was talking to them about that very thing when you and McCabe showed up."

A buzz came from Fuentes's phone. After glancing at the screen, he got to his feet. "I need to step out for a minute. Can I get you something to drink?"

Nora sagged in her chair. "Water."

As she sat in the empty room, she wondered what McCabe was doing. Would he look in on her when the interview was over? Was he anxious to hear what she'd said?

When Fuentes returned, another deputy followed him into the room. Nora was crushed to see that it wasn't McCabe. It was a woman with burgundy hair and a stern face. Her deep-set eyes studied Nora with thinly veiled hostility.

Fuentes said, "This is Deputy Paula Hollowell, our new K9 handler. She was on patrol with her partner last night and witnessed the scene between you and Ms. Walsh. She's going to listen in as we run through the events again."

Nora had a bad feeling about Deputy Hollowell. The woman was eyeing her as if she were a hardened criminal.

All you can do is tell the truth.

And then what? What would happen after she repeated her story? Would she be placed under arrest? Charged with murder? Manslaughter? Would they tell her how Kelly died? Would she be spending the night in a holding cell? Or would it be the first night of many nights behind bars?

Fuentes started the recorder and nodded at Deputy Hollowell. She turned her cold eyes on Nora and said, "How did you get those burn scars?"

Nora was thrown by the question. She looked to Fuentes for help, but he was busy scribbling on his notepad and didn't meet her gaze.

Seeing no other choice, Nora recited the events of that fateful night.

"Do you have a history of alcohol abuse?" Hollowell asked when Nora was done.

"No. I've always been a one-glass-of-wine-with-dinner type of drinker. I might have two drinks at a party, but only if someone else is driving."

"Did you consume alcohol before your altercation with Ms. Walsh?"

"No."

"What about when you got home?"

"I had a glass of red wine."

"That was all the alcohol you drank yesterday? One glass of wine?"

Her skeptical tone set Nora's teeth on edge.

Don't let her get under your skin. That's what she wants.

Nora said, "That's correct."

"Do you blame Ms. Walsh for your . . . disfigurement?" Hollowell flicked her eyes at Nora's pinkie finger.

Nora's dislike for this woman intensified. "I blame myself for my injuries. No one else is responsible for them. As I told Deputy Fuentes, I bore no ill-will toward Kelly. I liked her from the moment we met—"

"You mean, when you saw her with your husband?" Hollowell's pencil-line brows flew up her forehead. "You liked your husband's pregnant lover?"

"I didn't *meet* her that night. I caught a glimpse of her, that's it. I never knew Kelly's name until she introduced herself to me at the bookstore. That's the moment I'm talking about. I liked both Kelly and her son when I met them at the bookstore."

Hollowell's tone became acerbic. "You liked her so much that you struck her—a terminally ill woman. Is that correct?"

"I didn't—"

"You struck her in front of her son—a young boy you also *supposedly* liked. What were you thinking when Kelly grabbed your shirt? Here was the woman your husband chose over you, grabbing your shirt. Was this an opportunity for you? Did you dream of what you'd do to her if you ever saw her again? How you'd hurt her?"

The questions were fired with such Gatling gun speed that Nora couldn't possibly reply. At first, she was rattled, but then she realized that Hollowell wasn't interested in answers. She was trying to provoke—to incite an emotional reaction.

Nora pictured the wall of coffee mugs in the ticket agent's booth. One of those mugs featured an Oscar Wilde quote. It read, "Nothing is so aggravating as calmness."

Hollowell's lips were parted like she was getting ready to fire a new volley of taunts, but thanks to Wilde, Nora would not be goaded.

"I regret shoving Kelly," she said. "I wasn't trying to hurt her. I was only trying to get away. I've told you what happened twice now. I've answered your questions, but you haven't answered any of mine."

"We don't—" Deputy Hollowell began.

"No. I'm done." Nora folded her arms over her chest. "Either charge me with a crime or release me."

"If you think you'll get special treatment because of your relationship with the sheriff, you're wrong," snapped Hollowell.

Nora splayed her hands. "You're the one who brought up our relationship, not me."

Fuentes leaned over the recorder and announced that the interview was over.

"That's all for now," he told Nora.

Without waiting for permission, she pushed her chair back and walked out of the room. She heard the deputies following as she headed down the hall toward the lobby. When she reached the door to McCabe's office, she paused.

"He's in a meeting," said Deputy Hollowell.

Ignoring her, Nora knocked on the door.

"Come in!" McCabe called.

Opening the door, Nora saw that Hollowell was right. The ME, a middle-aged woman named Dr. Schuping, sat in one of the chairs facing McCabe's desk. When she saw Nora, she smiled.

"I was *just* thinking about you. Someone from work recommended a medical thriller and I wanted to call and see if you had it in stock, but I keep forgetting the title. I've asked my coworker twice, and I don't want to ask again, or they'll think I'm losing it." She chuckled. "I lost it a long time ago, but let's not go there. There's a girl in a nightgown on the book cover. It's blue, and I think the paperback came out pretty recently."

Nora clung to the topic of books like a lifeline. What a relief it was to picture the display table of mystery and suspense novels in her store instead of wondering if she'd inadvertently caused Kelly's death. She focused every ounce of her concentration on that book display. Most had black or red covers with white font, or white covers with blood-red font. A blue cover with a woman wearing a nightgown stood out among the rest.

"Is it *Insomnia* by Sarah Pinborough?"

Dr. Schuping slapped her thigh and cried, "You're *amazing*! Nothing wrong with your recall, that's for sure. Would you hold a copy for me?"

"Of course. Sorry to interrupt." Nora looked at McCabe. "Talk later?"

He started to stand and then checked himself. "Yes."

It was only one word, and a short one at that, but McCabe had infused it with warmth. Nora saw the concern in his eyes and knew he'd call or come to her as soon as he could. Until then, she'd have to wait to hear what had happened to Kelly Walsh.

Nora backed out of McCabe's office and closed the door. When she turned toward the lobby, Deputy Hollowell blocked her path.

"Don't leave town," she warned.

It was such a cliché that Nora almost laughed. But she was too drained to laugh, so she replied, "I won't. Everything I care about is here."

She didn't know why this woman disliked her so much, but she also knew that Hollowell would make a dangerous enemy. It was best not to provoke her.

Why did she say that I hit Kelly? Is that what she really thinks or is she lying?

It was clear that Hollowell wasn't going to step aside and let Nora pass. For a long moment, the two women stood there, coolly assessing each other. Nora wouldn't needle Deputy Hollowell, but she wasn't going to be intimidated by her either.

Fuentes put a hand under Nora's elbow and said, "I've got it from here, Hollowell."

"Suit yourself," Hollowell said with a casual air, but Nora could feel the deputy's eyes boring into her back as she and Fuentes proceeded down the hall.

When they reached the door to the lobby, Nora turned to Fuentes and said, "Am I a suspect?"

He shook his head. "You're a person of interest."

The line between those two things was often very thin, and Nora knew she had cause to worry.

Fuentes gave her arm a gentle squeeze and opened the door. It was a small gesture, but the kindness behind it meant the world to Nora.

Though her interview had taken a little more than an hour, it had felt much longer. As soon as she passed through the doorway into the lobby, she practically ran to where June and Hester were waiting.

They sprang from their chairs and reached for her. Nora let them draw her in close. She never wanted to leave the warm, safe circle of their arms.

"How bad is it?" Hester whispered.

Nora's composure broke. The tears she'd held back for the past hour raced down her cheeks. She clung to her friends like a frightened child.

"They think I had something to do with Kelly's death."

"*No!*" June hissed. "What about Grant? Isn't he going to set them straight?"

Nora's answer was a choked whisper. "What if he can't? What if I *did* kill her?"

Chapter 6

Your lawyer is always on your side. Your enemies are his enemies.

—Stephen King

June refused to drop Nora off at home.

"I'm taking you to my house. If I don't get some food in you, you're going to pass out."

"I can't eat."

Ignoring her protests, June bustled Nora into her car.

At the cozy two-bedroom house she shared with Sheldon, June led Nora into the kitchen and told her to sit down. She poured iced tea into four glasses and slid slices of bread into the toaster oven.

Sheldon materialized in the doorway and threw a puzzled glance at June. "*Buenas noches.* Am I interrupting?"

June waved him over to the counter. "Slice this banana, would you?"

"Yes, my liege."

The toaster pinged and June coaxed the slices of hot bread onto two plates. She spread peanut butter over the bread, placed the banana slices on the peanut butter, and topped the open-faced sandwiches with a drizzle of honey. After cutting the bread into triangles, she put one plate in front of Nora and the second in the center of the table.

"It'd be weird if we sat here and stared at you while you eat, so we'll join you," June said, pulling Sheldon into the chair next to hers.

Nora took a small bite of her sandwich. The salty peanut butter combined with the sweetness of the banana and honey was soothing. The scent of toast made Nora feel like a kid again. If she closed her eyes, she could picture the kitchen of her childhood home with its yellow wallpaper and checked curtains. She could hear the pop of the toaster and the crunch of the butter knife as her mother passed the blade over crispy slices of cinnamon-raisin bread. This had been Nora's favorite breakfast for years, and June's offering took her right back to that yellow kitchen.

She gave June a grateful nod and took another bite.

"Is someone going to fill me in or am I just here to cut bananas and look pretty?" demanded Sheldon.

Nora rubbed the crumbs from her fingertips and said, "Remember Kelly and Tucker? The mother and son who were in the shop on Friday looking for origami books?"

"Of course. They were so—wait. Please tell me she's okay."

Very softly, Nora said, "She died last night."

Sheldon clamped his hand over his mouth. "*Dios mío.* She went that fast?"

"You probably heard that I left Estella sitting at the diner counter, and that I left without saying goodbye." When Sheldon said that he'd heard all about it, Nora went on. "That's why Hester and June were at my place this afternoon. They were checking on me."

"Because you weren't answering your phone. And when one friend is worried, all friends get worried," said June.

"I was telling those two what happened, when Grant and Fuentes showed up at my house. They wanted to talk to me about Kelly, so they took me to the station. Fuentes interviewed me first. Then he was joined by a bulldog called Deputy Hollowell. I'm now a person of interest in their investigation."

Sheldon frowned. "Investigation?"

"Into Kelly's death."

"*What?*"

While Nora filled him in, Sheldon rhythmically stroked his silver mustache. By the time she reached the end of her narrative, he was shaking his head in dismay.

"This is crazy. Kelly. Your ex. The flowers." He passed his hands over his face. "Wait. Why did Grant haul you to the station? He knows you didn't hurt anyone."

Hester said, "He has to play by the rules."

Sheldon stared at Nora, his dark eyes swimming with concern. "Do you need a lawyer?"

June snapped her fingers. "I know *exactly* who you should talk to. Davis Godwin. He's in my knitting circle."

"Are you serious?" Sheldon smirked. "The world's sexiest knitter is a lawyer?"

Everyone at the table knew about Davis Godwin because June had been singing his praises for the past two months. She'd repeatedly told her friends about the devilishly handsome and incredibly charming forty-five-year-old man who'd joined her Wednesday night knitting circle. They'd heard how he'd never held a knitting needle before but took to it like a duck to water. They'd heard that Davis was smart, funny, and always impeccably dressed. He'd joined the knitting circle to relax. He'd tried yoga, meditation, jigsaw puzzles, and bonsai gardening, but none of those activities had lowered his stress levels.

However, the rhythmic motion of knitting had loosened something inside of him. He finished his first project, the obligatory scarf, in record time. He started a new project, a doggie sweater, right away. Two weeks ago, he'd rented a passenger van to take the knitting circle to their favorite yarn store,

Friends and Fiberworks. He'd also treated the group to lunch at Doc Brown's BBQ.

June had gushed about this man at every book club meeting, but she was clearly gearing up to gush over him some more. "Did I mention that he looks like a middle-aged version of that beautiful man from *Bridgerton*?"

Sheldon scowled. "Like two hundred times. But Nora doesn't need a sweater-making, cravat-wearing dandy. She needs a gladiator in a suit."

"Davis is stressed because he always has a full caseload. He has a full caseload because *everyone* wants him to be their lawyer, which is why I want Nora to talk to him."

Nora rested her hand on June's. "Thanks for looking out for me, but I'm done talking tonight. I just want to go home."

Two hours later, Nora was in bed. She'd taken a very long shower, put her pajamas on, and climbed into bed. She opened her book and tried to read, but there was no room in her head for words. She kept revisiting the moment when she pushed Kelly, and every time she pressed rewind, the same questions accompanied the playback.

What happened after I drove away?

Did she fall?

Am I responsible for her death?

The one person who could end her torturous speculation was McCabe, but as the night wore on and the silence of her tiny house closed around her, she began to doubt that she'd hear from him.

Nora rolled onto her side and glared at her phone, which was charging on the nightstand. Why didn't the damn thing ring? Why didn't the screen light up with a text?

"Why aren't you calling me?" she whispered into the dark.

She was in a twilight sleep when her phone finally rang. Her book was splayed open on her chest, the pages folded like the bellows of an accordion, and when she jerked in surprise, the book flapped like a startled goose and dropped to the floor.

Grabbing the phone, she murmured a hello.

"Did I wake you?" McCabe asked.

"Yes. No. I don't know," she stammered. "I guess I dozed off."

Nora picked up the book and tried to smooth its pages, but they refused to go flat. The folds had left deep creases, like premature wrinkles on a young person's brow.

"I'm sorry about today," McCabe said, sounding contrite. "I really am. I've never dealt with a situation like this before."

"You mean, you've never dated a suspect before?"

McCabe grunted. "A person of interest."

"From my perspective, they're the same thing. Especially when no one will tell me how Kelly died. You have to tell me, Grant. Did I kill her?"

Her question was met by silence. Nora kept smoothing the creased pages like she was running an iron over rumpled fabric.

The seconds continued to tick by. When McCabe still didn't speak, Nora's anger sparked.

"How can I wake up and function tomorrow without knowing what happened? How am I supposed to talk to customers or do errands around town? How can I look anyone in the eye? If I killed another human being, I need to know about it! It's wrong to leave me in the dark. Damn it, Grant. It's more than wrong. It's cruel."

A sigh feathered through her speaker, and McCabe finally gave in. "Kelly didn't fall. She was upset that you pushed her, but she wasn't physically hurt by that push."

The boulder that had been sitting in the center of Nora's chest rolled off, and she let out a choking noise that was halfway between a gasp and a sob.

"Thank God. I was so scared that I'd . . ." Her breath hitched and she was unable to speak.

McCabe remained silent.

Eventually, when she was calmer, Nora said, "I'm sorry that she's gone. I feel horrible for her family. Especially Tucker."

McCabe responded with a vague, "Hmm."

That's when the truth hit Nora like a hammer.

"I'm still a suspect, aren't I? I didn't hurt her, but there's more to this than you're telling me. Which means she must've died later—after I pushed her. No one can vouch for my whereabouts until I was seen at the flea market. I have no alibi for that huge chunk of time."

"I wish I hadn't been on call."

Nora let out a humorless laugh. "Yeah. Spending the night in bed with the sheriff would've made a handy alibi. What else can you tell me?"

"Nothing. I shouldn't even be talking to you now." After a pause, he said, "I know you didn't do this, but I'm an elected official. Plenty of people would like to see someone else sitting behind my desk. If I screw up, I could lose the next election. And believe me, Nora, you're *way* more important than my career, but the best way for me to protect you is to make sure my team solves this quickly, and by the book."

"And in the meantime, we can't communicate."

McCabe's reply was a mournful, "No."

After they said good-bye, they'd have to act like strangers. For the sake of appearances, they needed to behave as if they didn't love each other. They'd have to pack their true feelings away until it was safe to let them out again.

That's not how love works, thought Nora.

Love was like a fire. It needed constant tending. It needed oxygen and fuel. Without these, it would lose heat. Its light would grow smaller and smaller until it was nothing but embers in ash. Eventually, there would be only the memory of flames.

"Things will probably get worse before they get better," McCabe said. "But I need you to listen to me now. I love you. I trust you. I'm in your corner. No matter what it seems like, or what you hear, I'm with you. If you doubt anything in the upcoming days, don't doubt how I feel about you. Don't forget, okay? I love you, I trust you, and I'm in your corner."

McCabe's words loosened the knot of fear in Nora's chest. "I know you'll do what's right. I believe in you, Grant, and I love you too."

After wishing him a good night, she hung up.

Nora woke up long before her alarm was set to go off and shuffled into the kitchen to start the coffee. Even though she'd read that storing coffee grounds in the freezer didn't keep them any fresher than storing them in a cupboard, she did it anyway. The bag of coffee was wedged between a pint of ice cream and a bag of frozen blueberries.

"Since I'm up," she said, reaching for the berries.

An hour later, the air inside her tiny house was filled by the scent of baking muffins. Nora had filled the muffin tins to the top, yielding two-dozen oversized muffins. After sprinkling their golden domes with sanding sugar, she packed them in a box and set off for the shop.

Outside, the weather couldn't have been more Monday-ish. An early morning downpour had painted shadows on the ground and left the sky a dull battleship gray. The birds were quiet, and the parking lot was mostly empty.

Entering the store, Nora switched lights on but opted for silence instead of music. She walked among the books, straightened shelves, and carried strays to their proper places.

Her life was messy right now, and there wasn't much she could do about that. She could restore order in her store, however, and it was incredibly therapeutic to alphabetize, fill inventory holes, and line up spines.

Touching the book covers suddenly reminded her of one of her elementary school teachers. Mrs. Preston used to pat the head of each student as they entered her classroom. She'd smile, look every boy or girl in the eye, and wish them a good morning. At the time, it seemed like such a small, insignificant thing, but Nora remembered how special it had made her feel. She touched the books with the same tenderness and warmth.

Sheldon arrived at ten to find the coffee brewed and the pastry case loaded with muffins.

He dropped two loaves of his homemade Cuban bread on the counter and opened his arms. "Come here, *mi reina.*"

Nora moved into his embrace and breathed in his familiar scent of aftershave and peppermint gum. He wrapped his arms around her and squeezed.

When he released her, he said, "Your man didn't make it all better, did he?"

"Not yet, but he will."

Sheldon chucked her under the chin. "That's right. In the meantime, be a busy bee. You can start by showing me the flea market goodies."

Unlike most people, Sheldon loved Mondays. Only the worst flare-ups could prevent him from coming in to clean, price, and arrange the shelf enhancers Nora found at the flea market or from area tag sales. He loved pricing the items and had a decorator's eye when it came to displaying them with certain books. The idea was to lure a customer over to the shelf enhancer while simultaneously drawing their attention to a new hardcover, a stack of vintage paperbacks, or one of the rare editions Nora kept on a high shelf behind the checkout counter. She'd recently started carrying books with sprayed or stenciled edges, and they'd been so popular with the young adult crowd that Sheldon wanted her to order more.

After pouring coffee into a mug with a cartoon Ruth Bader Ginsburg face and the text, THE NOTORIOUS RBG, Nora went through her emails. There were several newsletters from publishers announcing upcoming releases, and Nora was inspired to order several titles. Next, she took care of special orders and phoned customers to let them know that the book they'd wanted was available for pickup.

Nora rarely finished a task without interruption, but such was the nature of retail. From the moment she unlocked the front door, people entered the store. Nora was always happy to hear the sleigh bells ring because she was always happy to have customers. She'd much rather put a good book in someone's hand than focus on computer work.

"Your muffins are going fast," Sheldon told her as she washed her coffee mug. "Will this be a new Monday thing?"

"Maybe. I only made them because I got up too early."

Sheldon poured milk into the frothing pitcher. "We're all insomniacs. I watch bad TV, June knits and goes on long romantic walks with a herd of stray cats, and now, you're going to bake muffins. We're such multitaskers."

"A new breed of zombies."

As Sheldon poured the steamed milk, he created a heart in the latte foam. When he was done, he whispered, "Take this to the couple in the Readers' Circle. She has a cute pixie cut and is wearing a purple top. Her hubby is going for hobo chic. Without the chic. He's been out of work for six months and she thought he might find a book or two to help get him back in the saddle. But he won't even put his phone down.

"I'll see what I can do."

Nora popped two muffins on a plate and picked up the mug. She served the latte to the woman in purple, who smiled in delight at the sight of the heart. Her husband was dressed in a tan T-shirt peppered with holes in the sleeves and light-wash jeans with frayed hems. He was overdue for a shave and a haircut, but those were easy fixes. His flat gaze and listless expression were more concerning.

"I was wondering if you'd be willing to sample a muffin," Nora said, perching on the edge of the chair next to the man. "I'm thinking of serving them on Mondays when the bakery's closed, but I'm not sure if they're good enough. I could use an honest opinion."

Seeing the muffin, the man showed a tiny spark of life. "Sure."

"What a nice treat," said the woman.

When Nora asked them if they lived in the area, the woman explained that they were from Asheville but were housesitting for a relative.

"My sister has a lovely house with a big deck and a hot tub, so it feels like we're on a mini vacation."

"Because we can't afford a real vacation, you mean," the man grumbled.

The woman shook her head. "That's not what I meant, Wyatt. A change of scenery is a good thing, and I've always loved this town."

"I can't remember the last time I took a vacation," Nora said, addressing Wyatt. "Trips are expensive."

He stared at his half-eaten muffin. "Especially when you don't have a job to pay for them."

"That makes it hard to enjoy lots of things," she agreed. "How long have you been looking for work?"

"Over six months."

Nora nodded. "There've been plenty of layoffs around here. So many, in fact, that a career coach gave a talk in the community center a few weeks ago. A friend of mine went and took notes. Would you like to hear some of the key points?"

The woman watched her husband with a mix of apprehension and hope. When he muttered, "I don't know," she visibly sagged.

"Why don't you walk with me to the stockroom? You can eat your muffin while I talk. I have a feeling you're a good listener."

"Go on, Wyatt," the woman prodded.

He sighed. "If it'll make you happy, Carol, I'll go."

Nora led Wyatt to the stockroom and told him to pull up a stool. She started unpacking books from boxes marked with the HarperCollins logo.

Without looking at Wyatt, she said, "It's got to wear you down. Not just the job search but worrying about your finances and wondering about your future too."

From the corner of her eye, she saw Wyatt nod.

"People are funny. We can get stuck feeling a certain way, even when we don't want to. We forget how to be anything other than down and defeated because feeling like that becomes a habit. Habits are hard to break. Something has to come along and kick us in the ass."

She shot a glance at Wyatt. He was chewing his muffin and staring at the bookcase on the back wall, but she could tell that he was listening.

"One of the things I love about books is how they make us feel less alone. Plenty of people have been fired, quit, changed careers, or spent too many years doing a job they hate, and I guarantee you that someone has a story like yours. It might help you to read other stories — to see what choices they made or how they learned from their mistakes."

Wyatt grunted.

"I have a list of titles for you to look over. I know you probably don't want to drop a hundred dollars on books, but I have used copies of most of them. Or you could just read them here. You can stay and read for as long as you'd like."

She winked at Wyatt before turning her attention to another box.

"What kind of books are they? Self-help mumbo-jumbo?"

"They're a mix of fiction and nonfiction. One's actually a graphic novel."

Wyatt looked suspicious. "What's that?"

"It's like a comic book for grown-ups. The title is *The Adventures of Unemployed Man*. It'll make you laugh."

"O-kay. What else?"

Nora stopped what she was doing and faced him. "One of the nonfiction books is called *Knock 'Em Dead Job Interview: How to Turn Job Interviews into Job Offers*."

A glimmer of interest appeared in Wyatt's eyes. "I'd look at that one."

"Excellent. I'll bring you back to Carol and round up the books for you."

Wyatt stood up and said, "This muffin's good. You should keep making them."

Nora smiled and led him out of the stockroom.

Other than a brief break for lunch, Wyatt spent most of the day in the bookstore. Carol left before noon and returned to collect her husband around four. When she walked in, the shop was full of high school kids and Nora was busy making drinks and Nutella on toast.

Carol apologized to the kid at the front of the line and then stepped inside the ticket agent's booth to present Nora with a bouquet of pink peonies.

"I just wanted to say thank you. For the first time in months, Wyatt feels hopeful. Neither of us expect anything to change overnight, but it's a start."

Later, when the line died down, Nora put the peonies in a white pitcher and placed the flowers on the checkout counter. As she looked at them, she thought about Estella and her father and wondered how they were doing.

Estella had been preparing for her father's release for weeks. She'd cleaned out the guest room and painted the walls a soothing shade of pale green. She'd bought new bedding and a small TV. Jack had stocked her freezer with meals, Hester had baked fresh bread and a cinnamon coffee cake, June had knitted a throw blanket, and Nora had provided a Miracle Books gift card so that Gus could pursue his love of reading.

When six o'clock rolled around, two people were still browsing. Nora never rushed her customers, but today, she wanted them to hurry up and leave. Now that the day was over and she was no longer busy, yesterday's stress had returned with a vengeance.

Finally, one of the customers approached the counter carrying Michael Connelly's *The Concrete Blonde* and said, "A friend of mine told me this was good. Have you read it?"

"I've read the whole series. Harry Bosch is one of my favorite detectives."

Satisfied, the woman paid for the book and headed for the door. As she reached for the handle, a man in a Nile blue suit opened the door from the outside and held it for her.

"Good evening," he said, flashing her a brilliant smile. He waited for her to exit before closing the door and smiling at Nora.

"Ms. Pennington? I'm Davis Godwin. June told me to see you before you left for the night, so here I am." He gestured at the stacks. "Any more customers back there?"

Before Nora could answer, the last customer rounded the corner of the Fiction section, a phone pressed to his ear, and hurried out of the shop.

Nora flipped the window sign from OPEN to CLOSED and turned to Davis. She tried not to stare, but he was so good-looking that it was hard not to. He was powerfully built with the shoulders and hands of a football player. His skin was the color of brown cashmere, and he wore his black hair in a low fade with a part to one side. Nora didn't think she'd ever seen such a well-tailored suit.

"Did June tell you what happened?" she asked.

"All she said was that you might be in trouble. Are you?"

Nora said, "I don't know. Would you like to sit down while I explain?"

"I would."

Unsure of how to start, Nora waited until they were seated before saying, "A woman died yesterday. On Saturday night, she and I had—I don't know what to call it—an argument? A heated encounter? Anyway, the sheriff's department questioned me, and after they were done, I learned that I'm a person of interest in their investigation."

"You'd better start from the beginning," Davis said, settling deeper into his chair.

Once again, Nora repeated her story. When she was finished, Davis studied her carefully.

"Is that everything? Do I now know all there is to know?"

"From my point of view, yes." Nora searched his face. "Am I in trouble?"

Davis looked thoughtful. "Legally? Not yet. I need to find out how Ms. Walsh died. Once I know that, I'll have a better idea of how to advise you. Until then, stay clear of her family. You might be tempted to stop by with a casserole and a condolence card, but don't. Give me your number. I'll call when I have more information."

He typed his passcode into his phone and handed it to her.

Nora hesitated. "I don't know if I can afford an attorney."

"Let's see if you need one first. Tonight, we're just two people talking, and that won't cost you a cent." He smiled. "I'll show myself out. Talk soon."

After Davis left, Nora locked the door and thought of how he'd told her to stay away from Kelly's family. She wanted to tell them how sorry she was but didn't know how. A food offering would fall way short, they didn't need flowers, and she couldn't show up at Tea Flowers in person. All she could do was write a note—something honest and heartfelt—but even that felt insufficient.

What comfort could her words give them? A few sentences on paper would hardly lessen their grief. In fact, a message from Nora might make them feel worse. She would always be the woman who'd pushed Kelly the night she died. She was the woman who'd yelled at her. Who'd refused to listen to her.

Feeling miserable, Nora completed her closing duties and trudged home. When she reached her moped, she stopped to take the origami flower out of the cargo compartment. Relieved to find the lily and the little bee hiding under its petals unharmed, she carried her treasure into her house and placed it on her nightstand.

When she got in bed to read later that night, she felt the quiet presence of the paper sculpture.

Later, after switching off the lamp, she stared at the delicate flower and thought of the little boy who'd made it. She imagined his fingers folding the paper, again and again—turning and flipping and creasing until the flat, lifeless sheet became art. What Tucker did was a kind of magic.

Nora wished she could perform magic too. If she could, she'd wave a wand and give Tucker the thing he wanted most.

She would give him his mother.

Chapter 7

*Time lost can never be recovered . . . and this should
be written in flaming letters everywhere.*

—Erik Larson

The next morning, Nora walked to the Gingerbread House
and knocked three times on the back door.

After Hester had opened the door and pulled Nora inside,
she whispered, "Estella and her dad are here. I told them you'd
be stopping by to get your pastries, but I wanted to give you a
heads-up."

The unmistakable aroma of cinnamon buns wafted through
the air and Nora inhaled a greedy lungful. Though she'd had no
appetite at breakfast time, she was suddenly hungry, and her
stomach betrayed the fact with a loud gurgle.

"I heard that!" Hester giggled. "Good thing I overcooked a
whole tray of cinnamon buns. You can eat one here and bring a
few extras to work for Sheldon."

Nora trailed Hester into the kitchen, where Estella and a
bald man with a neatly trimmed white beard were perched on
stools facing the prep table. Seeing Nora, Estella hopped down
from her stool and put her arms around her friend.

"June and Hester told me everything. I'm so sorry," she
murmured into Nora's ear. "I wish I'd come outside that night.

If I'd been there, I could've told McCabe what really happened."

Nora didn't want to talk about Kelly in front of Estella's father, so she gently detached herself and said, "It's okay. Really. McCabe will straighten it out."

Estella gestured at her father. "Dad, this is Nora."

Gus Sadler got to his feet and shook Nora's outstretched hand. "I've heard so much about you. I feel like I've known you, June, and this little lady for years."

He gave Hester a shy grin before returning to his seat.

Gus had a low, husky voice. He looked a bit like Patrick Stewart but with a thicker neck and darker brows and lashes. His skin spoke of a hard life. His forehead was etched with deep lines and his cheeks and hands were marred by a dozen small scars. His arms, sinewy and strong, were covered with tattoos.

Nora's eyes took in the Alice in Wonderland tattoo sleeve on his right arm. It began at the wrist with an elaborate pocket watch surrounded by flowers. His biceps featured Alice perched on a mushroom cap. Alice bore a striking resemblance to a younger Estella, and she smiled happily as she stroked a sleeping Cheshire cat. Cursive writing curled around Alice's head and disappeared under the sleeve of Gus's shirt.

Seeing Nora's interest, Gus said, "You can't see all of the letters because of my shirt, but it says, 'You might do something better with the time.'"

"Is that from the book?"

Gus nodded. "It's a reminder to me to never waste a minute. That's why the pocket watch doesn't have an hour hand. It's all about the minutes. Each one matters."

That's how Kelly must have felt. She had so little time left. Every moment was a treasure.

"Whoever tattooed this was really talented," she told Gus.

"Yes, he was. His other talent was robbing convenience stores."

Estella tapped her stool and said, "Take my seat, Nora. Hester already stuffed us with cinnamon rolls, so it's your turn. After you eat, I was hoping we could come with you to the bookstore. The gift card you gave Dad is burning a hole in his pocket."

As always, Nora was happy to steer the conversation to books.

"What do you like to read, Mr. Sadler?"

"Call me Gus. Only lawyers and judges call me Mr. Sadler." He gave Nora the same reserved, bashful smile he'd given Hester earlier. It was as if the expression didn't come naturally, which this didn't surprise Nora. A smile in prison was probably a rare thing.

Gus glanced at the ceiling as he contemplated Nora's question. "What do I like to read? Almost everything, I guess. I like fiction the most. For nonfiction, I stick with biographies and history. Oh, and cookbooks. I checked out all the cookbooks from our library a bunch of times. I used to write down the recipes I wanted to make when I got out. Estella's been such an angel, and I aim to cook for her as much as she'll let me."

"Aren't I the luckiest woman alive?" Estella asked her friends. "I now have *two* men making meals for me. Daddy— sorry—*Dad* wants pop in hit the grocery store right after he stocks up on books. I thought he'd take a few days to adjust, but this man wants to hit the ground running. Like he said, he doesn't want to waste a minute."

Gus beamed at her. "I've waited a long time to do things with you, baby girl. We could sit around watching paint dry and I'd still be a happy man."

"I think we can set the bar a little higher than that. Hester, my dad might be able to fix the display case that's been giving you trouble. Do you want to show it to him while I catch up with Nora?"

After plating a cinnamon bun for Nora, Hester led Gus to the front of the shop.

"*This* is overcooked?" Nora asked, turning the warm, soft pastry over to examine its golden-brown bottom.

"Didn't taste overcooked to me, but Hester could cover an eraser with icing and I'd probably eat it. I don't know what's come over me. I've never had much of a sweet tooth, but I've been craving sugar all week. Why don't my hormones want kale?"

Nora took a bite of the bun and moaned. "Kale doesn't make you feel like a choir of angels is singing in your mouth."

"You definitely need a dose of comfort food. I can't even imagine what you've been through since we had dinner together." Estella shook her head. "I wish I'd never told you the Walshes were there. And I hate that you can't talk to McCabe. You can talk to me or Hester or June, but I know it's not the same."

"Speaking of talking, Davis Godwin stopped by the bookstore last night. He's going to try to find out how Kelly died."

Estella scooted her stool closer. "Is he really all that and a bag of chips?"

"He totally is, and I'm glad June sent him my way. At least, I have someone to call if things get worse. And things can get worse. The new K9 deputy, Hollowell, has me seriously worried. She's gunning for me, but I have no idea why. I've never met the woman before she came into the interview room. She grilled me like I was Lizzie Borden."

"Are you talking about Deputy Hollowell? She's a piece of work," Hester grumbled as she returned to the kitchen.

Nora eyed her curiously. "Have you met her?"

"Oh, I've met her, all right. She comes in twice a week to buy donuts or cookies to take to the station. The last time she was in, she said, 'What do guys like the most?' as if the women she works with don't matter. Both times, she went out of her way to mention little details about Jasper—like she knows him better than me just because they both work for the sheriff's department. She asks too many probing, personal questions too. I mean, it's not like we're friends. Why does she want to know when Jasper and I started dating or if I've met his parents? I don't like her one bit, and I don't trust her either. She's bad vibes in a uniform."

Estella drummed her nails on the table. "I have her down for a cut on Wednesday. If she tries to fish for info on the men in my life, she'll end up with a mullet."

"She might not be her passive/aggressive self with you. I'm in a relationship with one of her coworkers and Nora's dating her boss. For whatever reason, she sees us as competition."

Crossing her arms over her chest, Estella said, "Honey, she probably sees *all* women as competition. I know her kind. She'll belittle or vilify another woman to make herself look better, but she won't *feel* better. I bet she doesn't have any female friends but secretly wants nothing more than to be part of a girl gang. So, I'll try to be her friend while she's in my chair. Maybe she'll come round."

"If not, there's always the mullet option," joked Nora.

The door chime rang. Hester smoothed her apron and said, "Time to serve the donuts."

It didn't take long for Nora to polish off the rest of her cinnamon bun. As she rinsed her sticky hands in the sink, Estella and Gus loaded their arms with boxes containing the book pockets and peach muffins. On the short walk to the bookstore, Nora told Gus about buying the former train station and converting a retired caboose into a tiny house.

"When I was a kid, I wanted to be a conductor. Now I'll take any job I can get and count myself lucky," Gus said.

The comment made Nora think of Wyatt, the customer who'd been out of work for six months.

After sharing Wyatt's story with Gus, Nora said, "I'll show you the books I showed him. Maybe one of them will help."

Gus looked apprehensive. "I haven't had a job interview in thirty years. How am I going to convince someone to hire me?"

"By getting them to see how much you learned while you were away," said Estella. "Any employer would be lucky to have someone as motivated and disciplined as you."

Gus shot her a sidelong glance. "You might be a little biased, darlin'."

Nora smiled at him. "Do you have a dream job? Other than driving a train?"

"I just want to earn enough to live a simple, quiet life and to spend time with my girl. I don't care if I'm emptying trash or flipping burgers. I just want somebody to give me a chance."

That's what we all want, Nora thought as she unlocked the delivery door and held it open for her guests.

For the next hour, Gus flipped through books on résumé writing, interviewing, and finding job listings online.

At one point, Nora overheard him talking to Estella about how complicated the process had become in the past two decades.

"Used to be, you'd find jobs in the paper. Then you'd call for an interview and after a little chat with the boss, you'd get hired or you wouldn't. According to this book, I need to jump through a hundred hoops before I can sit down and talk to a real person."

"Folks still find work by word-of-mouth, Dad. Someone will know someone who needs a cook or a dishwasher or whatever. There are plenty of restaurants, grocery stores, and hotels around here. When we get back home, we'll look online."

Gus grunted. "I wish I knew more guys who'd gotten out before me and found work. Way too many of them ended up back inside. You don't hear from the ones who turned their lives around. They want to forget the past and keep their eyes on the road ahead, and I don't blame them. If I saw a guy on the street from my old cellblock, I wouldn't say hello. I'd keep right on walking."

When Sheldon arrived, he brewed a cup of Cuban coffee for Gus and a cup of tea for Estella. By the time Gus used his gift card to purchase a stack of used paperbacks, the trolley from the Lodge had arrived and the shop was filling up with customers.

Estella eyed each visitor with suspicion.

"It makes no sense that someone from Miracle Springs would want to kill Kelly," she whispered to Nora. "She was a stranger to most of us. Whoever did it must be from out of town. Where did she and your ex live before she came here?"

"No idea. I never looked them up online. I know absolutely nothing about their lives."

"Maybe it's time you knew. What if your ex is involved in Kelly's death? The husband is always the prime suspect. Why isn't *he* being hauled in for questioning?"

Nora pressed her fingers to the back of her neck. A headache had sprouted at the base of her skull and was slowly fanning upward. "I don't want to think about him."

"This is your worst nightmare, I know. But isn't it better to know what's going on than to stick your head in the sand? Don't you want to avoid more surprises?" Estella curled her fingers around Nora's wrist. "If our roles were reversed, you'd tell me to arm myself with information. You'd remind me that knowledge is power and that I'm brave enough to face any challenge. Well, that's what I'm telling you to do."

Glancing at her laptop, Nora thought of all the information she didn't want to see. The photos. The status updates. The wedding and birth announcements. Anniversaries. Holiday posts.

But Estella was right. She'd been blindsided by Kelly's death, and she didn't want to be caught unawares like that again.

However, she wasn't about to exhume her past in front of an audience. It would have to wait until she was safe at home.

Opening a gateway to the past required privacy, as well as copious amounts of chocolate and wine.

Looking at Estella, she said, "I hear you. I'll learn as much as I can tonight."

Estella and Gus left, and Nora was so busy taking care of customers that she was able to forget the outside world for large chunks of time. Overcast days always drove people into the downtown shops, and once inside Miracle Books, they were rarely in a hurry to leave.

A woman carrying a stack of books told Nora, "My husband came here for physical therapy. I'm here for retail therapy."

Another customer staked a claim to the mustard-yellow chair in the Readers' Circle and spent the next four hours reading and drinking cappuccinos. When Nora stopped by to ask if he needed any help, he replied, "I have everything I need. Books, coffee, and a comfy chair. This place is a bibliovert's paradise."

Nora had never heard this term before but instantly loved it. Sheldon did too.

"We need to put that on a mug," he said. "And while I'm online ordering custom mugs, *you* should be shopping for a car. I need you to buy more shelf enhancers on the weekends so that my Mondays are even more exciting. I mean, you can't tote stuff in the rain and snow anymore. You've got to take care of yourself, *mija*."

Nora had completely forgotten about buying a car, but when the shop traffic slowed down between five and six, she pulled up the website for the local paper and clicked on the classified section. The ad for the used Ford Escape was still there.

While she was trying to decide if this was a good time to make the owner an offer, her phone rang.

"Miracle Books. This is Nora."

"Hi, Nora, it's Davis Godwin. I have some news, and I'd like to tell it to you in person. Any chance you can meet me at the Oasis after work?"

The location threw Nora for a loop. She was surprised that Davis wanted to talk about Kelly's death at a bar, but since he held all the cards, she readily agreed.

The Miracle Springs Lodge had several restaurants and bars, and the Oasis was Nora's favorite. She loved its tropical vibe. It had teak tables, wicker chairs with upholstered seats, potted palms draped with white lights, colorful paper lanterns, and music that could transport its patrons to a Caribbean beach café. All the drinks came with little umbrellas and pineapple stirrers.

Though the bar's dress code was casual, Nora was the only person wearing jeans. The other guests were country club chic in floral dresses, linen pants, and collared shirts. Davis, of course, wore another impeccably tailored suit.

After beckoning Nora over to his table, he pulled out a chair for her.

"I hope you're hungry because I ordered snacks." He gestured at the plates in the center of the table. "Haitian chicken empanadas, jerk shrimp, veggie kabobs, and sweet potato chips. There's a pitcher of mojitos on the way, but if mojitos aren't your thing, tell me what you'd like, and I'll get it."

"I love mojitos. This is—wow."

"Nah, it's just what happens when I'm hungry and someone hands me a menu. Lunch was a *long* time ago and there's nothing at my house except a few slices of petrified pizza."

A server arrived with a pitcher of mojitos and two glasses loaded with ice cubes and fresh mint.

"Should I go ahead and pour for you, sugar?" The server batted her eyes at Davis. "I wouldn't want you to spill on that nice suit."

"Thank you kindly."

After she'd finished pouring and returned to the bar, Davis

raised his glass and said, "There are good ships, and there are wood ships, the ships that sail the sea. But the best ships are friendships, and may they always be!"

Hoping that Davis's cheerful demeanor meant he had good news to share, Nora smiled and took a refreshing sip.

"Happy hour is the best hour of the day." Davis picked up the plate of empanadas and handed it to Nora. "Let's get some food in before I start talking."

It felt strange to be sharing a meal with a man Nora barely knew, especially since the last time she'd eaten at the Oasis, she'd been with McCabe.

This isn't a date.

But it wasn't exactly a professional meeting either. How many lawyers discussed a case with their client over mojitos? Then again, how many clients had a lawyer with enough magnetism to give Rick Castle or James Bond a run for their money?

He's not your lawyer yet, she reminded herself.

While they sampled food from every dish, Davis asked Nora what it was like to run a bookstore.

"I wouldn't want to do anything else," she replied. "It'll never make me rich, but nothing else could make me happier. What about you?"

He grinned. "I like money *and* happiness. I wish I was into reading for pleasure, but it's not my jam. I deal with words on paper all day, so in my downtime, I want to focus on things without words. Knitting's great, but a man can only make so many scarves and sweaters. I'm always on the lookout for a new hobby."

Nora thought about the paper lily pad sitting on her nightstand.

"If you like to keep your hands busy, you could try origami."

"Origami. That's Tucker Walsh's thing, isn't it?"

Heat crept up Nora's cheeks. "Yes. Do you know how he's doing?"

Davis laid his utensils down. "You know how he's doing. The kid just lost his mom. I can tell that you want to do something to make him feel better. You'd probably bring him a whole box of origami books if you could, or put together meals for Kelly's family, or find a way to support their business, but you can't. You need to keep your distance."

"Would you please tell me what you know?"

"Alright. For starters, Kelly Walsh didn't die because you pushed her. She had stage four cervical cancer and had three months left to live—best case scenario. But cancer didn't kill her either. Lack of oxygen did."

Nora stared at him. "She suffocated?"

"The official medical ruling is death by asphyxiation. There was bruising to the front of her throat. It's looking like someone came up from behind and used an arm or a hard object to cut off her blood flow at the neck. Have you ever watched a pro wrestling match?"

"No."

Davis said, "I take my nephews at least once a year, so I'm down with my wrestling terms. Do you know what a sleeper hold is?"

"A chokehold?"

He seesawed his head. "Yeah, but there are different kinds of chokeholds. For example, if you were an angry drunk and a bouncer thought you might harm yourself or others, he might grab you from behind with his Popeye forearm and squeeze. His goal would be to reduce the blood flow to your brain, lower your blood pressure, and force you to lose consciousness. The hold shouldn't last more than five seconds or so. If done correctly, the sleeper hold leaves no damage other than some tenderness to the throat."

An image of Kelly's thin, pale neck appeared in Nora's mind. "And if done incorrectly?"

"Anything from permanent injury to the throat to concussions, retina hemorrhage, loss of brain function, stroke, and in extreme circumstances, death."

"Is that what happened to Kelly?"

Davis splayed his hands. "I don't have access to the autopsy report—only the final ruling."

Nora imagined someone creeping up behind Kelly and cutting off her air supply. She must have been terrified, but Nora doubted she would've surrendered easily. She could see Kelly twisting her body, desperately trying to escape her assailant's hold. She probably clawed and kicked, fighting until the darkness closed in around her. For her son's sake, she would have called upon the last of her strength. But it wouldn't have been enough.

"Didn't the killer leave evidence? Skin under Kelly's nails? A strand of hair? Fibers from clothes?"

"I hope so. Because you're not off the hook. Not by a long shot. Kelly lived with her brother and sister-in-law in their house on Maple Street. The sister-in-law says that she was watching TV in bed when she heard noises coming from the backyard. When she opened her window, she saw Kelly standing on the patio, talking to a woman out on the lawn. According to Val, this woman was a brunette with shoulder-length hair. Her face was in shadow, but she held a helmet in her hand. Val thinks it was you."

"I wasn't on anyone's lawn that night. I drove home from the diner and didn't leave again until I went to the flea market the next morning. Did Val see this woman attack her sister?"

"No. She went downstairs to ask Kelly about her late-night visitor, but Kelly said the woman was looking for a lost cat and wanted permission to walk through the woods. Val didn't believe the story, but let it go. Later that night, she heard Kelly moving around in the kitchen. Then she heard the sound of a door closing. That must've been Kelly leaving, though no one knows why she went out or where she was going. Her body was found in between the parking lot of the Inn of Mist and Roses and the delivery entrance of the gift store on the property."

"Red Bird Gallery and Gifts. I know the owners of the inn and the gift shop. All three live on the property. Did they see or hear anything?"

Davis shook his head. "Nothing. Kelly was found early Sunday morning by a man walking his dog."

Nora's eyes welled up. Someone had killed Kelly and then dumped her body on the ground like a bag of trash.

There was no more delaying the question she'd been avoiding since she'd first heard of Kelly's death.

"Why was she living with Val and Kirk? Where's her husband?"

"In Vegas. With his girlfriend."

Their server appeared and began clearing their plates. Sensing the tension at the table, she stacked the dishes and hurried away without asking if they'd like another round of drinks.

"He and Kelly—they were divorced?"

Davis stared at her. "You really don't know about your ex, do you? He and Kelly got divorced seven years ago. Lawrence hasn't gone back to the altar since, but he's dated a string of women and has at least one other kid."

"Jesus," Nora whispered.

Had Lawrence cheated on Kelly too? Was their divorce amicable or full of animosity? Was he close to Tucker? Was he a good father? Or was he too busy jetting around the world with his latest fling?

As long as he's not in Miracle Springs, who cares?

Returning her attention to her own circumstances, Nora said, "Am I the only suspect? Or are there others?"

"I couldn't tell you. At this point, you know everything that I know. The most damning evidence against you is Deputy Hollowell's statement that you hit Kelly, and Val's statement that you showed up at their house at eleven at night."

"But neither of those are true."

After pulling out his wallet and signaling their server, Davis said, "The truth can be tainted by perception. There are people who believe that you threatened Kelly. However, the only undeniable facts are these." As he spoke, he ticked them off on his fingers. "Your marriage ended because your husband left you for Kelly. You yelled at Kelly outside the diner. You shoved her. As far as the investigation goes, those are the most pertinent facts in connection with you. The court of public opinion is a whole different ballgame."

"If the sheriff's department doesn't find the real killer, people will assume I was responsible. Even if I don't get arrested, I'll lose friends and customers for something I didn't do."

"You've probably heard that crime has a ripple effect, but a murder investigation doesn't ripple. It creates a damn riptide. Innocent people are pulled under. They get dragged miles away from safety. Some make it through with a few cuts and bruises. Others drown." Davis reached for her hand. "You're going to need lots of support in the days ahead, so lean on your friends. Ask for help. And call me whenever you have a question or you're feeling anxious. I'll do what I can to ease your mind."

Nora was touched by his kindness. He'd told her what he knew, paid for dinner, and offered her advice without asking for anything in return.

June was right. Davis Godwin is an incredible person.

As she drove home, she looked at the glowing windows of the houses and thought about how many of her neighbors were regulars at Miracle Books. She knew all of them by name. She knew what they liked to read. While serving them coffee or hunting for the perfect book, they'd tell her stories about their work and family life. They'd confess their secret fears and hopes. Again and again, they told her that her bookstore was the heart and soul of the town.

Would they still believe in her after the rumors finished circulating? Would they still shop in her store?

Nora thought she'd feel better after meeting with Davis. And though she was grateful to him, he hadn't been able to allay her fears. Unless Kelly's killer was identified and charged, Nora might lose everything. Her standing in the community, her business, and quite possibly, the man she loved.

She wanted to see McCabe. She wanted to sit with him on the sofa, close enough that their knees touched, and talk all of this over. They were good at talking. It was how they solved problems, made each other laugh, and planned for the future. The enjoyment they took just being in each other's company was Nora's favorite thing about them as a couple. They'd been friends before becoming lovers, and McCabe was the friend Nora needed most right now.

Before she realized what she was doing, she'd turned onto his street.

I'll just drive by, she told herself. *Just seeing his lights and knowing he's inside will be enough.*

But when she saw a car with the department seal and the words K9 UNIT parked in McCabe's driveway, she felt like the threads holding her world together were being cut, stitch by stitch.

Chapter 8

My mother's footsteps
Were so quiet
I barely heard her leave.

—John Green

Wednesday came and went with no word from McCabe.

On Thursday morning, Nora and Sheldon were in the Children's Corner preparing the storytime activity when Nora said, "I might be buying a car tonight."

"That's exciting." Sheldon handed her a piece of green felt. "Can you cut that into strips? Just follow the pencil lines. These are our plant stems."

"What are you using for flowers?"

"I'm *so* glad you asked." Sheldon upended a paper bag and a riot of colorful cupcake liners tumbled out. The bright hues perfectly matched the colors on the cover of Lois Ehlert's *Planting a Rainbow*.

Nora said, "Clever."

"And easy to glue. The felt will be harder for the little monsters, but I like how soft it is. Remember when we read *Elmer* and the kids made those patchwork felt elephants? It's one of my favorite projects ever."

"That was probably less about the felt and more about how

you identify with an elephant that's completely different from the rest of the world's elephants."

"Misfit characters are *always* more fabulous than the rest." He opened the packages of cupcake liners and began dividing them into colors. "I wanted to use buttons in the center of the flowers, but they'd never stick with regular glue and there'd be wailing, gnashing of teeth, and rending of garments. From me *and* our itty-bitty readers."

"If this craft involves glitter, *I'm* going to cry."

Sheldon laughed. "It's good to see your snarky side reemerging. It means that you're coping."

"They say people can get used to anything, but I can only adjust to this nightmare for a few moments at a time. I'm so desperate for a distraction that I'm actually looking forward to a shopful of sticky-fingered toddlers. The more chaotic the store, the more I can forget about being a murder suspect."

Sheldon threw her a sympathetic look. "This can't go on much longer. McCabe will move heaven and earth to clear your name. He'll arrest the real killer and then show up at your place with flowers and a box of truffles, begging for your forgiveness." Sheldon's eyes gleamed. "And just think of the things he'll be willing to do. You'll have him rubbing your feet and washing the dishes for months."

Nora tried not to fixate on the word "months." Murder investigations were rarely solved in a matter of days, but what would happen if the status quo dragged on for weeks?

I'll snap, that's what'll happen.

The sleigh bells rang, causing Sheldon to squeak in alarm. "No, no, no! I'm not ready yet!"

"You can put your apron on. I'll finish up here."

Because Sheldon's weekly story hour was always well attended by children and their parents and caregivers, Thursdays were one of the shop's most profitable mornings. And even though the toddlers and preschoolers left a wake of crumbs, trash, and messy bookshelves, Nora was delighted to see them. She loved fostering young readers and Sheldon reveled in playing dual roles of barista and circus master.

In his sweater-vest, polka-dot bow tie, and red Converse sneakers, he was a rounder, darker-skinned version of Mister Rogers. Like the beloved TV host, Sheldon used puppets to entertain and educate his audience. Today, the rabbit and butterfly puppets would do their best to convince their audience to eat their veggies.

Once their kids were seated "crisscross applesauce" on the alphabet rug, parents and babysitters were free to either watch the performance or wander the store sipping coffee. For the next hour, Nora divided her time between the ticket agent's booth and the checkout counter.

She'd just finished bagging a stack of historical romance novels for a mom carrying a sleeping baby in a sling when the infant stirred and mewled like a kitten.

The mother laughed. "He's in his cat phase—naps all day and stays awake all night. It's a miracle that I handed you the right credit card. The other day, I tried to unlock the door to my house with my car keys. Last week, I sat at a red light until everyone started honking at me. That's when I realized it wasn't a red light. It was a stop sign."

"Sounds like you could use a coffee. Why don't I keep your bag back here until storytime's over? You can grab it on your way out," she told the woman.

"I won't say no to a decaf. It's hard to get out of the house with both kids, but it's so worth it. Thursdays are one of the few times I get to talk to other parents about temper tantrums or picky eating. My husband cares, of course. He's a good listener too, but it's not the same. I need to be around people who are living what I'm living." She swept her arm around the space. "This is so great for the kids, but it's even better for the grown-ups."

Nora served the woman her coffee and returned to the front just as a man in overalls and a baseball cap approached the counter. His name was Josh and he and his son were storytime regulars.

"Hey, Nora. I wasn't sure if I should say anything, but there's a boy sitting on the floor in the back of the store. He seems upset. I don't know if he's someone's big brother or what. I asked him if he was okay, but he wouldn't answer. He didn't even look at me."

"Would you show me where he is?"

Josh led Nora past Sci-Fi and Fantasy to the YA section. When they rounded the final corner, Nora saw ahead to where the stacks ended at a painted bookcase filled with new young adult releases.

A brown-haired boy sat with his back to the bookcase and his chin lowered to his chest. Sheets of colored paper were piled on the carpet to his right and a dozen origami butterflies were scattered around his body like a fairy ring.

Turning to Josh, Nora whispered, "I know this boy. He's very shy, so I should probably speak to him alone. Thanks for coming to get me."

Nora waited for Josh to walk away before dropping to her knees a few feet away from Tucker. He continued to fold a lime-green piece of paper as if she wasn't there, tears dripping down his cheeks onto his shirt.

"Hi, Tucker," Nora whispered. "I don't know if you remember me, but my name's Nora. I definitely remember you. You like *Star Wars* and making shapes using paper. What's that called again?"

She waited for him to fill in the blank, and it took him so long to answer that she didn't think he would. Finally, he murmured, "Origami."

"That's it. Origami. You're really good at it, Tucker. These butterflies are beautiful."

"They're for my mom."

A vise clamped around Nora's heart and squeezed. She wanted to take Tucker into her arms and gently rock him. She wanted to wipe his tears away with a soft tissue. But this heart-broken child wouldn't welcome her touch, so she had to find a way to soothe him with words.

Brushing the wing of a butterfly, she said, "This is such a pretty color."

Tucker sniffed. "It's the color of Snoopy's doghouse. Snoopy is Mom's favorite, but I like Woodstock. Yellow's my favorite color too. My room in my old house was yellow."

"So many wonderful things are yellow. Honey, sunflowers, lemonade . . ."

Tucker kept folding.

"I saw a yellow seahorse once," he said. "In an aquarium. They're not very good at swimming, but they don't have too many predators because other fish don't like how they taste. The dads have the babies. The moms and dads stay together their whole lives."

Nora wanted to ask Tucker about his dad but bit back the question. "Do your aunt and uncle know you're here?"

Tucker shrugged.

"You can come to my store whenever you want if it's okay with your aunt and uncle. I can call them and tell them you're here, so they don't worry. How does that sound?"

"Okay."

"You know, I have a special drink for my favorite customers. It's called Harry Potter hot chocolate. It has whipped cream and lots of rainbow marshmallows. Would you like one?"

Tucker sniffled. "I don't like whipped cream."

"Fine with me. You can have extra marshmallows instead."

"Okay."

Nora hurried into the ticket agent's booth and pulled out her phone. She dialed Tea Flowers and pressed the phone to her ear while taking a Darth Vader mug down from the pegboard.

"Tea Flowers. How may I help you?"

"Kirk? This is Nora. Tucker's here, at the bookstore. I had a feeling you might not know."

Nora heard murmuring in the background. Then Kirk said, "We've been looking all over for him. I'll be right there."

As soon as he hung up, giggles erupted from the Children's Corner and Nora heard the high, singsong voice Sheldon reserved for the puppets. "But I don't want *carrots*! I only want *cookies*!"

Whatever he said next was drowned out by the gargle of the milk frother.

Nora didn't heat the milk as much as she would have for an adult. Their hot chocolate was more like very warm chocolate. Children also received twice as many marshmallows.

By the time she returned to the YA section, Tucker had made five more butterflies.

"Here's your Harry Potter hot chocolate," she said, setting the mug down on the carpet. "Do you have any paper that matches the colors of these marshmallows?"

Tucker set aside the lime-green butterfly he'd been folding and reached for the mug. "I have some marble paper like that. It's at Uncle Kirk's house."

"He knows you're here now."

"They said I had to stay at the store, but I don't like it there. I want to stay home, but they won't let me."

Nora nodded. "Where do you go to school?"

"Mom teaches me. We do math, science, reading, history, drawing, and computer. We have to go outside every day, even if it's raining. If it's really cold, I get to work on my LEGO city. That's what I wanted to do today, but Aunt Val said I couldn't."

Though Tucker wasn't looking directly at her, Nora saw the angry jut of his chin.

"The little kids will be leaving soon," she said. "You can stay here and drink your hot chocolate. I'll come back and check out your new butterflies after they're gone."

"They're loud," Tucker complained.

The giggles from the Children's Corner had escalated to shrieks and squeals, which meant Sheldon was nearing the end of his performance. Craft time was next, and because the parents always helped with the activity, the noise level would soon return to normal.

Nora said, "It'll be quieter soon."

Three customers were waiting at the checkout counter. Nora apologized for the delay and rang up their purchases as quickly and efficiently as possible. As a customer opened the door on his way out, the sound of church bells tolling the hour floated into the shop.

Eleven. The trolley will be here any minute.

Nora suddenly felt anxious. Between the children and the Lodge guests, the bookstore was about to get even noisier, and Tucker was clearly sensitive to noise.

Following on the heels of her departing customer, Nora stepped outside and glanced to the right, expecting to see Kirk heading her way. If she'd looked to her left, she would have noticed the woman in a sheriff's department uniform and a large, all-black German shepherd bearing down on her.

"Ms. Pennington!" Deputy Hollowell shouted.

Nora spotted the pair of deputies and felt a stab of alarm.

Don't freak out. You haven't broken any laws.

"Is the Walsh kid in there?" Hollowell demanded, jerking a thumb at the storefront.

"Yes. I already called his uncle. Kirk should be here any minute now."

Hollowell moved closer. When her K9 partner began to sniff Nora's sneaker, Hollowell's mouth twisted in a wry grin.

"Show me where he is."

Nora took a step back. "You're welcome to come inside, but the dog has to say out here."

"Are you preventing a deputy and his handler from checking on the welfare of a missing child?"

"I'm barring your canine partner, not you. Tucker isn't the only kid in the shop. It's our weekly storytime—I have at least twenty kids in there. Mostly toddlers and babies. A big, strange dog will scare them. Some of their parents too."

To Nora's horror, Hollowell responded by calling for backup.

A nanny with a toddler on her hip exited Miracle Books. When she saw Hollowell and the black dog, she froze.

"Doggie!" cried the child in the nanny's arms. "I wanna pet him!"

"No, Hiroshi. We can't. That's a police dog." The nanny leaned over to Nora and whispered, "Is everything okay?"

Nora forced a smile. "Absolutely. Did Hiroshi finish his craft already?"

The nanny shook her head. "We had to leave early because Hiroshi's visiting Mom at her office today. We'll do the craft later. Sheldon gave us a bag of supplies." She smoothed Hiroshi's dark hair. "Sheldon's the best, isn't he?"

Hiroshi was too fascinated by the police dog to answer.

After shooting a wary glance at the two deputies, the nanny walked away. Nora watched her cross the street and exhaled in relief when she saw Kirk Walsh on the opposite sidewalk.

"There's Kirk," Nora told Hollowell. "I'll take him to Tucker, and everything will be fine. No harm done."

Kirk was red-faced and panting by the time he reached the bookstore. Without waiting for him to catch his breath, Hollowell said, "Did this woman invite your nephew to her business without your permission?"

"*What?*" Nora spluttered. "I had nothing—"

Cutting her protest short, Kirk said, "All I know is that Tucker was in our stockroom one minute and gone the next." He looked at Nora. "Is he okay?"

"He's making origami butterflies in the Young Adult section. He was crying before, but he's better now. Let me take you to him."

"Mr. Walsh, I'll need to speak with you on your way out," Hollowell commanded.

Kirk nodded and entered the shop.

Finding herself alone with Kirk—if only for a few seconds—Nora couldn't stop herself from saying, "I'm so sorry about Kelly. I wish I hadn't acted the way I did outside the diner. I shouldn't have pushed her. Or yelled at her. I'm really sorry."

She didn't expect a reply and wasn't given one. Still, she was grateful that she'd had the chance to tell him how she felt. This wasn't the time or place to insist that she hadn't killed his sister, so she focused on reuniting him with his nephew.

Tucker was exactly where Nora had left him. He'd finished his hot chocolate and was busy creating a hot-pink butterfly.

Nora stood aside to let Kirk pass.

Squatting down, Kirk put a hand on Tucker's shoe. "Hey, bud. I've been looking for you. Why didn't you tell me you were coming here?" He waited a beat before saying, "Tucker? I need you to answer me when I ask you a question."

"I don't like how your store smells."

"I know that some of the teas and flower smells are too strong for you. I guess you like coffee better." Kirk picked up Tucker's empty cup. "I like it too. More than tea. But don't tell Aunt Val I said that."

Tucker didn't reply.

"We need to go back to Tea Flowers, Tucker. I have work to do and people won't be able to see the books if you're sitting here." Kirk tapped a book spine near Tucker's shoulder. "See these books? People want to take them home, just like they want to take my flowers home, but they need to be able to look at all of them before they make a choice."

Tucker's hands stopped moving. He glanced at the bookshelves as if seeing where he was for the first time.

"Look at these amazing butterflies," Kirk continued. "Any idea how we're going to get them all home?"

Nora said, "I have the perfect box for the job. I'll go grab it."

As she headed for the stockroom, Nora saw that the storytime activity was almost over. The kids had finished making their rainbow gardens and were now sampling baby carrots, cherry tomatoes, and celery sticks.

A child suddenly cried, "Ew!" and made a spitting noise.

I hope Sheldon has napkins and a trash can in there.

Pushing aside images of partially masticated tomatoes being ground into the alphabet rug, Nora ducked into the stockroom to fetch a display box from Scholastic. The box featured graphics of children reading on a bright yellow background.

"Will this work?" she asked Kirk when she returned to the YA section.

Kirk gave her a weak smile. "Yeah, thanks."

As he and Tucker loaded the butterflies into the box, Kirk whispered. "What do you say to Miss Nora?"

"Thank you."

Tucker's reply was robotic, but Nora saw how tightly he gripped his yellow box. His face was still puffy from crying and his upper lip was stained by a chocolate milk mustache. Again, Nora wished she could reach out and hug him.

"It was nice to see you, Tucker, and I hope you come back. Make sure to ask your aunt and uncle first, but I can always find a spot for you to sit whenever you visit."

Kirk put a hand on the boy's shoulder and steered him toward the front of the store. Suddenly, he paused and turned to Nora. "Dogs make Tucker nervous. He's more of a hamster guy."

"Would you rather leave out the back? After you're a few blocks away, I'll tell Deputy Hollowell that you and Tucker are gone." To Tucker, she said, "Would you like to go out through the delivery door? It's for staff members only."

Tucker peeked at her from under his lashes. "Where does it go?"

"To the parking lot. But if you look across the parking lot, you'll see a red caboose. That's where I live. The train passes right by my house."

Tucker brightened. "I like trains. There were tracks near my old house and Mom used to pull over so I could count all the freight cars. The longest was one hundred sixty-three."

"I always wonder what's inside all those freight cars, don't you?"

Nora escorted her guests to the delivery door and propped it open. Tucker went out first, but Kirk lingered in the threshold.

"I told Kelly not to spring the news on you the way she did. She gave you the flowers because she wanted you to come to the shop. Her plan was to talk to you there, in private, and I wish that's how things had gone. I don't blame you for getting upset."

Nora was nearly undone by the kindness in his voice. "I didn't see her again after I drove away, I swear. I went straight home and tried to sleep. I tossed and turned for most of the night, but I never left my house."

Kirk passed a hand over his face. Grief had left shadows under his eyes and deepened the lines around his mouth.

"My wife thinks you were mad at Kelly—for dragging up the past. Were you?"

"When she first told me who she was, yes. I moved here to start over, so it was a shock to be confronted by my past. My anger came from shock." She gestured around the parking lot. "This is my home. The place I ran to after the accident. I built a life here. I made the best of friends and fell in love with a wonderful man. I wouldn't throw all of that away because of what Kelly told me."

By this time, Tucker was halfway to Nora's house.

"I'd better go," Kirk said. He took two steps forward and then swung around again. "Would you come to our place tonight? I'd like for all of us to sit down and talk this out. We're at 127 Maple Street."

Nora was nodding before he had the chance to finish his sentence. She said, "I can be there by seven."

She returned to the checkout counter to find a group of parents waiting to buy books. Their restless toddlers were either fiddling with the bookmark spinner or examining the felt-and-paper rainbow gardens they'd just made.

Nora apologized and rang up sales as fast as she could. She managed to winnow the line down from ten to two people before McCabe entered the shop.

Shooting him a glance, Nora wondered, *Is he Hollowell's backup?*

McCabe acknowledged her by tipping his hat. It was such a familiar gesture that she almost smiled, but the solemn look in his eyes killed the smile before it could form.

She took care of the two remaining customers, and they left.

Nora and McCabe were now alone.

She pointed out the window. "Deputy Hollowell called for backup after I refused to let her four-legged partner inside, so if you're looking for Kirk and Tucker, they're already gone. They used the delivery door because Tucker's scared of dogs."

"Why was he here in the first place?"

Nora shrugged. "I think he's sensitive to smells. He told me that he doesn't like being at his aunt and uncle's shop, so he came here."

"Did you see him come in?"

"No, but I was probably working the espresso machine. He sat down on the floor and started making origami butterflies. He said they were for his mom."

McCabe closed his eyes and whispered, "Poor kid."

The sleigh bells jangled, and a pair of elderly ladies entered the shop carrying teal tote bags with the Lodge logo. The trolley had arrived. Nora peered out the window to find that Hollowell was still stationed outside the front door.

Nora's anger flared. "Can you ask your deputy to move away from my front door? She's bad for business."

"We'll both go. I want to follow up with Mr. Walsh."

"I'm doing just fine, by the way." Nora's tone was acerbic. "Kirk doesn't think I had anything to do with Kelly's death. He even invited me over tonight. If I can convince Val that I'm innocent, can you find someone else to investigate?"

McCabe let out a breath. "It's not that simple."

"I know that Val thinks I was in their backyard, arguing with Kelly, even though I was home, barely sleeping on my couch. I understand why she believes that woman was me. She had a helmet. I have a helmet. I yelled at Kelly earlier that night, so it had to be me out there on their lawn. But there's no way she saw *me*, and she needs to admit as much to you. It's the truth, Grant."

McCabe put a hand under Nora's elbow and steered her around the corner of the fiction section. A few steps into the stacks, he halted.

"I'm working as hard as I can to find the killer, but it's going to take time. There's nothing cut-and-dried about this case. We have no motive, no witnesses, and very few clues. The sooner we solve this, the sooner you and I can put this behind us. Trust me. I want that more than anything. I miss you."

Before Nora could reply, McCabe leaned in to kiss her. As his lips brushed against hers and she felt the warmth of his mouth, she closed her eyes. She wanted to savor the taste of him. It could be a long time before they touched each other like this again.

Their kiss deepened and McCabe ran his knuckle along her jawline. When she reached out to curl her hand around the back of his neck, he broke off the kiss and moved out of reach.

Without another word, he turned and walked away.

Chapter 9

Anger is an acid that can do more harm to the vessel in which it stands than to anything on which it is poured.

—Mark Twain

Kirk and Val's craftsman-style cottage needed a little TLC. The porch sagged, the paint was peeling, and there was rust on the gutters. Yet somehow, these signs of aging seemed to add to its charm.

A plaque affixed to the front door read SUGARBERRY COTTAGE—a fitting name for a pale pink house with a wide veranda, tapered columns, and a low-pitched roof.

Lights glowed from the windows and there was a sense of stillness to the house. Gathering her nerves, Nora pressed the doorbell. When Kirk had suggested they sit down and talk things over, it felt like the right thing to do, but now that she was here, she questioned the wisdom of meeting with the Walshes at their home.

The event had been on Nora's mind from the moment Kirk and Tucker left Miracle Books. She'd been practicing speeches in her head all afternoon, but her mind had suddenly gone blank.

I don't think I need to convince Kirk of my innocence. He wouldn't have asked me over if he thought I killed his sister.

Val was another matter. Val believed she'd seen Nora in their backyard. Later that night, Kelly had left the house. The next morning, she was dead. Of course Val thought Nora was guilty. It would be a major feat to change her mind, but Nora meant to try.

She'd spent most of her lunch break mulling over what sympathy gift to bring the Walshes. Flowers were out. As were books. A home-cooked meal would be lovely, but Nora didn't have time to cook. She barely had time to go grocery shopping. Luckily, a quick call to Hester had solved the problem.

"A grieving family needs wholesome, simple food," she'd said. "And there's nothing more comforting than homemade bread. One loaf won't be enough either. I'm thinking a loaf of cinnamon raisin, a loaf of farmhouse, and some buttermilk rolls. I'll throw in a jar of strawberry jam too."

When Kirk opened the door, Nora presented him with the bakery box and said, "I don't know if you've been to the Gingerbread House yet, but my friend makes the best bread in the world. She picked out a few of her favorites for you."

"Very kind," Kirk said. "Come on in."

Nora followed him through the hallway and into a living room with exposed beams and a stone fireplace. A pair of easy chairs, a sofa, and a coffee table occupied the center of the room, while a series of bookcases marched along the back wall. Nora was naturally drawn to the books, but as soon as she saw that the shelves also held dozens of framed photographs, she averted her gaze. She didn't want to see a photo of her ex-husband. She wasn't ready for that yet.

As if hearing her thoughts, Kirk said, "We don't have any pictures of Lawrence. I doubt this comes as a surprise to you, but he wasn't good to Kelly. Val and I were relieved when they got divorced. We knew she'd be better off without him, but it's been hard on Tucker. A boy needs his father. Too bad Tucker's is such a jackass."

"He has you, though."

Kirk nodded absently. "Sit wherever you'd like. I'll put this in the kitchen and get Val. Would you like anything to drink? Tea?"

"Sure. Thank you."

A minute later, Nora heard Kirk and Val arguing. Though their words weren't distinguishable, the timbre of their voices gave them away.

Val doesn't want me here.

To quell her anxiety, Nora focused on the books. She let her gaze travel slowly over the hardcovers and paperbacks. Most were contemporary fiction, but there were also slim volumes of poetry, oversized reference books, and a collection of classics. Nora was pleased to note that the books weren't just for show. The paperback spines were deeply creased, and the dust jackets bore signs of wear.

The collection told Nora that Kirk and Val were frugal people who valued their books. Every title on the shelf had been read—probably more than once—before being returned to its proper spot. Tears, dog-eared pages, or broken spines didn't matter to this couple. They cared about the contents.

They love their books. Each and every one.

Nora had been in the book business long enough that she could accurately judge people based on their home libraries. The Walshes' library told her that they were sensible, curious, and loyal.

All good traits.

By the time Kirk returned with Val in tow, Nora's apprehension had eased a little.

Val placed a tray with a teapot and three cups and saucers on the coffee table. She poured the tea and then sat down on the sofa. She didn't acknowledge Nora's presence but kept her gaze locked on the pile of magazines on the table. Her face could've been carved from wood.

Indicating the cup and saucer closest to Nora, Kirk said,

"This is one of Val's special blends. It's got spearmint, linden flowers, chamomile, and a pinch of anise. She calls it Evening Comfort. It helps us get to sleep."

"Nothing helps now," Val grumbled.

Nora breathed in the curl of steam rising from her cup and took a tentative sip. The flavors of the tea were as gentle and soothing as being tucked into bed by a parent's loving hands.

"This is really good," she said, speaking directly to Val.

Kirk turned to his wife. "Kelly was my kid sister, and I know she wouldn't want any enmity between us. She wanted to make peace with Nora, and since she can't, we're going to do it for her."

"Even if she's a murderer?" Val challenged.

Nora said, "I understand why you feel the way you do. You think I came here the night Kelly died, but the woman you saw wasn't me. I've never been to this house before."

Val's glance moved past Nora to where darkness was settling in outside the window. "You can't prove that you weren't here."

"No, but I swear to you that I drove straight home from the diner and didn't leave again until ten the next morning." Nora put her teacup down. "What about you?"

"What about me?"

"Are you one hundred percent positive that it was me you saw? Or that the voice you heard was mine? You saw a woman with a helmet. You saw a woman with shoulder-length hair. But could you put your hand on a Bible and swear that you saw *me*?"

Val jumped to her feet. "I don't have to answer—"

"Sit down, Valerie!" Kirk snapped. "My sister is *dead!* I need you to help me figure out what happened that night, and we can't do that unless we talk like civilized human beings."

When Val remained standing, Kirk hid his face in his hands.

Instantly softening, Val put an arm around Kirk's shoulders and whispered, "I'm sorry, honey. It's all been . . . too much. The move. Opening Tea Flowers. Kelly's illness. Worrying about her and Tucker. Worrying about money. And when we got the call about Kelly, I was scared. I just . . ." The rest of her words were lost as Val rested her forehead against Kirk's.

Kirk patted his wife's back and murmured into her hair.

Nora's heart hurt for the grieving couple. The dozens of framed photos on the bookshelves spoke of two people who cherished their family. Now, one of those precious family members was gone. They expected to lose Kelly to cancer, but she'd been murdered instead. Kirk and Val's grief was compounded by fear, anger, and uncertainty.

Val wiped her eyes with a tissue and passed the box to her husband. Then she looked at Nora and said, "I owe you an apology. Kelly knows so few people in Miracle Springs that, yes, I just assumed the woman I saw was you. I was mad at you because you pushed her. In fact, I've been mad at you for years."

Nora gaped at her.

"If your marriage had been stronger, then Lawrence wouldn't have met Kelly. He wouldn't have ruined her life—or *our* lives!" Val raised her voice. "If he hadn't gone into her flower shop because it was your birthday, then Kelly could've married a decent man. She wouldn't have been a single mom. She would've taken better care of herself and been less stressed. She might have discovered the cancer sooner or never gotten it at all. Things would've been better for me and Kirk too. If only Lawrence had stayed with you."

Nora stared at Val. "Are you serious?"

"It was easy to blame you because I didn't know you. My sister-in-law was an idiot to fall for such an asshole, but she was also a sweetheart. You were a stranger. It was safe to be angry at you."

Kirk shook his head in dismay. "Good Lord, Val. You have to call the sheriff right now and tell him how you've falsely accused this woman."

Val's eyes flashed with defiance. "She could be the woman I

saw. I mean, who else had a grudge against Kelly? I might not be able to swear it in court, but it *could* have been her."

Nora had had enough. Getting to her feet, she said, "I think we're done here. I'll show myself out."

"Wait!" Kirk rounded on Val. "I'm going to show her the books, but you should go upstairs. Check on Tucker. He could use the company."

Val began loading the teacups onto the tray. The porcelain clinked in protest as her hands shook. "My whole life has been about *your* family. Just once, it would be nice if someone cared about what *I* want!"

As Val stormed out of the room, Kirk closed his eyes. He was the picture of misery. And though Nora felt sorry for him, she was more than ready to leave.

"I apologize for my wife's behavior, and I'll be calling the sheriff tonight. You have no reason to help us after this, and I wouldn't ask if not for Tucker. You see, Lawrence's mom left Tucker her book collection."

Nora frowned. "Go on."

"Kelly wanted to make peace with you. She hoped that, over time, you two would be friendly enough that she could ask you to sell the collection on Tucker's behalf. She believed you'd get top dollar for the books, and the money would go toward Tucker's college fund. We're not wealthy people, Val and me. We'll do our best by the boy, but he's going to need more than we've got."

"What about child support?"

"Lawrence will pay right up to the day Tucker turns eighteen. After that, he's out. He made that crystal clear."

What kind of monster has he become?

Nora remembered the look of pride she'd seen on her husband's face the night he'd stood in Kelly's doorway. He'd seemed larger than life then—a man protecting his lover and unborn child from his deranged wife.

"Isn't he part of Tucker's life?"

Lowering his voice, Kirk replied, "No, he isn't. Tucker isn't the son Lawrence wanted. He wanted a boy who played football and soccer. Who'd go fishing and join the Scouts. He rejected Tucker long before the Asperger's diagnosis. Called him backward and weird. Said he acted retarded. His own kid. He wouldn't pay child support without getting a paternity test first. Lawrence said he'd make the payments but wanted nothing to do with a kid he was ashamed to have fathered."

Nora was aghast.

Kirk's eyes pleaded with her. "Tucker's a great kid, and I promised Kelly I'd look after him. So, can I show you the books?"

"Yes."

Kirk led her to a small room at the back of the house that was part office, part craft area. A desk and two file cabinets took up half of the space. The rest was devoted to a bookcase filled with board games, puzzles, sewing materials, and painting supplies. There were also two card tables. One held a jigsaw puzzle. The second was covered in plastic bins.

"Tucker was very close to Grandma Virginia. He called her Meemaw, and she called him Sparky. Did you know Virginia well?"

"Sadly, no. Lawrence never asked his parents to visit, and they rarely spoke on the phone. He told me they had a falling-out because he didn't want to go into the family business. They came to the wedding, and I thought they seemed like a nice couple, but I saw them only a few times after that."

Kirk put a hand on one of the plastic bins. "They were good people, and they both loved Tucker. They made provisions for him in their wills, but Lawrence gained control over his mother's assets before anyone realized she had dementia, and he made big changes. Lawrence's brother took him to court over the whole thing but lost. Those two were too busy fighting over money to pay attention to the collection Meemaw left Tucker.

I don't know what this stuff's worth, but I promised Kelly that I'd do whatever I could to see that Tucker got a college degree and a savings account."

Nora eyed the tubs with a mixture of excitement and apprehension. By the time Tucker finished high school, a college education would probably cost well over $200,000. Did these boxes contain books valuable enough to cover the expense? She doubted it.

"Is there a catalog of the collection?" she asked.

Kirk gave her a blank look. "Is that the same thing as a list of contents?"

"Yes."

"There is." He turned to his desk and grabbed the folder sitting on the blotter. "Since it's getting late and you've worked all day, you could just take this home if you'd like. I realize I'm asking an awful lot of you, considering what you've been through in the past few days. But if you'd look this over and tell me what you think, I'd be mighty grateful."

Nora accepted the proffered folder. "I will, but I don't want you to get your hopes up. For these to contain books of substantial value, they'd have to be very rare and very desirable books. I don't come across books like that very often. I'm not trying to bring you down, but it's better to have realistic expectations."

"My dad used to say that a lie could be halfway around the world before the truth got its boots on. You can be straight with me. I might not like the answer, but I'll appreciate it."

Maybe, thought Nora.

She'd been on countless house calls where she'd patiently explained why someone's book collection wasn't worth a small fortune. Perfectly reasonable adults had burst into tears or raged at her after learning that their literary treasures weren't coveted by the rest of the world.

If there's nothing good in those boxes, Val will have another reason to be mad at me.

Still, Nora wanted to help Tucker. If it took a whole village to raise a child, then Tucker's village was on the small side. He had his aunt and uncle, but they were grieving. Grieving families needed support. Did the Walshes have friends or relatives to lean on?

"Do you have kids?" she asked as Kirk walked her to the door.

"Just Tucker. From the day he was born, he's been partly mine and Val's. I'm the closest thing to a father he's ever known, and between Kelly and Val, he's had two moms."

Glancing at the staircase, Nora imagined Tucker in his room, quietly folding butterflies. She said goodnight to Kirk and left.

At home, she opened a fresh pint of Chocolate Therapy ice cream and grabbed a spoon from the drying rack. She carried the ice cream to the table and powered up her laptop. Then she opened the folder and began to read.

She was immediately impressed by the neatness of the enclosed list. Each entry contained the title and author, publication date, edition, overall condition, and original purchase price. An asterisk indicated that the sales receipt was stored in a separate folder.

The list dispelled some of Nora's pessimism. This level of detail and organization indicated that Virginia had a serious collection. Her hunch was confirmed when she reached the fourth item on the list.

"A signed first edition of Evelyn Waugh's *Love Among the Ruins*. Originally purchased for 725 dollars." Nora tapped the spoon against her lips. "Wonder what it's going for these days?"

Nora used three sites to look up book values: Abe Books, LiveAuctioneers, and WorthPoint. After finding the Waugh edition on all three sites, Nora felt a rush of adrenaline.

She punched numbers into her phone's calculator app and smiled. "Sells for an average of fifteen hundred. Not bad."

After reloading her spoon with ice cream, Nora moved to the next item on the list. The leather-bound edition of *The Love Affairs of Lord Byron* was heavily illustrated and included a portrait of the poet on the front cover. Virginia had spent a cool thousand on the book.

"Was she a big Byron fan? Because I bet she overpaid," Nora murmured as her fingers raced over the keyboard. "Yeah, it's leatherbound. But it's from 1910. There are older, finer, leather-bound Byrons and—whoa!"

A search result informed her that the same book had just sold at auction for nearly $7000.

"Nice one, Virginia."

Nora kept shoveling ice cream into her mouth without really tasting it. Her body was on autopilot while her brain fixated on titles and dollar signs.

She took a brief break to fetch a pen and notepad, and after jotting down the current market value of ten books, she added them up and whistled.

"Twenty grand."

The first page of the twelve-page list was made of classic English literature, but the first item on the second page was Ian Fleming's *From Russia, with Love.* When Nora read the description, she almost choked on a piece of chocolate cookie.

She put the ice cream back in the freezer and returned to the table with a glass of water. After rereading the description, she shook her head in amazement.

"A limited edition signed by Ian Fleming. She paid seven grand in the '80s. Now it's worth . . ."

It had been two years since a similar book had sold online. A signed first edition of Fleming's *You Only Live Twice* had realized $25,000 at a London auction house, but Nora believed Virginia's book was worth even more because her book was a first edition, first impression, presentation copy. The edition of *You Only Live Twice* was second state, which meant a small change had been made to the original printing. A single correction or a slight alteration in the book cover kept it from being labeled as a true original.

"Virginia's Fleming could be worth $30,000," Nora whispered.

She considered the rare and collectible books on display at Miracle Books. Her most expensive titles cost a few hundred dollars, and the books tended to move slowly. She sold the majority of her signed and first editions to online buyers, and she was a small fish in the world of rare book dealers.

I'm not the person for this job, she thought.

Virginia's books had to bring top dollar, which meant her collection should be sold by a reputable and experienced book dealer or auction house. Putting the collection into the right hands was key. Nora needed to recommend a business with a large reach and generous advertising budget. A reasonable commission fee was also a must. The profits from this sale would likely be used for more than Tucker's college education. With Kelly gone, Kirk and Val were now responsible for his welfare. They'd receive child support payments for another eight years, but Nora had no idea if those would cover all of Tucker's expenses.

Having finished her water, Nora switched to wine and continued to peruse the inventory list. Usually, collectors stuck to a certain genre, author, or time period, but Virginia's books ran the gamut from classic lit to contemporary romance. There were novels, plays, poetry, and a handful of children's books.

Nora was about to look up the value of Hugh Leonard's play *Love in the Title,* when she suddenly barked out a laugh. The theme of the collection was staring her right in the face.

"Love, love, love," the Beatles sang in Nora's head.

Scanning the titles on the third page, she saw Anthony Trollope's *An Old Man's Love*, Gabriel Garcia Márquez's *Love in the Time of Cholera*, Raymond Chandler's *Farewell, My*

Lovely, Toni Morrison's *Love*, Stephen King's *The Girl Who Loved Tom Gordon*, and more.

If the condition reports on the list were accurate, the collection could possibly sell for $200,000 or more.

Nora pictured the little room in the back of Kirk and Val's house. She saw the tidy desk, the incomplete jigsaw puzzle, and tableful of plastic bins. She thought of the strange woman showing up at their house. The woman with the helmet and the shoulder-length hair.

Are the books safe?

Suddenly agitated, Nora walked into her kitchen. She took out a dishrag and a bottle of Windex and began to clean the counter. It wasn't the least bit dirty, but she needed to move while processing her thoughts.

Someone had talked to Kelly the night of her murder. What if that person knew about the books? They were worth a lot of money. Had Kelly been killed because of them?

Nora picked up her phone. She couldn't call McCabe, but she could call Deputy Jasper Andrews.

I hope he's with Hester.

"He's out on patrol," Hester said when Nora explained why she was looking for him. "Try his cell. I just talked to him a few minutes ago and nothing's going on, so he'll be glad to hear from you. Don't tell him I said this, but he doesn't think you had anything to do with Kelly's death."

"Thanks, Hester. See you in the morning."

Andrews answered his phone with a professional detachment that he immediately dropped after listening to what Nora had to say.

"I'm off duty in an hour, but I'll put in a request for the next patrol to keep an eye on the house. Have you told the sheriff?"

"I thought it would be better to leave that to you."

After promising to relay the information, Andrews ended the call.

Abandoning her cleaning, Nora got a refill on wine and carried her glass and the inventory list to the sofa. As she sipped, she wondered how many people knew about Virginia's collection.

Did she leave it to Tucker in her will?

Hopefully, Kirk had the necessary legal documents. One set to prove that the books belonged to Tucker and another showing that he had the right to sell the collection on Tucker's behalf.

Nora uncapped her pen and wrote a short to-do list.

1. *Examine the books*
2. *Advise Kirk about legal docs*
3. *Is the collection safe? Do they have a security system? If not, does Tea Flowers?*
4. *Who knew about Virginia's collection?*

The high, jarring shriek of an owl broke her concentration. She put the pen down and carried her wineglass outside to the deck.

Moonlight leaked through the trees and oozed over the grassy slope behind her house. The owl screamed again—a primeval call of hunger that echoed through the silent night.

As Nora's gaze swept over the shadows amassing in the woods and down by the railroad tracks, she thought about the mysterious woman Val had seen on her back lawn.

Nora was suddenly struck by a thought.

What if there was no woman?

Val was angry. She admitted that she'd been mad at Nora for years. She hated Lawrence, and Nora had a feeling that she resented Kelly and Tucker too. She'd wanted a different life from the one she'd been leading—a life that seemed to revolve around Kirk's sister and her child.

"Was *she* the woman who'd argued with Kelly? The best lies are close versions of the truth."

Nora turned over several theories in her head but knew too little about Val to come up with a concrete idea.

Val was hiding something; she was sure of it. Maybe she'd pointed the finger at Nora to keep her away from Virginia's book collection. Maybe she had her own plans for it.

Whatever her secrets, Nora was confident that McCabe and his team would ferret them out. She'd done her part by reporting her findings. The rest was in the hands of the professionals.

It was too cool to linger outside, so Nora stretched out on the sofa and lost herself in her current read.

By the time she climbed into bed, the moon had risen to its full height. It cast a river of light over her quilt and to the edge of her nightstand, where it set the origami lily pad aglow.

Nora picked up the flower and unfolded the petals to reveal the little bee. Its yellow body shone like a tiny star, but it made her sad.

This bee had no queen. He was alone in his hive of paper.

Chapter 10

To a true collector, the acquisition of an old book is its rebirth.

—Walter Benjamin

The next morning, Nora brewed coffee and called Kirk. An hour later, she was knocking on his front door.

"I just got off the phone with the sheriff. He asked me lots of questions about Virginia's books. I assume you had something to do with that," he said as he led Nora back to the office.

"I did. If the condition of those books matches the description on the inventory forms, then that collection is worth a pretty penny. If so, they need to be in a safe place."

Kirk paused in the office doorway. "The woman Val saw in our yard—was she after the books?"

If there was anyone out there, Nora thought. Aloud, she said, "It's something to consider."

"I dunno. I can count the number of people who know about this collection on one hand, and none of them live within driving distance of Miracle Springs. Have you eaten breakfast?"

Nora had grabbed a banana on the way out the door, but when she saw a tray containing two steaming mugs of tea and a plate of golden-brown crumpets, she said, "I had a piece of fruit."

"That won't stick to your bones. Val's been making these for the past two weeks to see if we should add them to the menu. Help yourself to butter, jam, and honey. The tea is Earl Grey."

Kirk moved a pile of puzzle pieces aside and laid their plates in between sections of blue sky and flowering cherry trees.

"This is how Kelly liked to start her day. She'd wake up before the rest of us, make a cup of coffee, and come in here to work her puzzle. Sometimes, she'd listen to music or an audiobook. Other times, it was just her and her thoughts. I don't know what to do with this now. I can't put it away. But I don't want to finish it either."

"Does Tucker like puzzles?"

Kirk shook his head. "I know it sounds crazy, considering how many hours he can focus on origami, or LEGO, or drawing maps, but he doesn't have the patience for this."

Nora looked at the mound of flower pieces near her mug. "Maybe you could put in a piece a day. First thing in the morning. It could be your time with your sister."

Kirk smiled. "I like that."

"And I like this crumpet. Where'd you get the honey? It has such a unique taste."

"It's wildflower honey. Unlike processed honey, it has bee pollen and little bits of honeycomb. We buy our honey from a small company in Hendersonville. We're going to start stocking their lotion, lip balm, and furniture polish. If you have the chance to walk around during the festival, they'll have a booth outside Tea Flowers tomorrow."

"You haven't been here for a festival yet. You're lucky if you can use the restroom, let alone go outside."

Kirk's eyes went wide. "Really? I guess Val will be baking more crumpets tonight."

"You might want to have premade sandwiches ready to go too. Visitors will roll through like locusts. They'll eat anything you've got, but they'll leave your cash register stuffed."

"Sounds like we'll both be behind the counter tomorrow. It'll be a long day for Tucker too. He and Val already left for the shop. They're going to make the back room more Tucker-friendly."

I hope she's kind to him, Nora thought.

As if reading Nora's mind, Kirk said, "Val loves that boy and—this is no excuse—seeing him suffer has been really hard on her. She knows she lashed out at the wrong person. After she talked to Sheriff McCabe last night, I told him how you helped Tucker leave your shop without having to encounter that officer's dog. The sheriff knows we don't think you had anything to do with . . . what happened to Kelly."

Nora flashed him a grateful smile and gestured at the plastic bins. "I should wash my hands before I take a look at those."

"The powder room is across the hall to the left. I left scissors on the desk. Most of the books are in bubble wrap. I don't think they've been touched since Virginia packed them. I'll be in the kitchen if you need me. We're serving honeyed carrot soup with crunchy chickpeas for the next week, and I've got another million chickpeas to roast."

Once her hands were thoroughly washed and dried, Nora popped the lid off the first bin. Inside, she found a cache of books wrapped in bubble wrap.

The packages were secured by masking tape, so Nora didn't need the scissors. She picked up a book and carefully peeled off the bubble wrap, revealing a second layer of protection. A sheaf of white paper was secured with more masking tape. Nora carefully removed the paper and saw that she held a signed and dated copy of Erich Segal's *Love Story*. The near fine novel was protected by a clear, archival cover and perfectly matched the description on the inventory list. Nora had no idea if the signature was genuine, but the way the book was catalogued and stored inspired confidence.

After rewrapping the novel and setting it aside, Nora reached for the next book in the pile. She planned to examine three or four books from every box before heading to work.

Examining Virginia's books was pure bliss. Nora admired each one, cradling the spines in one hand while carefully turning pages with the other. Noises from the kitchen—running water, the clank of pots, a knife blade striking a chopping board—played like music in the background.

In what felt like no time at all, Nora was ready to survey a few books from the last bin.

She checked her watch and swore under her breath. She'd taken too long looking at the other bins, which meant she had about five minutes before she had to leave.

"Okay, Virginia. Let's keep the streak going."

The shapes inside the bin gave her pause. Instead of bubble-wrapped books, they appeared to be a collection of square boxes.

Nora took a peek inside one of the smaller boxes. It contained a set of enamel pins. Each pin featured a Disney character and a Valentine's Day greeting. Taped on the inside of the box lid was a note that said, DUO PINS, DISNEY, RARE.

That was it. There was no purchase history or additional description.

Her curiosity aroused, Nora opened another slim box. This one held a heart-shaped container. The red heart lid featured a cherub playing a harp. The inside was lined with gold paper. The item was described as, ANTIQUE GERMAN CANDY CONTAINER.

"Just one more," Nora vowed.

The object in the third box was completely foreign to her. It was a wooden octagon no bigger than her palm that was inlaid with tiny shells. In the center of the octagon was a portrait of a woman. She had porcelain skin, brown ringlets, and blue eyes. Her necklace looked to be made of tiny beads.

The note inside the box read, SAILOR'S VALENTINE, ANTIQUE, HAND-PAINTED PORTRAIT WITH SHELLS AND SEED PEARLS.

Nora carried the objet d'art into the kitchen, where Kirk was stirring the contents of a commercial grade stockpot.

"It smells great in here."

"You must like carrots." Kirk chuckled.

He dipped a small spoon into the soup and brought it to his mouth. Nodding in satisfaction, he turned the heat down and tossed the spoon in the sink.

"What've you got there?"

Nora placed the box containing the shell sculpture on the kitchen table. "It's called a sailor's valentine. It was in a bin along with a bunch of other valentine-themed collectibles."

Kirk smiled. "That was Virginia's favorite holiday. I don't know if you remember, but her maiden name was Love."

"Ah, that explains the theme of her collection," Nora said. "The valentine items are outside my wheelhouse, so let's focus on the books. From what I saw, it's an incredible collection. I only looked at three or four books per bin, but Virginia's descriptions seem accurate. If the rest of the books are like the ones I saw, there's some good money to be made *if* you send them to an auction house or to the right book dealer."

"Kelly thought *you* were the right book dealer."

Nora shook her head. "I don't handle many rare books—especially of this caliber. If you want to get top dollar, you need to ship those books to someone who has a huge client list, an advertising budget, and a name. I'm just a small-town, independent bookstore owner. I'm not the right choice, but I can recommend someone who is."

Kirk stared down at the valentine made of shells. "Will they sell the knickknacks too?"

"If you want one company to handle the books and the collectibles, it'll have to be an auction house. Knowing what the items are worth might help you decide. I have a friend who sells vintage items at the flea market. I could send her some photos and see what she has to say."

"That sounds great. I'll have Tucker take the pictures. If you give me your number, I can text you the images."

Nora glanced at her watch. "I should've left five minutes ago, so I'll put this back and show myself out." Kirk thanked her and she turned away. At the doorway, she turned around again. "I know it's none of my business, but are the books safe?"

Kirk spread his hands. "We don't have a security system here or at Tea Flowers. Val and I talked about getting one for the shop but decided not to. We really can't afford it."

"Not many shops use them. There isn't much cash in the registers since people tend to use credit cards these days, and most merchants make daily bank deposits." Nora shrugged. "I don't know where you could put the books. Too bad you can't rent a big, loud dog for a few days."

"If I did, Tucker would sleep in the treehouse. Oh, I almost forgot!"

Kirk scooped a brown bag off the counter and handed it to Nora. "Soup and sandwiches for two. It's the least I can do."

By the time Nora reached the shop, Sheldon had already picked up the day's pastries and prepped the coffee and espresso machines. Nora found him pulling books with yellow covers.

"I thought I'd get a jump on the black and yellow table. I cleared off the other books, but I didn't feel like putting them away. I can't waste my creative genius on menial tasks."

Nora proffered the brown bag. "Kirk Walsh made us lunch."

"Oh?" Sheldon peeked inside the bag. "That soup is an interesting color. What is it?"

"Carrot and honey."

Sheldon grimaced. "I'm almost afraid to ask about the sandwich."

"Where's your sense of adventure? Let me put this in the fridge and then I'll tell you about their book collection. It's why I'm so late."

Following her into the ticket agent's booth, Sheldon said, "I was hoping you'd stayed up to the wee hours with your man. Since he was here yesterday, I assumed he was done ghosting you."

Nora studied the wall of coffee mugs. Influenced by the carrot soup, she reached for a white mug with orange lettering that said, COFFEE. BECAUSE PRISON ORANGE ISN'T MY COLOR.

"I don't know what's up with Grant, but I do know that Tucker Walsh has inherited a collection that could be worth two hundred grand." Sheldon whistled and Nora opened the photo app on her phone. "That's not all. His grandmother, who had a thing for valentines and books with the word *love* in the title, also left him a boxful of antiques. Ever seen anything like this before?"

Sheldon took the phone from her and brought it closer to his face. "What am I looking at? Are those shells?"

Nora told him about the Disney pins, the German candy container, and the name of the object in the photo.

"Doctor your coffee while I turn to the great and powerful Internet for help."

Nora stirred half-and-half into her coffee and took one sip before Sheldon started tugging on her sleeve.

"This is interesting. Back in the Victorian era, there was this crazy thing called 'conchylomania.' Sounds like an STD, but it's not. It's the act of obsessively collecting seashells."

"Didn't they collect bugs too? And stamps? And bones? I think it was part of the whole cabinet-of-curiosities thing."

"Yeah, but no one's going to pay thousands of dollars for some creepy bug pinned to red velvet."

"Will they pay thousands of dollars for tiny shells?"

Sheldon raised a finger. "Patience. You need to hear the backstory first. And it *was* a story. A fictional tale worthy of a Grimm brother."

Nora put her hand on her hip. "I'm not following."

"Lots of people believe that sailors spent their solitary moments creating these works of seashell art for their sweeties back home. I get it. It's a romantic tale. You can almost see these grizzled men sitting on the deck of some huge ship, smoking a pipe while gluing tiny shells to a piece of cotton batting with a strong, scarred, tattooed hand."

"That's not what happened?"

"No. As much as we'd like to think that these rough-and-ready men combed the beaches for shells and sketched designs into the sand, they didn't. Sailor's valentines are the products of a cottage industry souvenir shop. Made in Barbados, baby. It's where most of the shells were found and lots of ships stopped at the island during their travels. As vintage pieces of art, they're beautiful, and the women who made them obviously put great care into their craft."

"So, they're more like something you'd pick up at the airport because you forgot to buy a gift for your sweetheart on your trip?"

Sheldon laughed. "Exactly. But like I said, lots of people cling to the romantic legend and have no idea that they're antique souvenirs. Now, let's talk money. One very similar to this sold last year for five grand."

Nora nearly snorted her sip of coffee. Forcing it down her throat, she said, "*What?*"

"Yeah. And get this! People are still making these things. Some of the twentieth-century pieces sold for even more." He started untying his apron. "That's it. I'm moving back to Florida to spend the rest of my days gluing shells to a little hexagonal box."

"I wouldn't let you do that to your hands."

Sheldon examined his knuckles as if expecting them to be inflamed. "Guess I'll stick to coffee art. Oh! I almost forgot to tell you. Gus got a job."

"Already? That's great! Where?"

"Ever heard of Midnight Chicken?"

Nora nodded. "It's not far from Pearl's. I've never been in, but isn't it attached to a twenty-four-hour truck stop?"

"That's the one. Starting tonight, he'll be frying chicken, baking biscuits, and seasoning waffle fries."

"I'm glad someone gave him a chance. Estella must be thrilled."

Sheldon gave her arm an affectionate squeeze. "She's going to tell you later, so pretend to be surprised. I just thought you could use a little good news."

A knocking sound came from the front of the shop and Nora cried, "It's after ten!"

Nora opened the door, apologized to her customers, and flipped the sign over to read OPEN.

After powering on her register, she moved the book cart Sheldon had left in the middle of the aisle dividing Romance and Mystery and continued to work on the bee-themed display. Though the one-day festival didn't start until tomorrow, visitors would be keyed up to buy bee-related items all weekend long.

Miracle Springs hosted festivals and street fairs every month of the year, but the second half of April marked the start of the true festival season. Nora was energized by the thought of all the new people she'd see entering her shop from now until October.

The tourists seemed equally invigorated. They roamed about the shop while sipping iced coffee and chatting. They pulled books from the shelves, piled books on tables and chairs, and carried shelf enhancers around only to put them back in the wrong spot.

Nora didn't mind. A messy shop was the sign of a busy

shop. As long as nothing was damaged, she could handle a little disarray.

She was helping two ladies pick out books for their grand-children when one woman whispered to the other, "For heaven's sake. That girl is practically naked."

Her companion kissed her teeth and said, "That's how they dress these days. Nothing left to the imagination."

Nora turned to see a young woman in a white midriff-baring top, cutoffs, and cowboy boots standing in front of the ticket agent's booth. She had toned, tanned limbs, long and lustrous brown hair, and huge breasts. Her eyes were glued to her phone, and she twirled a lock of hair around her finger while she waited to place her order.

"Did you ever dress like that?" one of the ladies asked Nora.

"No, but I never looked as good as she does," Nora replied. She didn't want to alienate her customers, but she wasn't going to belittle another woman behind her back either. Gesturing at a waterfall display of picture books on gardening, she pointed to *Planting a Rainbow* and told the ladies about Thursday's storytime activity.

"What a clever idea!" exclaimed the first woman. "My son's children are such fussy eaters. Maybe this will get them to try something made with vegetables. Besides ketchup."

The second woman smiled and said, "I'm going to paint a rainbow garden with my granddaughter. Do you have any kid-friendly cookbooks?"

And just like that, the young woman in the crop top was for-gotten.

Shortly after the two ladies left, their teal Miracle Springs Lodge tote bags laden with books, Nora decided there was enough of a lull to walk the shop and straighten the shelves.

Of all the genres, romance novels seemed most likely to sprout wings and travel to different parts of the store. Nora had gath-ered an armload of books with pastel covers—which she fondly referred to as Jordan Almond covers—and was starting to put them in their proper places when the young woman in the crop top appeared at her side.

"Do you work here?" she asked.

Nora slid a book into its proper place and said, "I sure do. Can I help you find something?"

"Um, maybe." She glanced over her shoulder to see if anyone else was within hearing distance before continuing. "Do you have books about getting guys to want you?"

Nora must've done a poor job at concealing her surprise, because the woman suddenly laughed and swept an arm down the length of her body.

"Not like, wanting to have sex with me. That's easy. I mean, like, falling in love with me."

"In other words, you want them to see past your outer beauty and get to know you as a person?"

The woman smiled, revealing a mouthful of straight, electric-white teeth. Her eyes were a lovely shade of greenish gray. They reminded Nora of moss-covered stones.

I'm totally staring at her.

To cover her embarrassment, Nora introduced herself.

"And I'm Justine. I'm here on vacay with my man. He's *so* amazing! He's smart and super rich. And he's been all over the world." After a pause, she added, "He's kind of a player too. I knew that when I got with him, but I want to be the only woman in his life. I want him to put a ring on it." The corner of her lips dipped in the semblance of a frown. "The thing is, I think he's getting bored with me. I see him checking out other girls. I need to make him obsessed with me and *only* me."

Nora's eyes roved over the shelves. "How much steam do you like? No steam or steamy enough to fog a mirror?"

Justine stared at her blankly.

"Do you prefer this?" Nora showed her Alice Clayton's

Wallbanger followed by Debbie Macomber's *The Best Is Yet to Come*. "Or this?"

"Um, I don't know. I haven't read a book in a really long time. Can you just find something short that'll tell me what to do to keep my man?"

"I can pull a few titles for you. Would you be interested in any nonfiction?"

A tiny line appeared between Justine 's pencil-lined brows. "Nah. I want a book that's like a movie."

"Okay. You can keep browsing or take a seat and I'll bring you a small pile to look through in a few minutes."

Justine walked away and Nora moved deeper into the stacks, her gaze skirting over titles as she made a mental checklist of romance tropes.

Older man. Second chance. Jealousy and possession. Mistress heroine.

As a reader, Nora tended to stick with rom-coms, historical romance, and romantic suspense, so she wasn't as versed in the tropes she was looking for as she needed to be. She found two suitable titles, and after a quick text to June, was able to add three more to the pile.

She carried the books to Justine. The young woman had her cowboy boots on the coffee table and was watching a makeup tutorial on her phone.

Nora placed the books on the table and said, "Take your time looking through these. I'll be at the checkout counter if you need me."

Five minutes later, Justine appeared. She fanned the books across the counter and said, "If you were me, which one would you pick?"

Nora glanced down at Christina Lauren's *Beautiful Stranger*, Lynda Chance's *The Mistress Mistake*, *The Marriage Bargain* by Jennifer Probst, Sylvia Day's *One with You*, and *This Man* by Jodi Ellen Malpas.

"I'd have to read the back cover blurbs before I made my choice. Did any of the summaries speak to you?"

"Are you married?" Justine blurted.

Nora shook her head.

"Have you ever been?"

"Once, a long time ago. It didn't work out."

Justine put both hands on the counter and leaned closer to Nora. "If you could go back in time, would you do whatever you could to stay married?"

Eager to put an end to the conversation, Nora simply said no before randomly selecting one of the books on the counter and showing it to the younger woman. "I think you should give this a try."

"I don't," Justine scoffed. "Books didn't work for you, so why should I waste my time on them? This place"—her pretty mouth twisted in derision as she waved a hand at the stacks— "is for people like you. *Old people. My* generation is all about action. If I want something, I buy it online. If I'm hungry, I have food delivered. And if I want to avoid ending up like you, I'll read threads on Reddit and focus on my self-care. Your coffee's good, but it's not good enough to make you relevant. Even coffee couldn't have saved Blockbuster."

The sleigh bells rang, signaling the arrival of a fresh batch of visitors.

Justine sauntered out of the shop, leaving Nora fuming behind the checkout counter.

Several hours and dozens of lucrative sales later, Justine's comments still rang in Nora's ear. As she locked the store, she spoke to the rude young woman as if she was there, but no matter how much she wanted to tell Justine off, she'd missed her chance.

On her way home, she called June to complain. "She said she didn't want to waste time, but she was fine with wasting *my* time."

"Honey, I smile at people I'd like to smack at least ten times a day. My mama used to say, 'Don't let anybody with dirty feet walk around in your head.' Take her advice and kick that girl out of your nogg. Think about something else. Like that book collection. Want to tell me about it, or are you saving the story for tomorrow night?"

Nora was all too glad to tell June about the love-themed books. In the process, Justine's remarks lost their bite. Nora knew the younger woman was wrong. There would always be a need for bookstores, just as there would always be a need for books. Both were necessary if mankind was to continue evolving.

Later, after dinner, Nora ignored her current read and combed over the books she kept at home. She wanted to flip through the pages of Jack London's *The Sea-Wolf* and tap into the feeling of nautical hardships experienced by generations of seamen. Despite the debunking of their romantic nature, she was still fascinated by sailors' valentines and wanted to lose herself in their world for the evening.

Her fingers were curling around the top of the book's spine when someone pounded on her door.

"Now what?" Nora growled.

She reached the door in three strides and peered through the little square window. Deputies Andrews and Hollowell stood on her deck.

Hollowell was about to knock again when Nora whipped the door open. Looking directly at Andrews, she said, "I take it this isn't a social visit?"

"We need you to come with us," Hollowell demanded.

Pointedly ignoring her, Nora said, "What's this about, Andrews?"

Hollowell sucked in a breath and was undoubtedly going to bark orders at Nora, but Andrews didn't give her the chance.

"There was a break-in at the Walsh place this afternoon. The thief had very specific interests."

Nora paled. "Not the books."

"I'm afraid so."

Hollowell's eyes gleamed. "We dusted every inch of that office for prints. I have a feeling we're going to find all ten of yours there." She paused to shoot a disgusted glance at Nora's pinkie and then added, "Oh, right. All *nine.*"

Chapter 11

We are bees then; our honey is language.
                    —Robert Bly

Nora told the officers to wait outside while she grabbed her purse and a sweatshirt. If she was going to end up in that chilly interview room again, she wanted to be prepared. She also wanted to call Davis Godwin from the privacy of her bedroom.

When he picked up, she said, "There's been a robbery at the Walsh place and officers are waiting outside my house to take me to the station. I don't know if I need a lawyer—"

"You do. Don't say a word to *anyone* about *anything*. Tell them you're not talking without your attorney present."

Oh, my God. I have an attorney.

In novels, people needed lawyers because they'd committed a crime, been falsely accused, or were trying to right a terrible wrong. But none of the characters in those novels were like Nora. She was a middle-aged book nerd whose greatest vices were wine and carbs.

Still, she was relieved to have someone in her corner. Davis wouldn't be intimidated by Hollowell, or anyone else for that matter. His knowledge of the law and confident manner would guide Nora through this ordeal.

How much will his services cost?

Again, Nora thought about book characters. She pictured Mickey Haller, aka "The Lincoln Lawyer," in his custom suits and chauffeured Lincoln Town Car and wondered how much Davis charged an hour.

Guess I won't be buying a car.

The unfairness of her situation made her angry, but she didn't tamp down the feeling. She embraced it. It was better to be angry than scared.

Someone pounded on her front door and Nora hurried back to the living room. If it had just been Hollowell, Nora might have let her stand outside and fume a little longer, but since Andrews was there too, she opened the door and said, "I'm ready."

The short ride to the station was marked by awkward silence. Nora and Andrews had always gotten along. They could talk about books, food, movies and the people they knew, so it was strange to be looking out the window while he stared fixedly ahead. The only noise was a brief exchange between the dispatcher and a deputy on patrol.

"That's the third coyote report this week," Andrews murmured.

"They're hungry. People with indoor/outdoor cats better wise up or Fluffy's going to end up as someone's dinner." Hollowell sounded pleased by the idea. "Do you have any pets, Andrews?"

Andrews shook his head.

"You seem like a dog man to me. A guy with a truck who can't wait to drive to the lake for some fishing or head to the woods to camp. Just you, the great outdoors, a stocked cooler, and your dog."

You deliberately left Hester out of the picture, didn't you? Nora thought.

A grin appeared on Andrews's face. "I had a chocolate Lab

when I was a kid. His name was Bear. He was the best fishing dog ever. I swear, he was part alligator. And he never got tired."

"See? You should get a dog. I know a bunch of breeders. I could introduce you and help you train your puppy too."

Nora rolled her eyes.

Andrews pulled up to the back door of the sheriff's department building and Hollowell leaped out. Nora exited the car before Hollowell could touch her. When Hollowell reached for her arm, Nora jerked it away and said, "I can walk without assistance."

Hollowell opened her mouth to argue but shut it again when she saw Davis Godwin waiting on the other side of the glass doors. He held a briefcase in one hand and a phone in the other, but his eyes were on Nora. As were McCabe's.

Here we go, Nora thought.

Davis gave McCabe a curt nod before marching forward to meet his client.

After politely acknowledging Hollowell with an "Evening, Deputy," he put a hand on Nora's arm. She instinctively moved closer to him.

"They're going to ask you some questions, but don't worry," Davis murmured into her ear. "I'll be with you the whole time."

Davis turned to Hollowell. "My client will cooperate, but tomorrow's a big day for area merchants. I don't want her here a minute longer than is strictly necessary. So, what do you need from us?"

"We need her prints," was all Hollowell had to say.

Hollowell led Nora and Davis to the conference room down the hall from McCabe's office.

Andrews and Hollowell sat across the table from Nora and Davis.

McCabe entered the room, nodded at Davis, and settled in a chair behind his deputies. He leaned back, crossed an ankle over his knee, and placed a legal pad on his leg.

Nora felt a twinge of indignation. Couldn't he muster a congenial glance? A dip of the chin or a quick wink? Couldn't he find some way of telling her not to be afraid? That he believed in her innocence? That he loved her?

The interview began with Andrews saying, "Tell us how you came to be at the Walsh residence yesterday."

Relieved to be speaking with Andrews instead of Hollowell, Nora replied to his questions with clear, concise answers. Davis listened carefully and interjected only to request that a question be clarified or rephrased. He sat upright in his chair, his head moving back and forth like he was watching a tennis match. His sharp gaze never faltered, and Nora was comforted by his proximity.

Andrews moved through his initial questions quickly. He took a brief pause before asking, "Did you leave the store during business hours today?"

"No. Kirk made lunch for me and Sheldon, so I didn't need to go out for food. We were busy all day. I didn't even have time to water the plants out front."

Hollowell drummed her thumb against the table. "What about your employee, Sheldon Vega? Did you tell him about the book collection?"

"Yes."

"What time did he clock out?"

Though Nora sensed danger in this line of questioning, she had to respond. "Around 3:20."

Hollowell arched her brows and said, "How does Mr. Vega get home from work?"

"He usually walks. If the weather's bad, his housemate will pick him up at the store when she gets off."

"Did he walk home today?"

Nora had marched right into her trap. "Yes."

Hollowell looked a question at McCabe. He dipped his chin once and her eyes flashed with triumph.

Poor Sheldon, Nora thought. She wished she'd never told him about the books.

"After leaving the Walsh residence, you said that you went home and started researching how much the books were worth," Hollowell continued. "Why the rush?"

"Two reasons. I wanted to help Tucker and I was curious."

Hollowell nodded encouragingly. "How long did it take you to realize that the books were worth a lot of money?"

"By the time I got to the end of the first page of the inventory list, I knew the collection could be very valuable. I couldn't confirm this without seeing the books first. Condition is really important. Here. I brought the list with me." Nora pushed the thin stack of paper across the table. "I wrote down the prices I found."

Andrews put the list where he and Hollowell could look at it at the same time. They both studied it for a minute.

When Hollowell glanced at Nora, her mouth was turned down at the corners. "How was this partnership supposed to work? Were you going to take all the books, sell them, and give Mr. Walsh the money? Did you two sign a contract?"

"No. I went to his house this morning to take a quick look at the condition of some of the books. When I saw that they were as good as that list said they were, I told Kirk that I wasn't the person to sell the collection. A rare book dealer or auction house would net a higher profit. I told him I could recommend a few names."

Hollowell cocked her head. "Would you get a commission or a finder's fee for hooking him up with one of these businesses?"

"No."

"So, let me get this straight. After seeing this incredibly valuable collection of books, you told Mr. Walsh that you couldn't sell them for him. Did you also warn him to move the collection to a secure location?"

Nora sensed another trap, but since that's exactly what happened, she said, "Yes."

"Ms. Pennington, how long have you been saving money to buy a car?"

Davis held up his hand. "My client's finances aren't up for discussion. Unless you have specific questions about my client's movements or her opinions on Mr. Walsh's book collection, we're done here. Sheriff? Can we wrap this up? My client has a long day ahead of her tomorrow."

Addressing his deputies, McCabe said, "Get her prints and let her go. I'll speak with Mr. Vega."

He stood up and moved to the door while Andrews announced the termination of the interview and turned off the recording device.

Nora got to her feet and spoke to McCabe. "Sheldon will be in bed by now. With his conditions—sleep is so important."

"He doesn't need to come in. I'll go to him," McCabe said. In a softer tone, he added, "Thank you for your cooperation. I'll see you at the shop tomorrow."

With those words, Nora knew that all was well between them.

After she'd been fingerprinted, Davis offered to drive her home.

When they were alone in the car, he loosened his tie and relaxed his shoulders. "They're going to find your prints all over those plastic bins. As long as they don't find them on the back door, which is how the thief got in, they can't pin this on you."

Hearing this, Nora's fear evaporated. "I never went near the back door."

"Good."

Nora let out a sigh. "I'm relieved for myself, but not for Tucker. Without the money from that collection, his future isn't nearly as bright. Did the thief take everything?"

"At this point, it's unclear what's missing. Someone tossed a rock through the glass in the back door, got inside, and unwrapped every single book. Until Kirk compares what's there to what's on the inventory sheet, he won't know what was taken. The room's a mess."

"On the night Kelly died, a woman came to their house. It was late, and this woman talked to Kelly from a distance—in the backyard. Maybe she was there because she wanted something from the collection. Maybe Kelly was killed because she didn't hand it over."

Davis pulled in front of Nora's house and put his car in park. "That's for the sheriff to find out. My job is to look after you. And *your* job is to stay away from the Walshes. You're already tied to an open murder investigation, a B and E, and probably larceny too. You've got to be smart, Nora."

"I'll keep my distance. I promise."

Later, when she climbed into bed, she examined the inventory list of Virginia Love's books. She'd taken photos of the list in case she needed to send it to a book dealer or auction house, but now, she might be able to use it to identify the thief.

However, no title stood head and shoulders above the rest. Some were worth more than others, but not by a staggering amount.

Too tired to think clearly, Nora turned off the light and rolled onto her side.

Was something hidden in the pages of a book? A treasure inside a treasure?

This was her last lucid thought before sleep carried her away.

Nora dressed in the yellow T-shirt she'd received from the Miracle Springs Chamber of Commerce. The shirt featured a cartoon bee hovering over the word HAPPY. Sheldon's bee smiled over the word KIND.

"What if I don't feel kind or positive?" he grumbled as he scooped coffee grounds into the brew basket. "I vote for an alternative text. How about BEE QUIET? Or BUZZ OFF?"

Smiling wryly, Nora said, "Or BEE-WARE: I'M UNDERCAFFEINATED."

Sheldon slipped his apron on. "I get to cover mine up. *You* have to be happy *all* day."

"After last night, that's going to take a double espresso and a shit-ton of book sales."

"And sugar. Thank gawd for Hester. She gave us a few of her mistakes." He pointed at a small bakery box. "Honey-glazed donut holes. I may or may not have eaten a solid dozen already."

Nora reached for a donut. "How'd you manage that while carrying the bakery boxes?"

"Ever seen a horse feedbag?"

Nora dropped the donut back in the box, and despite Sheldon protesting that he was only kidding, she ate a peach muffin instead.

Despite last night's trip to the sheriff's department, Nora was energized. She looked forward to a hectic day of putting books into readers' hands.

She breezed through the Children's Corner, straightening the waterfall display of board books about honey, and repositioning the wooden chest filled with Winnie the Pooh plush toys. Honeybee, ladybug, and butterfly puppets occupied every branch of the puppet tree and boxes of a game called Honey Bee Tree were stacked in between the bookcases.

Satisfied by what she saw, Nora walked to the front of the store. The yellow and black book table was done, as was a large waterfall display of fiction, which contained titles like *The Secret Life of Bees*, *Bee Season*, *The Beekeeper of Aleppo*, *A Taste for Honey*, and *The Honey Bus*.

Nora spent the next hour rearranging the Romance endcaps

with books with yellow covers or references to honey. It was harder to find mystery novels to display, but she managed to find several cozy mystery titles as well as Laurie R. King's *The Language of Bees* and J. A. Jance's *Kiss of the Bees.*

The YA section contained a whole row of Kathe Koja's *Kissing the Bee* and Mobi Warren's *The Bee Maker.* Nora stood in front of Warren's book, which featured a group of origami bees on a blue background. She'd ordered the title weeks before meeting Tucker, but she couldn't look at the book without thinking of him.

Brushing her fingertips over the cover, she whispered, "Poor kid."

Turning away from the display, she pulled a few books about the healing power of plants as well as a cookbook with over a hundred honey-based recipes and slid them into acrylic book holders on top of one of the low bookcases. After distributing an assortment of bee-print book sleeves between the display books, she stood back and admired the effect.

"We're ready," she told Sheldon as she returned to the ticket agent's booth to collect her espresso. "Except for tunes. What music goes with today's festival?"

"We could put 'Flight of the Bumblebee' on repeat."

"I'd kill someone by ten thirty."

Sheldon pointed at her shirt. "I'll find some *happy* music. You drink your magical elixir and get ready to sell all the books."

For the next three hours, that's what Nora did.

Customers entered the shop smelling of funnel cake, honey lotion, and sunshine. They had bumblebees painted on their cheeks or bee antenna headbands in their hair. Some of the kids were in full costume. They zipped about the shop, fueled by honey donuts, chocolate honeycomb cookies, and honey banana smoothies while their parents guzzled iced coffee or collapsed into reading chairs.

At quarter to one, June's son, Tyson, entered the shop carrying a brown paper bag in each hand.

"Hey, Ms. Nora. My mom told me to drop these off for you and Sheldon. She wanted me to tell you that you've got to eat, even if you have to hide behind the counter."

"Your mom's the best," Nora said, accepting the bags. "Did you wade through the crowds just to bring this or are you working at the theater today?"

Tyson jerked his thumb toward the door. "I'm here with Jasmine, but she's buying jam and spicy pickles from the booth outside the hardware store and she's gonna be there a while."

"Do you want an iced coffee? I could make one for Jasmine too," Nora said, referring to Tyson's girlfriend.

"No, thanks. After she buys up half the farm stand, we're heading back to my place to chill. See ya!"

Nora took the bags back to the ticket agent's booth. "June is a saint."

Sheldon leaned against the counter and wiped his flushed face with a damp paper towel. "Actually, *I'm* a saint. Why? Because I didn't smack the bejesus out of the man who complained that I used sour milk in his latte. I didn't argue. I just made him a fresh one with a new carton of milk. And even though he *watched* me make it, he still asked for a free pastry so he could get the sour taste out of his mouth."

"I think you need a T-shirt that says, DON'T *BEE* AN ASS-HOLE."

Sheldon cracked a smile. "Our customers are beautiful people, *mija*, but every now and then, we get a real—no! I'm going to listen to June and refuse to let that jerk walk around in my head with his dirty feet for another second. What's for lunch?"

Nora insisted Sheldon take a thirty-minute break in the stockroom. He needed to put his feet up and rest if he was going to make it until three. Nora would grab fifteen minutes when he was done. Until then, she was determined to make drinks and ring up books without missing a beat.

Things were going just fine until she looked up to see Mc-Cabe standing in front of her.

"Can I buy you a coffee?"

Normally, the familiar line would have made Nora smile, but she was distracted by the number of customers milling about. Every reading chair was taken. The Children's Corner was crammed with little bodies, and six people were waiting to order coffee.

"Can you come back here?" she asked McCabe.

The next customer wanted an iced latte, and while Nora fulfilled his order, she made two ice waters for McCabe and herself.

Accepting his cup, McCabe said, "Are you doing okay?"

Nora nodded as she guzzled water. She then took a bite of turkey and cheese sandwich and chewed furiously.

McCabe's eyes took in the dirty dishes in the sink and the succession of milk rings on the counter. "Where's Sheldon?"

"Stockroom," Nora said before taking another bite.

A woman's face appeared in the order window and McCabe touched the brim of his hat and said, "What'll be, ma'am?"

"Oh! I've never been served by a sheriff before!" The woman giggled. "A large Wilkie Collins, please."

McCabe turned to Nora. "Keep eating. I've got this."

After he served the woman, she placed a five-dollar bill on the ledge and told him to keep the change.

The next customer wanted a cappuccino, which was beyond McCabe's abilities. While Nora made the drink, McCabe wiped off the counter and hung the dry mugs back on the peg board. She finished half of the sandwich while he served an Agatha Chris-Tea. When the next customer asked for two hot lattes, McCabe began washing dirty mugs.

Sheldon returned to find a very tidy workspace.

"You go above and beyond when it comes to serving your community, Sheriff. Can you take this woman to the stockroom and make her sit down? She's got to be in Energizer Bunny mode for five more hours."

Nora grabbed the rest of her lunch and followed McCabe down the hall.

"Is it safe to be here with me?" she asked when they were alone.

"I'm just making the rounds—same as I always do with every festival. I already stopped by the Gingerbread House. Hester looks like she might keel over any second. I thought she was going to hire someone to help her out."

"She hasn't found the right person yet." Nora began peeling the tangerine June had given her. "We don't have much time, so can you tell me where things stand?"

"Between us or with the investigation?"

Nora piled the bits of peel on a napkin and said, "Both."

"You and I are fine. I wish I could say the same for the investigation." His shoulders fell. "It's stalled. We have no suspects in either case."

"Except me."

Nora popped a tangerine segment into her mouth. The bright, sweet juice felt like a jolt of sunshine.

McCabe said, "Val's holding something back. There's more to that story about Kelly talking to a woman the night before she died. I was going to call her back in and make her go through it again—pressing harder this time—but then the robbery went down."

"It wasn't a random break-in. The thief knew about the collection. An old friend or relative? Someone who knew Virginia Love?"

"Your former mother-in-law."

"I probably saw her five or six times in my entire life. I never went to her house, and she never mentioned books to me. She knew I was a librarian, but she never told me about her collection."

McCabe was listening intently. "What did she talk about?"

"She mostly asked her son about his work and hobbies and stuff. She was pretty quiet. But someone knew her collection well enough to steal it. Have you seen her will?"

"Yes, and while it seems straightforward enough, there are reams of documents from the court case contesting it. Those aren't straightforward. I've talked to both of her sons. Roman's the youngest, right?" At Nora's nod, he continued. "He had the key to the storage locker where the collection was kept until the Walshes picked it up on their way to Miracle Springs. We checked the records, and no one's been in the locker for three years—not until Kirk and Val collected the bins."

"Maybe Roman needed money."

"I don't think so. He's an oral surgeon with a thriving practice. His wife's a successful architect."

As Nora unwrapped the other half of her sandwich, she said, "And Lawrence? People say he's rolling in it. Is that true?"

"He spends money like a sheik, but without access to his financial records, I don't know how much he's got. Same goes for Roman. As for the Walshes, Kelly was Kirk's only family and Val's people are all on the West Coast."

Nora could tell by the way McCabe turned the brim of his hat around in his hands that he was getting ready to leave. She put down her sandwich and said, "Kelly was dying. What would motivate her to leave her house in the middle of the night? It had to be something related to Tucker. She would've done anything to protect him. He was her world. And she was his."

McCabe got to his feet. "I wish I had more to tell you. Hell, I wish I had a lead to chase. I don't like having to act like we're strangers."

"Come here," Nora whispered, opening her arms.

They held each other for a full minute. Then a kid in the

Children's Corner began to wail and Nora took a step back and said, "I've got to go."

McCabe donned his hat. "I know you're going to do your own investigating—and I don't blame you. Just be careful, okay?"

He tucked her hair behind her ear, gazing at her as if her face was the loveliest thing he'd ever seen. Then he kissed his fingertips, pressed them to her lips, and walked away.

The rest of the afternoon flew by, and the infusion of energy Nora had felt after seeing McCabe was thoroughly exhausted by four o'clock.

She was behind the counter, bagging books for a young couple, when she heard a woman moan, "Ugh! These are gonna *break*! I need to wrap them in something."

The woman's Minnie Mouse voice sounded familiar, but when Nora glanced at the curly-haired brunette in a black Metallica T-shirt emptying the contents of her purse onto the counter, she didn't recognize her face.

The woman lined up three glass bottles of honey, a set of keys, and a lipstick, all while manically chewing a piece of gum.

"Hey," the woman said to Nora in between chomps. "Do you have a plastic bag I could wrap these in?"

"We only have paper." Nora gestured at the bag stamped with the Miracle Books logo she'd just packed for her customer. She then grabbed yesterday's newspaper from under the counter and pushed it toward the woman. "Help yourself."

"Thanks," she said.

The woman may have sounded like Minnie Mouse, but she looked like Stockard Channing's Rizzo. The high, squeaky voice was incongruent with the squished package of cigarettes sticking out of her jeans pocket, the cheap silver ring stacks on every finger, and the cow-grazing movements of her jaw.

Nora took care of her next customer while Rizzo wrapped

the honey jars in newspaper. She then stuffed everything back in her purse and pulled out her phone. Pressing it to her ear, she said, "Hey, babe. Do you still want coffee? Okay, *okay*! Chill. I'll meet you on the corner right now!"

She scooped up her purse and headed for the door, leaving a jar of honey on the counter. "Wait!" Nora called, but Rizzo kept walking.

She was halfway out the door when Nora touched her arm and showed her the jar she'd left behind.

The woman signaled for Nora to drop it in her purse while simultaneously promising the person on the other end of the phone that she was going as fast as she could.

The moment the jar was safely in her purse, Rizzo pushed through the crowd and hopped on the back of a black motorcycle idling next to the sidewalk. Though she barely had time to put on her helmet before the driver pulled away from the curb, she still managed to turn toward the bookstore and flip someone the bird.

For some reason, Nora thought that someone might be her.

Chapter 12

Thinking of the past is like digging up graves.
—Nathan Filer

"Are you getting up or should I grab a funnel and pour your cocktail straight down your throat?"

Nora opened her eyes and gave June a weary smile. "Funnel."

Estella peered at Nora over the back of her chair. "That carpet isn't the most hygienic place for a nap."

"I know, but my back is sore and it feels good to lie down on a hard surface." Nora let out a groan. "Okay, I'm going to sit up now. Give me another hour and I might make it to a chair."

"Don't hassle her," Hester scolded. "You and June don't understand what festival days are like for the two of us. My feet hurt, my shoulders hurt, and my face hurts from smiling. Also, I don't want to see, smell, or taste anything made with honey for the rest of my life."

"Not even a honey spritzer?" asked June.

Hester winced. "Please tell me that isn't what we're drinking."

Estella darted into the ticket agent's booth and reemerged carrying a tray of drinks. "Don't worry, *honey.* Since we're discussing *Silent Spring* tonight, I wanted to make a drink that looked and tasted clean. Rachel Carson really got me thinking about the chemicals in food, so *this* is my Spring Purity Spritzer. Stop laughing, June. I'm talking about the cocktail, not my sexual history! It's made with fresh mint and lime, elderberry syrup, sparkling water, and prosecco."

June passed a glass to Nora. "You obviously need a medicinal cocktail. Or four."

"Anyone have a toast that doesn't sound like a platitude from our ridiculous bee T-shirts?" asked Hester.

Estella opened her copy of *Silent Spring* and recited, "'The balance of nature is not a status quo; it is fluid, ever shifting, in a constant state of adjustment. Man, too, is part of this balance.'" She raised her glass. "To balance."

"To balance," Nora echoed and sipped her drink. The bright mint and lime flavors and the invigorating bubbles of prosecco danced on her tongue. Estella's spritzer was as crisp and refreshing as the cold, clean water of a mountain lake.

"Estella, you are a woman of many talents," said Hester. "How's the week of sobriety going?"

"Fine. I didn't even miss my nightly nips. Except for last night. After my dad started talking about his new job, I really wanted a drink. Beer, wine, cold medicine—I almost chugged Listerine."

Nora hauled herself up from the floor and took the chair next to Estella's. "What's going on?"

"I'm not sure. My dad's working with a few other ex-prisoners, and though he hasn't shared details, he definitely knows one of them. He said the man's a snake in the grass and anyone with sense should steer clear of the guy. When I dropped my dad off at the truck stop earlier, he looked . . . worried."

June clucked her tongue. "Your daddy doesn't want any trouble, so he'll figure out how to deal with this man. He's probably going to face lots of challenges like this. All you can do is trust his judgment and support his decisions."

Estella pulled a face. "Which is what I do. It's just that I had a bad feeling when I drove away. I was tempted to roll down the window and shout for him to get back in the car. Maybe he should find a different job. There must be a place for him to work where he doesn't have to be around people who, I don't know, make him feel like he's still incarcerated."

"Tell him how you feel and see how he reacts," Nora suggested. "It's no good to hold this stuff in."

Estella pushed her glass away. "I must be internalizing my stress because my stomach is nothing but knots. Here's my chance to have a drink and I don't even want it."

Hester put a hand on Estella's arm. "Everything will work out. And you'd better load your plate with food now because there might not be anything left when I'm done. I'm hungry enough to eat the mint right out of your glass."

"Come with me, hangry girl. I made mac and cheese in the slow cooker." June led Hester into the ticket agent's booth.

When Nora made to stand, Estella said, "Stay put. I'll fix you a plate. If anyone has a reason to stress eat, it's you."

She came back a minute later with a steaming bowlful of mac and cheese. Nora told June it was the best she'd ever had.

"The secret is Parmesan cheese and mustard powder. You can't taste the mustard, but it gives the cheese sauce an extra zing. After the week you've had, Estella and I figured that booze, books, and comfort food would do you good."

"Is there anything else we can do? Like figure out who the real killer is so your life can go back to normal?" asked Estella.

Nora let out a wistful sigh. "If only."

Hester said, "We should at least try. I'd do anything to repay you—all of you—for saving my life a few months ago, so I'm in. The question is, how do we succeed when law enforcement hasn't?"

"Let's just talk things out like we do with all of our problems," June suggested. "You're probably sick of telling your side of the story, Nora, but we might pick up on some tiny detail that could make all the difference. Start by telling us about the day Kelly and Tucker came into the store and keep going until you were questioned about the break-in."

In between bites of food, Nora did as June asked. When she was done, Estella said, "After all this, you *still* haven't stalked your ex on social media?"

Nora shook her head.

"That needs to happen right now." June pulled out her phone. "Sorry, Rachel Carson, but we'll have to get riled up about the environment another time."

Hester pointed at June. "You take Lawrence. I'll take Roman. Nora, where's your laptop?"

Estella pushed her cocktail across the coffee table toward Nora. "Here. This'll take the sting off whatever you're about to see."

"I honestly don't care about Lawrence or what he's done with his life."

"I'm not talking about that fleabite of a human. I've known men like Lawrence. Whatever he did to you, he did to Kelly, and to the woman after that and the woman after that. Whether he left Kelly, or she kicked him out, she ended up as a single mom. Tucker ended up as a kid with an absentee dad. I know what it's like to grow up in a broken home, and I know Kelly had her family's support, but I bet she went through some hard times."

Nora had been trying not to think about Tucker because every time she did, she felt paralyzed by sadness. Since no one wanted to interact with a depressed bookseller, she'd spent the past seven hours trying to live up to the slogan on her T-shirt. But that didn't mean that she wasn't sad, worried, and tired.

June broke the sudden silence by saying, "We need to write down the names of anyone who could have known about Virginia's book collection. Kelly must've been killed because of those books. The woman who came to the Walsh place obviously wanted something, and I take it Kelly didn't give it to her. After getting Kelly out of the way, the woman went back for it. That would explain the break-in."

Hester put Nora's laptop on the coffee table and positioned it so that Nora could see the screen. "Virginia's maiden name was Love. But what was her married name? What was *your* married name?"

"Townsend."

Armed with this information, June and Hester began their searches. While they clicked and scrolled, Estella volunteered to clean their dinner dishes.

Hester had no trouble finding Roman Townsend online. Because he was a practicing physician, his profile was listed on several medical directories. These profiles included his education and training, credentials, journal publications, and patient reviews. His Arizona-based oral surgery practice included recent photos of the physicians, and Nora recognized Roman right away.

"He has less hair and more lines on his face, but he hasn't changed much. He always looked rumpled—like he just woke up. But he was smarter than he looked and didn't have a mean bone in his body. He had a great sense of humor. I never saw him after he moved to Arizona."

June said, "Lawrence and Roman are both on LinkedIn and Facebook, but they don't follow each other. They probably stopped talking after Roman took Lawrence to court."

Estella's head appeared in the pass-through window. "Why don't you ask Davis to review the lawsuit? The answers everyone's looking for might be somewhere in those documents."

"I can't afford it. McCabe told me that there are reams of paperwork from that case," Nora said.

Over the sound of running water, Estella shouted, "If we knew which state Virginia's will was filed in, we could get a copy and comb through it on our own."

Nora shouted back, "Unless she moved before she passed, her will would've been filed in Maryland."

"We'll get to that when we're done with the brothers, and I don't think there's much more for me to find on Roman," Hester said. "He's married with three kids and coaches a Little League team. His wife, an architect, runs marathons and is on the board of the local animal shelter. They have a joint Facebook account, and there's lots of photos of kids playing baseball and soccer or at dance class, holidays, birthdays, and family trips. This man couldn't kill anyone. He doesn't have the time."

"We're looking at his life through a filter, but from what I see, he's got it pretty good. A family. A long-term marriage. Friends. Fulfilling career. Big house with a pool. He and his wife seem like upstanding members of their community." Nora pointed at a photo of Roman and his daughter grilling burgers. "Look at the date. This was posted the night Kelly died."

Hester turned to June. "Let's use the laptop to look at Lawrence so we can all see the screen. I bet *he* wasn't cooking burgers when Kelly was killed."

"He probably has a private chef," June grumbled.

Estella asked them to wait until she made herself a cup of tea. While she was busy doing that, June took their dessert out of the fridge and placed it in the center of the coffee table.

"Strawberry-lemon cheesecake bites. No bake, no fuss. And before you go thanking me, I can't take credit for these little lovelies. Jasmine made a huge batch for work—one of the other nurses was having a birthday—and she accidentally tripled the recipe instead of doubling it."

"She and Tyson are the sweetest couple. I hope they stay together forever," Hester said.

June clasped her hands together and gazed at the ceiling. "From your lips to God's ears."

For once, Nora wasn't tempted by dessert. The mac and cheese sat in her stomach like a brick, and as Hester typed Lawrence's name into Google's search box, that sense of heaviness intensified. It felt like an unseen force was pushing down on her shoulders.

Estella reemerged from the ticket agent's booth carrying two cups of tea. She set one down in front of Nora. "If we're going to figure this out, we need to be as sharp as my steel-toe stilettos."

"Lawrence is going to be a tricky case," said June. "He doesn't use social media like your everyday Joe. As the CEO of Windward Management, his image is carefully curated. I found a bunch of articles on his business in *Bloomberg*, *Wall Street Journal*, *Money*, et cetera. Most of these talk about how he got in the cryptocurrency game. The only interview that even touched on his personal life was a piece from the Georgetown alumni magazine, and all they got out of him was that he divides his time between his houses in Northern Virginia, South Beach, Aspen, and Westchester, New York."

Hester whistled. "Little Lord Fauntleroy in the flesh."

"That's an insult to Lord Fauntleroy, who taught his grandfather the true meaning of gentility," corrected Nora. "Lawrence was only philanthropical when he wanted a tax write-off. He wasn't stingy, and we never fought about money, but he wasn't a charitable man. He was a hard worker, and he was ambitious. Back then, I thought these were good qualities in a husband. We split up before I realized that he cared more about status and material goods than anything else."

June snorted. "And the adoration of younger women. Don't forget that."

Hester ran a new search for Lawrence by combining his name with the word *dating*. This resulted in dozens of hits from gossip rags. Thumbnail images of Lawrence with a different woman on his arm, each more beautiful than the last, marched across the laptop screen.

"Naomi, Paloma, Daphne, Justine, Ana—look at all of them. He's dated a string of models, actresses, and social media influencers. Do we really need to research all these women? Some of these relationships had the shelf life of a loaf of bread."

"What about his third wife?"

Hester started typing. "Robyn. She was a flight attendant when they met. According to this celebrity gossip blog, Lawrence and Robyn had a Vegas wedding after dating a few months. This was right before he made it big in cryptocurrency, but she still signed a prenup. Lawrence tried to annul the marriage within the first month. He accused Robyn of getting pregnant as a way of trapping him."

"Bastard," Estella muttered.

"When annulment didn't work, Lawrence filed for divorce. According to a source close to Robyn, Lawrence pays child support but has never met his daughter." Hester closed her eyes and murmured, "A son and a daughter. He abandoned both of them."

Nora was feeling overwhelmed. She walked away from the Readers' Circle and rested her head against a bookshelf. She breathed in the subtle wood, grass, and vanilla scent of the books until she felt calmer. Then she turned back to her friends and said, "We should make a timeline. Hester, can you open a new Word doc? After that can you look up when Lawrence and Kelly got divorced?"

After running a quick search, Hester recited a date. "Robyn came next. She met Lawrence on a trans-Atlantic flight when he was still married to Kelly."

Estella rolled her eyes. "Of course he did."

"What's Robyn doing now?" Nora asked Hester.

"She works for the same airline, but she's a guest service agent now. And a part-time fitness coach. Here's her Instagram account. Damn! Check out her six-pack."

The four friends were equally impressed by Robyn's toned physique. Scrolling through her feed, they learned that she was a brand ambassador for a line of protein shakes and that her daughter loved gymnastics and ballet.

June said, "Cute kid."

"She looks just like her mom. I can see a little bit of Law-rence in Tucker, but not a trace of him in this little girl," said Nora.

Hester pointed at the screen. "Robyn's bio says that she's a single mom. Maybe Lawrence put her off marriage."

"He seems to have that effect on people," Nora muttered. "Does it say where she lives?"

Hester nodded. "Yeah. Atlanta."

"Did she post the weekend Kelly died?" asked Estella.

"No, but let me see if she's on another social media site."

Nora didn't want to look at any more photos of Lawrence's exes. Seeing them made her feel even lower.

It wasn't jealousy. She was disappointed in herself for having fallen for Lawrence in the first place. Disappointed and embar-rassed. How could she have been so blind to his shortcomings?

He wasn't a bad man for your whole marriage, a small voice chided.

Their marriage hadn't been perfect—no marriage was—but it hadn't been awful either. For the most part, Nora had been content, and she thought Lawrence had been equally content.

She felt sorry for all the women he'd duped. He'd leap-frogged from one woman to the next, spending less and less time with each one. He'd blown three marriages, fathered two children, and traded in girlfriends like they were used cars.

This wasn't the man Nora had known for most of their mar-riage, but it was possible that she'd never known him at all.

A hand touched hers and she looked over to find Hester staring at her.

"You okay?"

"I can't do this anymore tonight. I'm pretty wrecked."

June closed the laptop lid. "To be continued another time. By us, not you. *You* need to sleep late and then go to the flea market. You need a day off from your worries. I'll be praying for you at church tomorrow, and when the three of us are done putting our heads together, we'll stop by and let you know what we learned."

Nora wiped her suddenly damp eyes. "Thank you."

"You don't need to thank us. This is what friends do." Estella took the empty mug from Nora's hands and hugged her. "Turn off the lights, sweetie. Your long, long day is done."

As she parked her moped outside the big red barn at ten the next morning, Nora felt more like herself. She'd slept soundly, woken to sunshine and birdsong, and spent a luxurious hour drinking coffee and reading the paper.

Unlike last week, she was one of the first people in line to shop the flea market and was delighted to find a pair of vintage ceramic magnolia-blossom bookends for a reasonable price. When she expressed interest in a second pair of bookends— hand-painted cast-iron kittens—the vendor offered her a robust discount.

Nora found more treasures deeper in the barn, including a vintage globe, an old library sign, a small Victorian birdcage, a copper tea caddy, and a porcelain chocolate pot with a floral motif.

By the time she reached Bea's booth, she had three shopping bags.

"Did you spend all your money, or do you want to see what I brought in for you?" Bea teased.

"I keep funds in reserve for you," said Nora.

Laughing, Bea waved for her to come around to her side of the booth.

"I figured you could use these for Mother's Day. I bought the whole lot from a sweet old lady in Danville."

Nora squatted down and unwrapped the yellowed newspaper surrounding an antique coffee cup with the word MOTHER.

"There are six cups altogether. They're German, 1910 or thereabouts. Gold paint. Not a chip or crack in sight."

"Very nice," Nora said. "What else have you got in here?"

"Two real pretty glove boxes. They belonged to the same lady and are about the same age as the mugs. And that funny shape in between the boxes is a brass vanity mirror. It needs cleaning, but it's a showy piece. French. Double-sided. Lots of little roses around the outside."

Unwrapping the mirror, Nora held it up and gazed at her reflection.

"Vintage female. Moderate shelf wear. Notable creases and lines. Some age spotting. Overall condition: acceptable."

Bea smiled at her. "I'd bump your rating from acceptable to very good. Anything that's been around for forty-plus years is gonna show some age. Gimme wrinkles every time. They tell me a person has lived long enough to tell the kind of stories I wanna listen to."

"You remind me of Dolly Parton. She said something about not having time to get old—that she couldn't stop long enough to get old. That's you."

"And every other woman on the planet!" Bea cackled. "Now, what are you gonna pay me for these goodies?"

They were in the second round of haggling when Nora remembered that she wanted to ask Bea about the sailor's valentine in Virginia Love's collection.

"I know what they are, but I've never seen one in person. My cousin works at an auction gallery up in Radford. I'll ask him how much they're worth and what makes some rarer than others. If he knows, I'll text you."

Bea's attention was caught by a sudden shift in the crowd. Since she was barely five feet tall, she couldn't see much, but Nora had a clear view of the center aisle. She saw people moving aside, eager to get out of someone's way.

"They're as nervous as cats in a room full of rocking chairs," Bea said.

As an elderly man leaning heavily on a cane paused to catch

his breath, two deputies in brown and khaki uniforms stepped around him. A black German shepherd was glued to the female deputy's right leg.

Bea heard Nora's sharp intake of breath and cocked her head. "Are you in trouble?"

"I hope not. I've spent more time trying to convince people that I'm neither a murderer nor a thief in the last week than I've spent reading."

"That's not good," Bea said, sounding grave. "Neither is the look the woman with the dog is giving you."

Deputy Hollowell's face was a stone mask, but the laser-beam glint of triumph in her eyes filled Nora with an icy dread.

"She doesn't like me."

"No shit," said Bea. "Do you need to sneak out of here? I can distract them by breaking a few plates. You know I'll do it."

Nora almost smiled. "I appreciate that, but I'm not going to run. I haven't done anything wrong." She shoved some money in Bea's hand. "Sorry, but I'm going to leave my stuff with you. I have a feeling I'm not going straight home."

Deputy Fuentes was the first to reach her. "I need you to come outside with me, Nora."

"Why?"

"One of the items stolen from Mr. Walsh's house has your prints on it. Let's not get into that here. We'll talk outside where there's less of an audience."

Nora couldn't speak. She felt like she'd swallowed sand.

"Are you arresting her?" Bea demanded.

"Outside," Fuentes repeated.

With a fearful nod, Nora left the booth and fell into step next to Fuentes.

Hollowell gaped at her partner. "You're not going to re-strain her?"

"No, I'm not. Lead the way, Hollowell."

As they proceeded to the exit, heads swiveled. Nora heard

whispers and felt the prickle of a hundred stares. Her body flamed with heat. Sweat beaded her brow and dampened the hair at the base of her neck.

"Almost there," encouraged Fuentes.

When they finally made it outside, Nora put her hands on her thighs and bent over. She took a great gulp of air and fixed her gaze on the ground.

"I told you"—she said in between breaths—"that I un-wrapped some of the books. Twelve or so."

Fuentes opened the back door of his cruiser. "The item we recovered isn't a book. It's from the other bin. You said you didn't touch anything in that bin, but your prints are all over this item."

And there, in the parking lot outside the big red barn, Deputy Fuentes read Nora her rights.

Chapter 13

Now I've changed things. I've left my own finger-
prints on the world, no matter how small, and it's
upset the equilibrium . . .

—Markus Zusak

The drive to the station was a blur, and Nora was in a daze when they arrived. She was told to stand there, sit here, sign this. As she moved like an automaton, a single thought kept repeating in her head.

How did my prints get on an item from the bin of valentine collectibles?

Yes, she'd opened several boxes. The Disney pins, the German candy box, and the sailor's valentine, but she hadn't handled any of them. She'd looked at each one, replaced the lids, and returned them to the bins. Could they arrest her for finding her prints on the boxes? No. It had to be a mistake.

Nora had been in this building countless times, but never on this floor. The basement level was cold and daunting. This was the side of the law few members of the public would ever see. It was the stark, matter-of-fact place where suspects and known offenders were processed. Phones rang, keys rattled, and security buzzers sounded at regular intervals. Officers spoke in serious tones. It was an austere and scary place.

I don't belong here.

The thought shook Nora from her daze. She needed help. She needed Davis Godwin.

"Do I get a phone call?" she asked the booking officer.

"Yes, ma'am. As soon as we're done here."

He made her pose for mug shots and then handed her a list of her possessions and asked her to verify that the form was correct. Next, he led her to a wall phone and stood back to give her privacy.

At the sound of Davis's voice, Nora lost her composure. "I've been arrested. Please help me."

She started to explain what had happened when he interrupted her. "I'll be there in ten minutes. Don't talk to anyone. They'll put you in a holding cell after this call, but don't worry. You won't be there long."

Nora replaced the receiver and turned to the booking officer. "I'm done."

He seemed surprised. "You don't want to call anyone else?"

An image of McCabe's face appeared in Nora's mind, and she almost turned back to the phone. But surely, he knew she was here. Was he on the floor above her right now? Sitting at his desk or meeting with his deputies?

She could call the Secret, Book, and Scone Society members. She had no doubt that all three would rush to the station and demand to see her, but she saw no sense in upsetting or alarming them when they really couldn't help. Davis was the only person she could rely on now.

"No," she told the deputy.

He nodded and led her to a holding cell.

The cell, which was mercifully empty, smelled of unwashed bodies and old beer. There was a sticky residue on the bench running along the back wall, which dissuaded Nora from sitting on it, but when the door slid behind her with an echoing clang, she put her forehead to the bars and closed her eyes.

Keep it together. Davis will get you out. Just keep it together.

Someone stirred in the next holding cell, and Nora realized that a man was stretched out on the bench. He let out a groan, bobbed his head up and down, and fell still again.

Noticing the man's jumpsuit, Nora felt a fresh jolt of panic. Would they commandeer her clothes and make her put on a similar jumpsuit? Would she have to spend the night on a sticky, foul-smelling bench?

That would make Hollowell happy.

Nora recalled the triumphant look in Hollowell's eyes as she and Fuentes had approached her at the flea market. She revisited every encounter she'd had with Hollowell, growing angrier and angrier by the moment. She wanted to blame someone for the position she was in, and Hollowell was the perfect choice.

Is she responsible for this? Did she plant my prints on the stolen item?

It didn't seem likely. She and Nora didn't even know each other. Why would Hollowell incriminate someone she'd just met?

But then Nora remembered the night she'd driven past Mc-Cabe's house and seen Hollowell's car in the driveway. She also remembered Hester's wariness regarding the new sheriff's department hire. Hollowell was incredibly friendly to all the male officers. She offered them baked goods and tried to get to know them. But for what purpose? Did she hope to advance her career by cozying up to the men, or was she motivated by something else entirely?

As Nora turned these ideas over, her hatred for Hollowell grew until it burned with the white-hot intensity of a star.

A heavy footfall echoed down the hall. The booking deputy appeared in front of Nora's cell and said, "Your lawyer's here."

"May I see him?"

The man spread his hands. "That's why I came to get you."

His affable manner had such a calming effect that Nora didn't even mind when he took hold of her arm to lead her to a small room containing a boxy wooden table and a pair of metal chairs.

"Thank you, Tony," Davis said to the deputy, who dipped his chin in acknowledgment and backed out of the room. Davis pulled out a chair for Nora and she dropped into it.

"I don't understand how this happened," she said. Her voice shook, but she couldn't control it. "I didn't handle any of the collectibles. Just the books. Do you know what it was? Or where it was found?"

Davis said, "My priority is getting you out of here so that you can spend the night in your own bed, which is why I'm asking them to release you on your own recognizance. You've never been arrested, you're not a flight risk, and you'll show up for court right on time. Correct?"

Nora wished she could nod in agreement. Instead, she said, "There's something you should know."

Davis studied her. "I'm listening."

"Ten years ago, I was charged with a DUI. I pled guilty. At the time, I couldn't be taken into custody because I was in a burn unit. Thanks to my attorney, I didn't go to jail. He got my sentence reduced to a fine and community service hours. That was ten years ago, and I haven't had so much as a parking ticket since then, but I almost killed two people that night. It was the same night I found out about Lawrence and Kelly."

Placing his fingertips within a centimeter of Nora's scarred hand, Davis said, "This happened that night?"

"Yes."

His fingers curled around the bubbly skin. "Is there anything else I should know?"

Nora shook her head.

"Okay, then." He gave her hand a squeeze and released it.

Without warning, the door swung open and Fuentes and Hollowell entered the room.

Davis waited for them to sit down before calmly explaining

that his client would cooperate. He went on to say that he expected her to be released on her own recognizance when they were done with their interview.

Hearing this, Hollowell snorted like a sullen bull.

Fuentes smirked and said, "Come on, Davis. We're looking at a felony here. B and E and larceny."

Davis grinned as if he were genuinely amused. "Nah. We're looking at a Class 1 misdemeanor at most. You can't pin the B and E on my client because her prints were on a single item. And are you trying to tell me that a valentine made of shells is worth a grand or more?"

"Could be. We're waiting on an appraisal, but some have sold for close to two grand."

Nora stared at the tabletop and reviewed every movement she'd made in Kirk's office. She hadn't touched the sailor's valentine. She was absolutely sure about that.

"My client shouldn't spend the day in a cell while you're waiting on that info. She's not a flight risk. She's an upstanding member of the community. Do you have anything else on her other than her prints on this shell thing?"

"She was the only person to touch those bins other than the Walshes," Hollowell said.

"Which she explained to you the last time she was here. She was invited to examine the collection, so she handled it. Could she have touched some of the items in the bin that didn't have books? Maybe." Davis held up a finger. "Where did you find the valentine? Was it in my client's shop? On her property?"

Fuentes waved off the question. "If you're done, we'd like to talk to Nora now."

"By all means." Davis laced his hands together and settled back in his chair.

Once again, Nora was forced to recount her visit to the Walsh house. She was asked a dozen questions about the valentine-themed collectibles, most of which focused on the shell and paper valentine. Hollowell seemed absurdly pleased by her answers, which frightened Nora.

Next, she was asked to describe her movements on Saturday down to the smallest detail. Hollowell was particularly interested in McCabe's visit to the shop.

"Tell us again why the sheriff came to see you," she demanded.

Nora was no longer fazed by her abrasive tone. "He didn't come to see me. He was making his rounds, same as he does for every festival. He walked through the store, said hello to some visitors, and left."

Hollowell's expression was openly skeptical, but Fuentes moved the conversation forward by asking Nora to list the number of times she left the bookstore on Saturday.

"I didn't put so much as a toe outside the door until after my book club meeting was over at around nine fifteen. I didn't even take the garbage out until six thirty. That was the first time I stepped out of the building since I came in at nine."

"You don't have security cameras, so there's no way to prove that, right?" Hollowell folded her arms over her chest and shrugged her brows.

Davis touched Nora lightly on the arm, wordlessly telling her that he'd take it from there.

"Feels like we're on a merry-go-round. Round and round we go. I'm getting dizzy, Deputies. Please. Where was the stolen item found?"

"On the windshield of a deputy's SUV. Someone put it in a plastic baggie and tucked the corner of the bag under a windshield wiper."

Davis cocked his head. "You don't say? Do you think my client stole this item, took it home for a spell, changed her mind about keeping it, and snuck out of her crowded shop in the middle of a festival to leave it on the hood of a patrol car? Unless you have a witness to confirm this, all you've got are her prints, which she might have left when Kirk Walsh *invited her* to examine Virginia Love's collection."

"She said she didn't touch the sailor's valentine," Hollowell argued.

"Maybe she did, maybe she didn't. If she doesn't remember correctly, it's probably because she's rattled from spending too much time in this building."

Fuentes leaned forward. "The valentine we found her prints on isn't the one she described. This one doesn't have a painting of a lady. It has a different painting."

Davis threw out his arms in frustration. "Come on! You shouldn't have charged her or booked her if this is all you've got. I'll be in court, first thing in the morning, seeing that any charges against my client are dismissed."

Hollowell opened her mouth to speak, but Fuentes beat her to it. Staring hard at Nora, he said, "Is there anything—anything at all—you want to tell us? Because now is the time."

Nora asserted that she had nothing to add.

An hour later, she was home, curled up in bed and having a good cry. She hadn't looked at her phone since it was returned to her at the station, but once she'd cried herself out, she glanced at the screen.

A text from Bea said, **Will swing by on my way to Sunday supper. If you aren't there, will come to the shop tomorrow. Hope all is ok.**

"It's definitely not okay," Nora told the screen.

She didn't want to see Bea. She was grateful to her friend for delivering her flea market purchases but inwardly cringed at the idea of having to talk to anyone. All she wanted to do was find a very big rock to hide under until her life returned to normal.

There would be no normal unless Kelly's murder was solved, and Nora knew she'd have to take an active role in proving her own innocence. Crying, hiding, and feeling sorry for herself would get her nowhere, so she went into the bathroom and washed her face. After that, she replied to Bea's text, started a load of laundry, and made a grocery list.

When Bea arrived, Nora welcomed her with a plate of homemade muffins still warm from the oven.

"To thank you for bringing my stuff," she said.

Bea laughed. "Wild horses couldn't keep me away. You know I wanna be the only one at the supper table who can explain why you left the flea market with an armed escort."

Bea came from a very large family, and every Sunday they got together to share stories and trade information. Whoever shared the most interesting tidbits earned the most respect, and was also exempt from the cleanup detail. Since Nora had used this network to her advantage in the past, she knew she'd have to spill the tea to her friend.

Nora waved Bea inside. "I just brewed half a pot of decaf. Would you like a cup?"

"Why not? I've got a little time."

Nora poured coffee into two pottery mugs and carried them to the kitchen table. She then gave an abbreviated version of how her life had imploded from the moment she met Kelly Walsh.

"Damn," Bea said when Nora was done. "I asked my cousin about those valentines. The last one sold at his auction house went for five hundred. Nice but not earth-shattering. He said they don't see them very often. The real rare ones end up at Christie's or Sotheby's."

"Thanks for asking."

"Not to change the subject, but how's Gus Sadler adjusting to life on the outside?"

It was one thing for Nora to talk about herself, but quite another to gossip about Estella's father, so she simply said, "He got a job."

"I know. My brother-in-law's a trucker and his route takes him by that truck stop every other day. He loves Midnight

Chicken and has already seen Gus in action. Said he thought there was tension between him and the manager. They were out back, howling at each other like a pair of tomcats."

Is this why Estella was worried about Gus's work situation? Gus called one of his coworkers a snake. Had he been referring to his boss?

"That doesn't sound good," she said.

Bea's eyes fell on the newspaper poking out from under Nora's laptop. "Not much going on today," she said. "Tomorrow'll be a different story."

"More bad news?" guessed Nora.

"Protests over the casino deal. The Cherokee didn't get the contract, and folks think there's been much greasing of palms. They're gonna march in front of the government offices in the morning, and since most of the Cherokee will be in ceremonial dress, there'll be lots of media attention."

Nora sympathized with the Cherokee but was too emotionally drained to respond to their plight. She and Bea finished their coffee in companionable silence and then unloaded Nora's flea market finds.

Bea drove away and Nora carried her purchases into the bookstore's stockroom. Afterward, she returned home, put her laundry away, and was mulling over her grocery list when Estella called with a dinner invite.

"Dad got up this morning and marinated four pounds of chicken thighs for me to throw on the grill tonight. He made four pounds because he's used to prepping meals for a crowd, so I need to gather a small crowd. June and Sheldon are free, but Hester has plans with Jasper."

Nora was done with people for the day. She didn't want to talk anymore or listen to other people talk. She wanted to flop on the sofa, open a book, and slip inside the skin of a character whose life was nothing like her own.

"I can't tonight," Nora said. And before Estella could protest, she explained why she'd be lousy company.

"God, Nora! You were in a holding cell?" Estella sounded as shaken as Nora felt. When she next spoke, her voice was steady and confident. "Things are getting worse for you, which means we have to figure out who killed Kelly. You should come over. June and I have continued the research we started last night, and by the time you get here, we might have a lead. I know you feel hollowed out, but I don't want you to see the inside of a holding cell ever again."

Nora said, "I'll be there in an hour."

The sun looked like a punctured egg yolk as Nora drove through town. Yellow oozed between the mountain peaks, and the first stars were appearing in the indigo curtain inching down the rest of the sky.

When she arrived at Estella's, Sheldon met her at the door. He pulled Nora into a fierce bear hug and cried, "*Mi querida niña!*"

She went limp in his arms. It felt so good to surrender to the warmth and comfort he offered.

Rubbing circles on her back, he said, "My mother used to say, 'Worries go down better with soup than without.' Or in this case, grilled chicken."

Nora and Sheldon walked back to the kitchen, where Estella was tossing a salad while June poured herself a glass of white wine.

"Nora?" she asked, holding the bottle over an empty glass.

"I'll stick to water, thanks."

Estella put the wooden salad bowl on the table and said, "Have a seat. I'll grab the chicken from the grill, and we'll see if Gus's Grilled Teriyaki Thighs live up to the hype."

Not only was the chicken delicious, but no one asked Nora to rehash the details of her arrest. June talked about her son and his girlfriend, Sheldon complained about the plot holes in the movie he'd watched the night before, and Estella shared her concerns about her dad.

"Something happened at work last night, but he won't tell me what," she said.

"How can you tell?" asked June.

Estella laid her knife and fork down. "He does this thing with his jaw when he's holding something back. It's like he's locking his teeth together to keep the words from getting out."

Sheldon said, "You think he's having trouble with that guy? The sketchy one?"

"I do. The problem is, the sketchy guy happens to be the manager." Estella's shoulders moved in a semblance of a shrug. "Dad's off tomorrow, so that's good. He can putter around the house and relax while I'm at the salon. Maybe he'll tell me what's going on when I get home."

Nora considered sharing what she'd heard from Bea but decided against it. There was no sense in adding to Estella's worries. She and her dad would talk things out soon enough.

Dessert was a choice between several gelato flavors. Sheldon picked hazelnut and milk chocolate, June and Nora chose peach, and Estella went for vanilla caramel swirl.

"Does this smell off to you?" she asked, thrusting the gelato container under Nora's nose.

"No. Want me to try it?"

Estella nodded, so Nora skimmed her spoon through the creamy gelato and popped it in her mouth.

"Tastes fine."

"Good." Estella passed out napkins. "Let's sit on one side of the table so we can all see my laptop screen."

Once they were settled, June touched Nora on the arm and said, "This might seem a little weird, but the best way we could figure out how to keep track of Lawrence's life was to make a slideshow of his relationships."

"*No*," Nora moaned.

Sheldon patted her hand. "Pretend it's a novel about someone you don't know, except this guy goes way beyond any unlikable character. He's just badly written. His novel is a reverse harem meets psychological thriller. Kind of like *American Psycho* without the serial-killer aspect."

"There's a killer in this plot too," she said.

June looked at her. "Which is exactly why we need to do this."

Estella's finger hovered over the space bar. "The timeline starts a few months after Lawrence and Kelly were married. That's the year he started his company, Tradewinds. At first, the company was a traditional investment firm. After divorcing Kelly and meeting Robyn the flight attendant, Lawrence hired a dozen new employees and began investing heavily in the cryptocurrency market. He'd already divorced Robyn and was dating Naomi the model when he bought a foundering IT company and transformed it into a cryptocurrency mining operation."

"A what?" Nora and Sheldon asked simultaneously.

June chuckled. "Trust me, I had to look up three definitions and watch two videos to understand it, myself. The short answer? It's how new bitcoins are entered into circulation. It verifies cryptocurrency transactions and requires superfast computers. Anyway, it's this company, Batten Technologies, that jettisoned your ex into the filthy-rich category."

Sheldon frowned. "But are his companies legit? Are his transactions aboveboard? Because you only have to look at his personal life to know that Larry is a shady character."

"Funny you should say 'aboveboard,'" Nora said. "Lawrence's first company was called 'Tradewinds,' and the IT company is 'Batten.' They're both sailing terms."

"He's got a bunch of companies now, including Windward, another sailing term. Tech stuff, hedge funds, real estate—Larry's fingers are in lots of pies," Estella said. "I like calling him Larry. I bet he'd hate it."

Nora cracked a smile. "He would."

"Moving on to the next unlucky lady, we have Daphne, the

British actress. She's filming on location in Ireland, which means we can cross her off the suspect list."

Clicking the next slide, Estella explained that Paloma had been in Italy for the past month and Rosie had gotten married shortly after breaking up with Lawrence.

She went on to add, "She just had her second baby, so I doubt she left her husband and kids at home to murder an ex-boyfriend's ex-wife."

"That's the thing—why would any of these women come after Kelly?" asked Nora.

June said, "We were trying to see if any of them knew about Virginia's collection. It's hard to tell if people are facing financial hardships by stalking them on social media, but if any of the exes need money, it's Robyn, Ana, or Justine. We already ruled Robyn out because she was clearly at home in Florida the night Kelly was killed."

"That leaves two ex-girlfriends. Or is one a current girl-friend?" asked Sheldon.

Estella held up a single finger. "Justine is the current girl-friend, but rumors are circulating that she's about to get dumped. Larry is being linked to a swimsuit model. As for Justine, she's a fashion and beauty influencer who made fifty thousand last year. According to the online gossip sites, she lost a ton of fol-lowers last month when Larry said that she looked older than her actual age. Look at her! Does she look a day over twenty?"

The image of a beautiful, fresh-faced brunette appeared on the screen, and Nora gasped.

"She was in my shop! She asked for books on how to keep a man interested but didn't buy any."

June and Estella exchanged shocked glances.

"I remember her," Sheldon cried. "She ordered iced coffee, and when I handed it to her and wished her a lovely day, she grabbed the cup without looking away from her phone. She might be pretty, but she's *rude*."

Staring into the middle distance, Nora said, "She asked me if I'd ever been married, and when I told her that I was divorced, she said that she wasn't going to buy books to fix her relationship problems because they obviously hadn't fixed mine. She also said that bookstores were for people of my generation because young people, like her, didn't waste time reading."

Sheldon blurted, "What a little bi—"

"We don't use that word, remember?" June cut in before he could finish. She then turned to Nora. "Lawrence's girlfriend was here! Not only did you see her, but you *talked* to her! Do you know what this means?"

A current of hope electrified Nora's body. She took out her phone and said, "Yes, I do. It's high time the sheriff's department picked on someone else."

Chapter 14

When the bee sucks, it makes honey, when the spider, poison.

—Spanish Proverb

Nora didn't call Andrews or Fuentes. She called the man she trusted above all others. When McCabe didn't answer, she left a message and went to bed.

Not long after her alarm went off the next morning, her phone rang.

"I'm standing on your deck," McCabe said. "I brought breakfast."

Nora made him wait while she ran a brush through her tangled hair and gargled mouthwash. She was still in her pajamas, and when she opened the door to see McCabe in uniform, she felt oddly exposed.

He held up a white bag and a paper coffee cup. "Breakfast croissant and a latte."

"Have you already eaten?"

He nodded. "I had an early start. I thought I'd sit with you while you ate if that's okay."

"Sure."

Nora took a grateful sip of the latte. "Where'd you get this?"

"The truck stop that has Midnight Chicken. I was up before dawn because a body was found there at five this morning. It's not my jurisdiction, but Quentin's stretched so thin with this casino business that I offered to help."

"A body? It wasn't . . ."

McCabe quickly waved his hands. "No, no, it's not Gus. He'd been home for hours before Quentin called me. The victim is Justine James."

"*Lawrence's* Justine?"

"Yes. I listened to your message, so I know that she came to the bookshop."

Nora wrapped her palms around her coffee cup. Twenty questions raced through her mind at once, but self-preservation caused one to rise above all the others.

"Am I a suspect for this too?"

McCabe covered her hands with his own. "No, love, you're not. I know you had nothing to do with this, just like I know you had nothing to do with Kelly Walsh's death. Or the break-in at her house."

"But don't you need to keep your distance? I'm still . . ." Nora trailed off as hope bloomed in her chest, as warm and vibrant as the sunrise. "Did you catch the killer?"

"Not yet. But—and this is just between us—we think Kelly and Justine were killed by the same person. They were both asphyxiated. Both women had bruising here." He touched the front of his neck. "The ME believes the killer incapacitated them from behind using a sleeper hold. After that, a plastic bag over the head or pillow to the face finished the job. We'll see what Justine's postmortem indicates, but since there were no fibers found in Kelly's mouth or nasal passages, it was most likely a plastic bag."

Nora raised her coffee cup to her mouth and drank. It was a mechanical movement, and when she realized that the coffee was tepid, she frowned.

"Let me pop that in the microwave," McCabe said, taking the cup from Nora. He also scooped up the bag with the breakfast sandwich.

Nora heard beeping as he set the microwave timer followed by the clink of a plate landing on the counter. These small, domestic noises were comforting. They represented the effortless compatibility that existed between her and McCabe. They might not live together, but they knew each other's houses as well as their own. McCabe kept a toothbrush, razor, and one of his favorite coffee mugs at Nora's house. She had a toothbrush, her favorite shampoo, and a pair of PJs at his place. They took turns cooking and tidying up, no matter where they were. They slept soundly in each other's beds. Nora had learned to love McCabe's cats, and McCabe had gotten used to the sound of freight trains passing behind Nora's home at night.

All of these things were a constant reminder of how well they worked together.

McCabe returned with Nora's breakfast, and as soon as he put her cup and plated sandwich on the table, she held his arm to prevent him from moving away from her.

"I've missed you."

The smiled reached his eyes first, and just as it was tugging the corners of his mouth upward, he bent down to kiss her.

He kissed her on the lips and then pressed his cheek to hers. "I'm sorry," he whispered. "I never hated my job until last week. If I thought quitting would have spared you pain, I would've walked out the first time you were brought to the station."

"That wouldn't have done either of us any good," Nora said as she put her arms around him.

"Maybe not, but you would have known that you meant more to me than my job."

Nora pushed on his chest until he had to step back and look at her. "Your job is a part of you, just like books are a part of me. You wouldn't be you without the law."

"Does that mean I can never retire?" McCabe asked with a grin as he slid into his chair.

"You'll never retire. They'll have to vote you out, and if that ever happens, you can be the town's first private eye."

McCabe laughed. "Just what Miracle Springs needs. Listen, I need to go soon. You eat and I'll tell you what I can about Justine."

The croissant sandwich was egg and cheese and immensely satisfying. There was nothing special about the combination of scrambled egg, melted cheddar cheese, and flaky pastry—other than the fact McCabe had brought it to her—but it was one of the best breakfasts Nora had eaten in ages.

"We have two suspects—a man and a woman. The woman approached Justine's car and spoke to her through the window. Justine passed her an envelope. The woman looked inside and removed a wad of cash. Then she shook her head and tossed the envelope back into the car. Because of the way she threw it, some of the cash landed on the ground outside the car. She walked away without turning around."

"How do you know this? Does the truck stop have cameras?"

McCabe held out a hand. "Five. They're not the best quality and we could barely make out Justine's face in the feed, but Andrews is working to reduce the noise and make the picture sharper. The suspects knew about the cameras. They were both careful to turn away from them and to keep their heads down while walking. Both wore camo sweatshirts, jeans, and black baseball hats. The woman had long, blond hair that looks like a wig. The man has close-cropped dark hair. The only identifier that might help us trace him is a tattoo on his neck. The film is too grainy for us to see what it is, but I'm hoping Andrews can perform a little tech magic on the feed."

The croissant was almost gone, so Nora took her time eating what was left because she wasn't ready for McCabe to leave. Besides, sharing meals with McCabe was one of her favorite things. It was what first brought them together. For years, they'd had platonic lunch dates. They'd taste each other's dishes and swap stories, and with every meeting, they grew closer.

That's why sitting across the table from McCabe felt natural to Nora. It was as comfortable as a favorite blanket or cozy sweatshirt.

"I think I'm missing something. What happened after the woman threw the envelope back into the car?"

"Justine got out of the car to pick up the money that fell on the ground. There's no sound on the recording, but she was obviously angry. She yelled and shook the envelope. While this was going on, the man slipped into the back seat. As soon as Justine sat in the driver's seat, the man's arm snaked around her neck. She struggled, but he had her in a sleeper hold. In a matter of seconds, she went limp. He pulled her into the back seat and, a few minutes later, he exited the car. It was nighttime, and the back windows are tinted, so we really couldn't see what happened. There was no movement inside after he walked away, and Justine never left the car."

McCabe glanced at his watch and stood up. He held out his hand and Nora slipped hers into his.

"Who found her?" she asked as he headed for the door.

"A trucker. He peeked inside the car as he was walking to his rig. At first, he thought someone was sleeping in the back seat, but when he thought the woman's eyes might be open, he went into the truck stop to tell the clerk."

Nora gazed up at McCabe. "Why do you think these people were responsible for killing Kelly?"

"We can't prove anything yet, but Val said that Kelly was talking to a woman out on the lawn. Right now, we're working on a theory that points to Justine as the ringleader. She may have paid the Camo Couple to kill Kelly and rob the Walshes. Then the Camo Couple turned on her."

"Where does that leave me?"

A pained look crossed McCabe's face. "Now that we have

new avenues of inquiry, the heat's off you." Mustering a smile, he said, "You might be at the bottom of the suspect list, but you're still at the top of my list."

"And what list is that?"

McCabe slid his arms around her waist and pulled her in close. "All of them," he said before tilting his head down to kiss her.

When Sheldon breezed into the bookstore, he found Nora reshelving the black and yellow books taken from the front display table.

"You're humming! Does this mean you're no longer one of America's Most Wanted?"

"It might."

Nora eased a book into its proper place on the shelf and reached for another. As she moved through the fiction section, she told Sheldon about McCabe's visit.

"*Gracias a Dios*! I thought they'd never leave you alone." Sheldon twirled his left mustache tail. "But this truck stop incident worries me. Gus works there and something is obviously going on with him. Do you think he knows these people? The camo couple?"

The thought made Nora go cold. "Lord, I hope not." She cradled the hardback in her hands, reassured by its firm edges, precise corners, and smooth, clothbound cover.

"Uh-oh, you have that look—the one you get when you want to fix things." Sheldon waggled a finger in front of her face. "Gus is a grown-ass man. He just got out of prison. If he comes to you for book recs, fine. But why should he open up to you about his personal issues? And why would you try to make him? That's for Estella to do."

"What if his job issues are connected to Justine's murder?" asked Nora.

Sheldon put a hand to his heart. "What exactly are you saying?"

"Look. I don't want to be a suspect or a person of interest

ever again. If I can help McCabe apprehend the real criminals, I can go back to living my life. I know that's selfish. I should absolutely leave Gus alone, but I just want to talk to him. If he doesn't want to tell me anything, I'll back off."

"You should call Estella first, and don't be surprised if she says no." Sheldon walked away, muttering to himself in Spanish.

Since Estella never answered her phone when she was with a client, Nora sent her a text.

She watched the three dots appear on her screen and waited for Estella's reply. The three dots blinked and blinked. Then they disappeared.

Five minutes later, Estella wrote, **Dad's at the bakery, working on that leaky faucet. He won't talk on the phone. You'll have to walk down.**

"I'm going to the Gingerbread House. I'll be back by ten," she told Sheldon.

Sheldon shot her a disapproving glance before returning his attention to the espresso machine.

The door to the bakery was unlocked, so Nora entered and called out, "Hello! This is an unannounced visit from the health department."

A projectile flew through the air and hit her squarely in the chest.

"Health department jokes are *not* funny!" Hester cried.

"Jeez. How old is that roll?" Nora rubbed her chest.

Hester was instantly contrite. "Pretty old. Did it hurt?"

"No, but you threw that like a major leaguer. Are you moonlighting as a pitcher for the Miracle Springs Mountain Cats?"

"I should. Their record couldn't get any worse." Hester turned and yelled, "Hey, Gus! Do you like a baseball?"

They heard a muffled grunt from the front of the bakery followed by, "Been a Braves fan all my life. Why? You giving me tickets?"

"Not for the Braves, but I can get you really good seats at the next Mountain Cats game."

Gus snorted and said, "That's a hard pass."

The comradery between Hester and Gus surprised Nora.

Seeing the unspoken question on her friend's face, Hester said, "We've been here for hours already. I gave Gus a lesson in bread making in exchange for a plumbing repair, but I definitely got the better deal. He's a natural baker."

"Don't you ever take a full day off?"

"Do you?" Hester retorted, her eyes dancing. "Wait. You're awfully perky for someone who may or may not have been arrested yesterday."

After Nora filled her in on McCabe's visit, Hester pointed to the front of the bakery and whispered, "Are you going to ask him if he saw anything?"

"Sheldon doesn't think I should. What do you think?"

Hester smoothed her apron as she considered the question. "I know what it feels like to be a suspect. I was in your shoes a few months ago, and I wouldn't wish that experience on my worst enemy. I understand how desperate you are to put an end to this. I couldn't sleep, I didn't want to eat, and my anxiety was through the roof. I was a total basket case. I didn't feel like I could take a full breath until my brother was locked up."

"I've been so wrapped up in myself that I haven't asked about Lea. How is she?"

Hester sighed. "I've already missed the first twenty-two years of my daughter's life, and even though I don't want to miss another second, she wants to keep exchanging letters instead of getting together in person. She writes every few days, and I can hear her voice in my head, but I really want to see her face."

"I'm sorry."

"Me too, but I get it. She craves peace and predictability, and she's found that with her Mennonite family. I really can't blame her for making me wait. I might have been forced to give her up, but I never looked for her. That hurt will take a long time to heal, if ever. Our relationship has to be on her terms, but that doesn't mean that I wouldn't give a kidney to spend the day with her."

"It'll happen," Nora said. "And it must be such fun to get real letters in the mail."

Hester brightened. "It is! Lea makes all of her own cards. I never know what I'm going to get. One day, there'll be a little watercolor painting or a pen-and-ink drawing. Or she might glue flower petals to the front. Or sketch a cow. I can't draw, so I just send cookies."

"What kind of bread did you and Gus bake?"

"Oh, I've been experimenting with a protein bread. It's whole wheat made with powdered oat milk." She laughed. "I know, it doesn't sound too appealing, but it's actually light and fluffy and good for you. I made it with Estella in mind."

Nora walked over to the cooling rack. "Her stomach's been bothering her for weeks now. Do you think it's stress?"

When Hester didn't reply, Nora turned to look at her.

"Do you know something I don't?"

Hester screwed up her lips and shot a quick glance to the front. Lowering her voice, she said, "I have a theory."

When she mimed a round belly, Nora's first thought was, *She's bloated?*

And then it hit her.

"*No!*"

Whispering now, Hester went on. "It's not just the wonky appetite, but her aversion to certain smells and afternoon fatigue too. Honestly, I don't think it's dawned on her yet."

Nora sank down on a stool. "Whoa."

At that moment, Gus entered the kitchen. "Morning, Nora."

"Morning." Nora pointed at the toolbox in his hand. "I see where Estella gets her work ethic."

He smiled. "I don't see any lazy people in this room, do you? I'm guessing you aren't here to bake bread, though."

"I'm not much of a baker, but I'm good at eating. If you need an official bread taste-tester, I'm available."

Gus jerked a thumb at the cooling racks. "Help yourself to a loaf. Estella eats like a bird. Always worrying about her figure, that one. She could weigh a thousand pounds and that man of hers would still think she hung the moon."

Hester put her hands on her hips. "So would you. Now, what's the diagnosis on my faucet?"

"It won't give you any more trouble. I'd better take a look at your oven next. I don't think they put the bulb in right the last time your thermostat was calibrated. One side is running a bit hotter than the other."

"You don't need to do that. It's your day off," Hester protested.

Gus knelt in front of the oven's kickplate and looked at her and Nora. "You gals have been like sisters to Estella. June too. Any friend of my girl's is a friend of mine."

Nora joined Gus on the floor. At his quizzical glance, she put a hand on his toolbox and said, "You're the oven surgeon, and I'm here to hand you your instruments."

"Alright. Let's start with a screwdriver. Phillips head."

Nora passed it to him. While he removed the kickplate, she said, "The sheriff stopped by my house this morning. Did you hear that a woman's body was found at the truck stop?"

"I heard," Gus said.

His tone made it plain that he didn't want to discuss the topic.

For the next few minutes, Gus worked in silence. Then he asked Nora to hold on to the screws while he shone his flashlight into the cavity behind the panel.

"The bulb looks okay," he told Hester. "You might be dealing with a heating element that needs replacing."

Hester wound her apron string around her wrist. "If I do, I'll have to pay for overnight shipping. I can't run a bakery without an oven. Can you tell if I need one?"

"I sure can."

The two women watched Gus work. Hester's eyes were fo-

cused on Gus's fingers, but Nora's attention was drawn to his Alice in Wonderland tattoos. They were so unique. What if the man who killed Justine also had a unique tattoo?

Nora hated to distract Gus while he was working, but her time was running out. She needed to get back to the shop.

"I have to get going," she said. "Could I ask you something before I do? It's important."

Gus turned to face her. "Go on."

Nora filled her lungs with air as if she was about to dive into the deep end of a pool and let it out again. Then she said, "The woman found at the truck stop? Her name was Justine. She was dating my ex-husband. She probably knew something about the crimes I've been accused of, but she can't help me now."

Words crashed around in Nora's head like bumper cars, and she grimaced in frustration.

Just tell him what you need! her inner voice shouted.

"Maybe you can help me," she went on. "The man who killed Justine was caught by the security cameras, but he must have known they were there because he kept his head lowered. He also wore a baseball cap. But he had a neck tattoo. Do you remember seeing anyone with a neck tattoo at the truck stop?"

Gus clenched his jaw so tightly that Nora expected to hear it click. She fought to remain silent—to patiently wait for Gus to speak.

Finally, he let out the ghost of a sigh. "If anyone else asks, I'm going to play dumb. I have to, understand? But between you and me, it might've been a spider web."

"Thank you."

She was about to get up when Gus grabbed her arm. "Be careful, girl. Keep your eyes open. And don't go anywhere alone. Especially at night. This is not your friendly neighborhood Spider-Man. This one's a killer."

Chapter 15

I begin to love this little creature, and to anticipate his birth as a fresh twist to a knot that I do not wish to untie.

—Mary Wollstonecraft

The following evening, Hester plopped a bakery box on June's kitchen counter and said, "This has to be the weirdest intervention ever."

June scowled. "It's not an intervention. It's just supper."

"How many suppers have you been to that ended with someone peeing on a stick?" Hester asked as she sat at the kitchen table where Nora was busy chopping cucumbers.

Nora poured Hester a glass of iced tea from the pitcher by her elbow and began slicing tomatoes.

Hester watched her work for a few minutes before asking what she could do to help.

June pointed at the oven. "Sprinkle cheese over that casserole and broil it for five minutes. I'll set the table."

June laid four place settings in the dining room, and Nora asked if Sheldon was at home.

"No. He and Tyson went to see a movie. It's supposed to be nothing but car chases and explosions with zero plot, and yet, those two were as giddy as preschoolers on a seesaw when they left."

Hester removed the casserole from the oven and placed the glass dish on a trivet.

"Be careful," she told Nora. "That dish is molten."

Following a perfunctory knock of the front door, Estella called out, "Something smells good!"

When she breezed into the kitchen a moment later, looking just like Ann-Margret in *Viva Las Vegas*, her friends stopped what they were doing to stare at her.

Estella glanced down at her butter-yellow dress. "Do I have a stain?"

"It's like the sun just came out from behind a cloud," said June. "You're glowing."

"Must be the new moisturizer I'm using. I'll order samples for all of you." After helping herself to iced tea, Estella asked, "What are we having?"

"Southwest chicken casserole. It's got black beans, corn, chicken breast, rice, and lots of cheese. It's also messy as hell, so I'll dish it out in here," June said.

While they ate, Hester told Estella about Gus's bread-baking lesson.

"You know I'm not comfortable having people in my kitchen, but I liked having your dad there. He doesn't talk much, which is a must-have when it's that early in the morning, but it was more than that. He handled the equipment with respect. The dough too. He seemed so at home in my space that it felt natural for him to be there."

"He texted me twice to tell me how much he loved his lesson." Estella turned to Nora. "Don't be surprised if he comes in to order a bunch of bread cookbooks. The man is obsessed right now. Who knew yeast could be so fascinating?"

Before Hester could reply, Estella winked at her. Then she looked at Nora again. "Were you able to talk to him?"

"Yes, but I promised to keep what was said between the two of us."

Estella smiled. "Barely out of jail and he's already baking with one friend and sharing secrets with another. Is this what sibling rivalry feels like?"

"Speaking of only children, I want to do something for Tucker Walsh," June said.

"Like a Night Angels delivery?" asked Hester.

Years ago, when the Secret, Book, and Scone Society had first formed, they'd made it part of their mission to show kindness to neighbors going through a tough time. This kindness came in the form of a tote bag stuffed with books, baked goods, socks, and self-care products.

Once or twice a month, the four friends would hop in the car and drive to a neighbor's house. Under the cover of darkness, one of them would carry the tote to the recipient's front door, ring the bell, and sprint back to the car. The women wanted to remain anonymous so that no one felt indebted to them, and even though they'd been chased by dogs and soaked by sprinklers, they'd never been identified.

The local paper had dubbed them "The Night Angels," and the women still referred to themselves by this nickname.

"That family won't welcome us ringing their doorbell after dark and running away," Nora said.

June folded her hands as if in prayer. "No, they won't, and I'd love to get more folks involved this time around. Kirk and Val are new residents with a new business. They're grieving Kelly's loss and are now responsible for her son's future. That's too much weight to shoulder alone."

"I'll schedule Val for a month's worth of pampering sessions—on the house," said Estella.

Hester nodded. "I can supply them with bread and breakfast pastries for a couple weeks, but what about their other meals?"

"Between my knitting circle and Bible study group, they'll have plenty of food," said June. "But what can we do for Tucker?"

Nora had been wondering the same thing for days. She'd ordered several sets of origami paper, but the boy had just lost his mother. He needed more than paper. He needed a friend.

"He likes the bookstore," she said to herself.

She'd spoken quietly, but not quietly enough because Estella gestured for her to keep talking.

Nora shrugged. "I'm not sure if he'd want to, but maybe he could hang out with us for a few hours each week. If he got comfortable enough, he could even make origami for one of our storytimes."

Her friends agreed that this was an excellent idea, and Nora decided to stop by Tea Flowers the next day to talk it over with Val and Kirk.

Hester got to her feet. "I made mango and coconut mousse for dessert, and I know you're all going to say you're too full, but by the time we clean up our dinner stuff, you'll have a room for a spoonful or two."

Nora laughed. "You say that like we're actually capable of stopping. I have never *not* finished one of your desserts."

While Nora and Estella washed dishes, June brewed a pot of decaf and lined up mugs, a creamer, and a sugar bowl on the counter. She then placed spoons and a fresh round of napkins on the table. Hester served the mousse in glass dessert cups.

"This tastes like a Caribbean vacation," June said. "I can practically hear ocean waves and steel drums."

Nora sighed in delight. "It's *so* good."

Estella was clearly less enamored of the dessert. She'd eaten the whipped cream off the top and was now shifting the mousse around with her spoon until the neat layers of mango and coconut formed a tie-dye pattern.

"You don't have to eat it if you don't want to. I won't be offended," Hester told her.

Estella groaned in frustration. "I don't get it. You know how certain canned foods have a metallic aftertaste? Half of what I eat tastes like that. Especially dairy. Even my coffee tastes like a tin can."

Nora glanced down at her coffee cup. "I'd be very upset if my coffee tasted like tin."

"I thought it was a fluke, but it's been going on for weeks, so I made an appointment with my GP. She managed to squeeze me in tomorrow morning. It'll be tight making it back to the salon for my nine o'clock client, but I have to know what's going on."

June took hold of Estella's hand. "Honey, I think I know."

Estella's eyes went wide. "You do?"

Instead of replying, June got up, walked over to the sideboard, and opened the top drawer. She removed a plastic bag from the drawer and gave it to Estella.

"What's this?" Estella asked.

June pointed at the bag. "Open it."

After shooting a quizzical glance at Nora and Hester, Estella reached into the bag and pulled out a home pregnancy test.

Her face broke into a smile and she began to laugh, but when her friends didn't join in, her smile slipped. "You don't seriously think that I'm—no. No way."

"I'm not saying I'm right, but I've been around enough women to recognize the signs," June said gently. "The fatigue, the aversion to certain foods, the headaches. And you complained about your bra the other day, remember?"

"Just because the fabric was bothering me doesn't mean I need this." Estella flicked the test away. It pinwheeled to the middle of the table and stopped.

No one could take their eyes from it.

Finally, Estella waved her hands as if warding off a blow. "I can't be pregnant. I'm forty years old. Jack and I use protection, and we've never talked about having kids."

Nora saw the fear in her friend's eyes and touched her lightly on the hand. "I read an article that said that over a hundred thousand women are having babies in their forties."

"Are they career-oriented, unmarried women who never planned on having a kid? I doubt it," Estella snapped.

Hester scooped up the test and examined the small print on the box. "This takes three minutes. Go pee on the stick and leave it in June's bathroom. We'll talk about whatever you want for three minutes and then see what the stick says. If there's a plus sign in the box, you're pregnant. If it's a minus sign, you're not."

"Fine, but this is ridiculous!" Estella grabbed the kit and strode toward the bathroom. It wasn't long before she rejoined them and said, "Start the clock."

Hester pulled up the stopwatch feature on her iPhone and pressed the green button. The milliseconds passed in a blur and the seconds began to accumulate.

Estella glared at the phone. "I do *not* want to stare at that thing for another two minutes and thirty-nine seconds, so somebody needs start talking."

Nora leaned closer to her friend. "No matter what shape appears in that test window, we've got your back. You know that, right?"

Estella nodded.

"If it's negative, will you be relieved or disappointed?"

Without a moment's hesitation, Estella said, "Relieved. I'm not cut out to be a mother. I wouldn't know how. My mama did her damnedest to ruin my life and her mama wasn't much better. Some women are meant to be child-free. I always thought I was one of those women."

Hester cocked her head. "Is there a 'but' coming?"

"I used to believe that I'd never find a good man. But I did. Jack's the man I've waited for my whole life. I thought I didn't deserve to be loved by someone like him, but he proved me wrong. Maybe I was wrong to assume that I'd fail as a mom too."

Tears sprang to Estella's eyes and she whispered, "I never really thought about having a family with Jack, but—oh God— I don't know what I want that stupid test to say. I've missed two periods in a row, but that's happened before. It never crossed my mind . . . what does that damned timer say?"

"The test should be ready."

Estella's hand flew to her mouth. "I'm scared."

"Do you want us to come with you?" Nora asked.

Locking her hands together to keep them from shaking, Estella said, "No. Either way, I'm going to need a minute alone."

As she walked to the bathroom, she threw her shoulders back and held her head high. When the door closed with a firm click, Nora, Hester, and June scooted their chairs closer together.

"I remember how I felt when I saw that plus sign," said Hester. "I was terrified. That feeling never went away, either. The whole time Lea was growing inside me, I was scared by what was happening to my body. I was scared of what would happen during the delivery and after she was born. I was so young, and no one told me that everything was going to be okay. That fear made me think she'd be better off without me, but I was wrong. For the rest of my life, I'm going to be making that up to her."

June wore a wistful smile. "When I found out I was pregnant with Tyson, I felt this *huge* tidal wave of love. At that moment, something unlocked inside of me. I didn't know I could feel so much joy and anxiety at the same time, and those feelings grew as my baby grew. That's why it hurt so much to spend all those years estranged from him. When we reconciled, I finally felt whole again."

Hearing footsteps in the hall, the three friends instinctively reached for one another's hands.

Estella appeared in the doorway. Her skin was blotchy from crying and her eye makeup was smudged. She held a wad of toilet paper in one hand and the pregnancy test in the other.

"It's positive," she said, pressing the plastic stick to her chest. Her lips quivered as tears raced down her cheeks. "I'm having a baby."

Her friends rushed over and enfolded her in their arms.

As they held her, they murmured, "You're having a baby," and "You're going to be an amazing mom," and "We'll be the best aunts in the whole world."

Leaning into them, Estella cried harder.

"Can I really do this? I don't know if I can."

June stroked her hair. "Honey, if it takes a village to raise a child, you've got one right here."

"Jack's going to be over the moon!" Estella was now laughing through her tears. "He never thought . . . *I* never thought. I just can't believe it!" She put her palm to her belly and, in a voice choked with wonder, whispered, "A baby."

The next morning, Estella sent a group text from the doctor's office confirming her pregnancy. She asked her friends to keep the news to themselves until she'd had the chance to tell her father.

Nora didn't know how she was going to hide such momentous news from Sheldon. Nothing escaped his notice, and when he asked why she was humming while she dusted or grinning as she pulled titles from the Pregnancy and Parenting sections, she told him that she was relieved that her life seemed to be returning to normal.

When he gave her a look that said he wasn't buying what she was selling, she said, "It's not all rainbows and sunshine. Every time I think about Tucker, I want to hide in a corner and hug my knees to my chest."

"Nobody puts Baby in a corner."

"Thank you, Patrick Swayze. How would you feel about Tucker hanging out here a few hours a week?"

A tiny crease appeared between Sheldon's brows. "Does he want to?"

Nora shared her idea to invite Tucker to join one of their storytime events. "Not every week," she added when she saw the look of alarm on Sheldon's face. "Just once to see if he enjoys it. He might not want to do it at all. Being with a bunch of little kids and their parents might be torture."

"Besides making origami, what else could he do here?"

"I don't know. I'm hoping to walk up to Tea Flowers after lunch to see what Kirk and Val think."

Sheldon let out a low whistle and muttered something in Spanish. Nora caught the word *loco* before Sheldon retreated into the ticket agent's booth.

In the end, Nora didn't speak with Val or Kirk because Tea Flowers was closed. Knowing the couple couldn't afford to take the day off without good reason, Nora got worried. She popped into the sheriff's station on the off chance that McCabe knew what was going on.

She'd nearly reached the front desk when the door to the inner offices opened, and Deputy Hollowell appeared in the lobby.

"Crap," Nora grumbled.

There was no way to avoid the truculent officer, so Nora fired off a text to McCabe and strode up to the front desk to await his reply.

Hollowell sauntered over to her and flashed her a humorless smile. "Back so soon? I'd have thought you'd had enough of this place for a while."

Nora shrugged. "As long as Grant is the sheriff, I'm happy to be here. I'd just rather avoid the interview rooms and holding cells in the future."

Hollowell's smile vanished. "The sheriff's in a meeting."

"Okay," Nora said, and glanced at her phone. McCabe hadn't read her text yet.

"Is the bookstore closed today?" Hollowell asked as she leaned on the counter. To a casual observer, the two women looked like they were having a friendly chat, but there was nothing friendly about Hollowell's cold stare. It was how a viper looked seconds before it struck.

"No. Why? Were you interested in buying a book?"

"Books aren't for me, I'm too active to be a reader. I'd rather run five miles or practice at the shooting range. When I have a day off, I'll hunt with the dogs. It's good training for them and I get to blow off steam. You ever been hunting?"

Nora shook her head. "I could never kill an animal, but to each her own. And even if you don't want a book, feel free to come in for a cup of coffee sometime. First one's on the house."

Hollowell seemed flummoxed by the offer. Before she could come up with a retort, Nora's phone buzzed with a message from McCabe.

After quickly scanning the text, she said, "Grant's waiting for me. Have a nice day, Deputy."

Though she tried not to let it, the interaction with Hollowell had unsettled Nora. She couldn't understand why the woman was so hell-bent on antagonizing her, or why Nora kept allowing herself to be goaded by the churlish officer.

The door to McCabe's office was open, and Nora found him standing in front of his whiteboard, studying a series of photographs. One of them showed a blown-up image of a spider web tattoo.

"Is that the man who got in Justine's car?"

Startled, McCabe swung around to face her. "Good Lord, woman. I want you to make my heart race, but not like that."

"Like what, then?"

McCabe tossed a file folder onto the table and leaned in to kiss her.

"I didn't expect to see you," he said as he pushed a strand of hair off her cheek. "Not here, anyway."

"Actually, I left Sheldon alone so I could pop into Tea Flowers, but when I got there, it was closed."

"That's because Kelly's body was released to her family. They're burying her today."

A heaviness settled in Nora's chest as she pictured two adults and a little boy standing next to an open grave.

Her eyes strayed to the whiteboard. The photos and documents taped to its shiny surface told the story of how Kelly's life had ended, but the villain of the story had yet to be named.

Nora's gaze was caught by a photo of a sailor's valentine. It wasn't the valentine she'd unwrapped. That one had a woman's portrait in its center. This one had a map showing an island surrounded by a cerulean sea.

She pointed at the photo. "Were my prints on that?"

McCabe nodded.

"I've never seen it before, let alone touched it. I can't understand how my prints got on something I've never laid eyes on. Me. Kelly. Justine. We're all connected to Lawrence. Are you sure he has nothing to do with any of this?"

McCabe's response was lost on Nora, for at that moment, she caught sight of the glass bottle on his worktable. The drink, which was half tea and half lemonade, was the same shade as the honey inside the bottle Rizzo had left on Nora's checkout counter. The bottle Nora had dropped into Rizzo's purse.

Had Rizzo left the honey behind on purpose? She had a helmet. She was thinner than Nora, but they were about the same height. Was she the woman who'd spoken to Kelly the night she died?

"Hey." McCabe gently tapped her temple. "What's going on in there?"

Nora told him about Rizzo.

"She might be the woman in the video," McCabe said as he jotted some notes on a legal pad.

"I didn't see the man who picked her up from the bookstore. All I know was that he drove a black motorcycle. I wish I'd gotten a good look at his neck. How many people have spider web tattoos on their neck?"

"He might be an ex-offender. There's been an increase of ex-offenders hanging out at the truck stop, notwithstanding those employed by Midnight Chicken and the convenience store. That's not to say that every person with a spider web tattoo has done time, but a forensic scientist specializing in tattoos confirmed that our guy's web was produced by a homemade tattoo gun."

Staring at the photo, Nora asked, "Homemade?"

"Someone used the motor from a beard trimmer, a pen, a toothbrush, and the spring of a lighter or a retractable pen. The spring is sharpened and becomes the needle. Ink is made from soot, water, and a liquid binder like shampoo or dish soap."

Nora searched McCabe's face. "Are you going to interview Estella's dad?"

"Yes."

"He doesn't have a neck tattoo."

McCabe rested his hands on Nora's shoulders. "But he might recognize the killer. That's why we're talking to all the employees." After a brief pause, he said, "When did you last see Gus?"

"Yesterday morning, at the Gingerbread House. Why?"

Sparks ignited in McCabe's eyes—the feverish glint of a hound catching the rabbit's scent—and his hands tightened on her shoulders. "What was he doing there?"

Nora pushed his arms away and snapped, "I'm done with interrogations. Call Hester if you want to know why he was there."

"Nora—"

"I have to get back to work."

McCabe blocked her path to the door. "Please. I need to find Gus. Do you know where he is?"

Nora frowned. "You make it sound like he's gone missing. How long you been looking for him?"

"Since this morning. He isn't at Estella's, and she doesn't know where he is. She had a doctor's appointment first thing. After that, she drove to the salon. The location services on Gus's phone are turned off and he's not answering Estella's calls or replying to her texts. The only person who's heard from him since Estella said goodbye to him this morning is the manager of Midnight Chicken."

Dread pooled in Nora's gut. "What did Gus say to him?"

" 'I quit.' That's all he said."

Nora's mouth hung open as questions darted around in her head like shiny minnows.

Gus quit his job? Why? Does Estella know what's going on, or is she in the dark too? If she hasn't talked to him since she went to the doctor, then he doesn't know about her pregnancy.

"There has to be a simple explanation for this," Nora reasoned. "All I can tell you is that he was happy yesterday. Hester showed him some of her bread-making techniques. In return, he fixed her sink. He was working on her oven when I left. He seemed good. Settled. He and Hester get along really well."

Nora didn't mention Gus's warning about the man with the spider web tattoo. It would only hone McCabe's interest, and though Nora didn't know Gus Sadler well, she was so sure that he'd had nothing to do with the murders of two women that she'd stake her store on it.

At that moment, Nora's phone pinged. She pulled it out of her pocket and glanced at the screen. Sheldon had written a single line of text. Nora read it and blanched.

"I have to go."

She was out the door before McCabe could say a word.

Chapter 16

This is why we call people exes, I guess—because the paths that cross in the middle end up separating at the end.

—John Green and David Levithan

Nora heard Tucker long before she saw him.

She opened the back door to noises that were more animal than human. Tucker's cries cracked the air like thunder, each note bursting with pain and anger. She caught the word *"No!"* but little else.

A man in a black suit stood at the end of the hall, his back turned to Nora. His finger was pressed to his ear as he shouted into his cell phone.

Nora ignored him and ran toward the Readers' Circle.

Val sat hunched in the mustard-colored chair, her face in her hands. Her shoulders pulsated as she quietly sobbed.

Nora hurried into the stacks, drawn by Tucker's wails and the cajoling voices of two men.

In the YA section, Kirk and Sheldon were trying to get between Tucker and the bookshelves. They held out their hands in supplication, shuffling to the left and right to block Tucker's reach.

The floor was covered in books.

Most were splayed open, their spines broken. Some had been

trampled. Others had been torn apart. Loose pages were scattered across the carpet like teeth knocked from a giant's mouth. Dust jackets lay like flightless butterflies around Tucker's feet.

While Nora watched in horror, he scooped a paperback off the ground and ripped off the front cover. Hurling it at his uncle, he cried, "*I want my mom!*"

Sheldon shimmied closer to Nora and gestured between the boy and the ruined books. "We don't know what to do!"

Kirk added, "I'm so sorry! We came in because he wanted a hot chocolate, and I was ordering our drinks when he started screaming. I've tried everything Kelly usually does, but nothing's working!"

Nora had no idea what to do. Kids had had meltdowns in the shop before, but they'd all been little kids and had either calmed down after a few minutes or been carried outside by their parents.

Tucker was a ten-year-old boy with Asperger's. Nora didn't know if she should try to talk to him, touch him, or leave him alone. She was completely out of her depth.

Petrified by helplessness, the three adults saw Tucker drop to his knees and gather a pile of loose books to his chest. His face was streaked with tears and snot and his body was as rigid as a board.

The blare of a siren added to the cacophony, and Sheldon went pale.

"*¡Dios mío!* He actually called an ambulance!"

"Who?" Nora asked, but her question was lost in the din.

With his back plastered to the bookshelves, Sheldon looked like a victim awaiting the firing squad. He pointed to the left and said, "I locked the door to keep customers *out*, but now the paramedics can't get *in*."

Nora swung around and headed for the front door, but when she turned the corner of the Fiction section, she saw that the man in the black suit had beat her to it.

A paramedic she knew—a woman named Isabel—entered

the bookstore with a man wearing khaki shorts and a MELLO YELLO T-shirt close on her heels.

"Hey, Nora. I hear you've got an unhappy little boy back there. Can you take us to him, and we'll see what we can do to calm him down?"

Isabel's calm, unhurried manner inspired confidence. Nora flashed her a grateful smile and led her into the stacks. The man in the MELLO YELLOW T-shirt also followed them back.

The moment Sheldon saw Isabel, he left the YA section and retreated to the Readers' Circle. Isabel briefly questioned Kirk about Tucker. When she was done, she beckoned for the man in the MELLO YELLO T-shirt to come forward.

"This is my brother, Derrick," Isabel told Kirk. "He's a child psychologist who specializes in treating neurodiverse kids. In my opinion, he's better equipped to handle this situation than anyone in emergency response. Are you okay with him talking to Tucker?"

Looking like he'd just been thrown a lifeline, Kirk nodded vigorously.

By this time, Tucker's shouts had deescalated to a soft, hiccupping moan. His body was still stiff, and his eyes were hollow. The poor kid was bereft and exhausted. Every hitch of his breath made Nora feel sick with pity.

Derrick cleared away a small pile of books and squatted down close to Tucker. He then hugged his knees to his chest and began speaking to him in a conversational tone.

"Hey, Tucker. My name's Derrick. I know you're not feeling too great right now, but I'm going to try to help you feel better, okay? I've got some cool sunglasses here. Do you want to try them on? Your eyes might like a little break."

Derrick held out a pair of sunglasses with neon yellow frames. When Tucker didn't reach for them, Derrick asked if he could put them on Tucker's face. When Tucker shook his head, Derrick placed the glasses on a crushed book near Tucker's hand.

"I'll just leave them here in case you want them." Derrick

waited a beat before continuing. "Wow. It looks like you're really strong. Do you know what? I have a special pen here, and if you're as strong as I think you are, you *might* be able to bend it. It's right here in my pocket. And now, it's right here in my hand. Do you want to see if you can bend it?"

Derrick held out a shiny, iridescent metal pen.

Snuffling, Tucker looked first at Derrick and then at the pen. After a moment's hesitation, he picked up the pen and fisted it in his hand. He squeezed it a few times before he began to fold it from both ends.

It's like an origami pen, Nora thought as she watched Tucker manipulate it.

Derrick said, "Do you like that pen?"

Tucker nodded. He was growing quieter and calmer by the second.

"Would you like to keep it?"

Tucker nodded again.

"I'll make you a deal. If you agree to sit in a chair and drink a glass of water, you can have that pen." Derrick tapped the face of his smartwatch. "You don't have to move right now. I could set my stopwatch for a certain time, and then you could move when you're ready. You tell me how long to set it. One minute? Two minutes? Or three minutes?"

When Tucker chose three, Derrick set the stopwatch app and stretched out his arm so that Tucker had a clear view of the numbers.

"When the time is up, you'll hear ducks quacking. That's my alarm. It's kind of silly, but I like ducks. I like them so much that I collect rubber ducks. I have a hundred and forty-two ducks in my office."

"I collect pennies," said Tucker. He reached under the collar of his shirt and pulled out a chain. At the end of the chain was a penny. "This is from the year I was born. My Meemaw gave it to me."

Isabel signaled for Nora and Kirk to follow her to the Readers' Circle. She sat next to Val and spoke to her in hushed tones while Nora sagged against a bookshelf.

"I'm so sorry about this," Kirk said. "It's been a long time since he's had a meltdown. Kelly told me how to handle it, but I obviously didn't do it right. The books—oh, God. I'm sorry. I'll pay for all of them, of course."

Nora waved this off. "That's what insurance is for." When it looked like Kirk would protest, she laid a hand on his harm. "I care about the books, but they can be replaced. What matters now is Tucker."

"What triggered the meltdown?" Isabel glanced from Val to Kirk. "Were you at a funeral?"

Kirk nodded. "We buried my sister, Tucker's mom, today."

"That must've been really hard. For all of you," Isabel said.

"Kelly had terminal cancer, so she started preparing Tucker for her death months ago. She even wrote out a set of flashcards full of answers to questions she knew Tucker would ask. Val and I memorized every single one." Kirk smiled at his wife before turning back to Isabel. "Kelly made sure Tucker was part of her send-off. His involvement was really important to her. He was supposed to make a hundred origami butterflies and sprinkle them over her coffin. They even used the bathtub to practice. Kelly would lie down in the tub . . ."

The rest of his sentence was lost in a sob. Val moved to her husband's side and put an arm around his shoulders.

"Tucker was doing fine until his father showed up outside the cemetery," Val said, her eyes blazing. "He hasn't seen his father for nine years, so when some strange man tried to hug him, he freaked out. After telling Lawrence to back off, we tried to distract Tucker by promising him hot chocolate from the bookstore. Lawrence followed us here. He kept saying that he wanted to come to our house and spend time with his son. He kept whispering to Tucker. It was all too much."

Val's voice receded until it was only a vague buzzing in

Nora's ears. She suddenly felt like she was on a boat deck in rough seas and had to grab the back of a chair for support.

The man in the black suit is Lawrence.

Lawrence is here. In my shop.

A strong arm encircled her waist.

"It's okay, *querida*," Sheldon whispered. "Miracle Books is yours. Say the word, and I'll kick his ass to the curb."

She shook her head. "I need to find out why he came here. The *real* reason."

"Do you expect him to tell you the truth?"

"No, but I'm going to ask anyway."

Lawrence was barking into his phone as he paced from the checkout register to the door and back. When he caught sight of Nora, he said, "I'll call you later," and pocketed his phone.

After all this time, here he was in the flesh.

This was a more polished version than the one she'd known. This Lawrence had groomed brows, moisturized skin, and stark-white veneers. His nails were manicured, his suit was custom-tailored, and his silk tie probably cost more than everything Nora had on. He'd always borne a slight resemblance to George Clooney and had clearly spent a fortune honing that resemblance.

Lawrence's hair was sparrow-brown with gray sneaking in at the temples and along the gel-slicked wave cresting over his forehead. When he smiled, laugh lines fanned out from the corners of his eyes. The expression was well practiced and probably charmed most people. But Nora wasn't most people.

"Am I supposed to call you Nora?" he asked, giving her the once-over. "I thought you'd have more scars, but you look good. Really good."

"Why are you here?" she demanded flatly.

"I came for Kelly's funeral. It was the right thing to do."

Nora's eyes narrowed. "Since when have you cared about that?"

Lawrence clutched his heart as if he'd been wounded. "Not pulling any punches, are you? Okay, fine. I have business in the area, so I thought I'd pay my respects and see my son. I'm his father, after all."

"You share DNA, but you're not his father any more than you're a father to your daughter."

"I see you've been keeping tabs on me." He sounded pleased. "What about you? Did you ever have a kid?"

Keeping her expression blank, Nora replied, "No. Anyway, the funeral's over and you've seen Tucker, so I guess you'll be on your way."

"I'm in no hurry to listen to any more of that"—Lawrence jerked his thumb toward the back of the store—"but I *am* dying for a coffee. Why don't we grab a cup and catch up?"

I'd rather walk barefoot over burning coals, Nora thought.

But Lawrence was the common denominator between herself and two murdered women, so Nora bit back an acerbic reply and said, "Are you staying at the Lodge?"

"I am."

"We can catch up there. I'll meet you at the outdoor bar at seven."

A gleam appeared in Lawrence's eyes. "You want to meet at my hotel, eh? You little minx."

Nora smirked. "We're meeting at your hotel because copious amounts of alcohol and a public setting will force me to be civil."

Lawrence laughed. "You're a breath of fresh air. Okay, *Nora*, see you at seven."

Unlocking the front door, Nora waved Lawrence through it. Before she could close it again, one of her regular customers approached. Pointing at the ambulance, she asked if everything was okay.

"Yes, but we'll be closed for a just a few more minutes. Do you mind coming back?"

"Not at all. I'll just pop into the hardware store."

Nora locked the door and returned to the Readers' Circle.

When she noticed that Sheldon's face was still pale, she quietly told him that his workday was over. For once, he didn't protest. He simply hung up his apron and left.

Isabel and her brother were the next to go.

"See you next week," Derrick said as he shook hands with Kirk. He then waved to Nora and headed outside.

"That man couldn't have picked a better moment to walk into our lives." Kirk put a hand on Tucker's shoulder. "We're going to visit him at his office next week, and if all goes well, he and Tucker will be spending a lot more time together."

Val put her arm around her nephew. "Let's get you home, sweetheart. You must be awfully tired." Glancing at Nora, Val mouthed a thank-you and exited the shop.

Kirk watched them leave but made no move to follow.

"I'd like to help you clean up."

"That won't be necessary. And I meant what I said about the insurance. I'm covered for the damage. Really. It's fine."

Kirk nodded. "Okay, then. Would you let me put together a flower arrangement for your checkout counter?"

"As long as none of the flowers mean 'sorry.' We're friends now, so there's no need for that."

"Friends," Kirk repeated.

He smiled warmly at Nora before hurrying outside to catch up to his family.

That evening, Nora took a quick shower, slipped on a sundress, and laced up a pair of white Chuck Taylors. Without telling McCabe or the other Secret, Book, and Scone Society members what she was doing, she drove to the Lodge to meet her ex-husband for drinks.

He was already seated when she arrived but got to his feet and pulled out a chair for her.

"You look stunning," he said, his hand lingering on her bare shoulder for just a second too long. "I've ordered some appetizers, but feel free to add to the order."

Nora picked up the cocktail menu. "I might. I'm hungry enough to eat a gas station sandwich."

Lawrence laughed. "Oh, you're so refreshing. The girls I date seem to survive on lettuce and air."

"If their livelihoods are tied to their looks, I imagine the *women* you date have to be very disciplined. I'm a middle-aged bookstore owner. If I'm fifteen pounds overweight, nobody cares." She dropped the menu on the table. "I'm glad you brought up your romantic partners because I'm curious about them."

"You and every tabloid in the country," scoffed Lawrence.

Their server appeared and Nora ordered an Aperol spritz. Lawrence chose a classic gimlet.

"With Hendrick's," he added gruffly. "If you don't have that, give me your top-shelf gin, and tell the bartender not to be stingy with his pour."

"I'll be sure to let her know," the server said as he turned away.

Nora grinned. "I bet you make friends wherever you go. So, what business brings you to this quiet corner of the world?"

Lawrence settled deeper into his chair. He'd always enjoyed talking about himself, and Nora could see that he still did.

"How much do you know about what I do? Aside from what you've seen in the media."

"This might come as a surprise, but I knew nothing about your life until Kelly was killed. I only googled you because of her."

Their appetizers came, and the server described each dish as he placed it on the table.

"Goat cheese crostini with honey and thyme. Fried chickpeas. Hawaiian barbecue quesadillas. Marinated olives. And soy-glazed chicken wonton cups. Enjoy!"

"Not bad," Lawrence said as he loaded food onto a small

plate. In between bites, he told Nora about his career. She knew he was trying to impress her, but she had a hard time following the cryptocurrency references. When he started talking about subsidiaries, she decided it was time for a more direct approach

"I noticed that your companies have nautical names. Do you still like to sail?"

Lawrence's carefully curated veneer slipped, and he looked genuinely sad. "I haven't been out on the water for years. Even when I travel, it's all about work. I need to wine and dine the right people. Be seen with the right people. It's part of the game."

"Who do you need to be seen with in Miracle Springs? This town is known for its slow pace, natural beauty, and restorative properties. We don't get many tycoons here."

Lawrence caught their server's eye and signaled for another round. Then he used the side of his fork to slice a wonton cup in half. "I'm going to build a casino. Not here, exactly. A few towns over."

Nora thought of the photos she'd seen in the paper. The protest against the "outsider" gaming corporation had drawn a crowd of thousands. Protesters had carried signs complaining of corruption and demanding justice for the Cherokee. Many of the Cherokee had attended in ceremonial dress, as had people from the Lumbee, Choctaw, Chickasaw, Catawba, Creek, and Seminole tribes. The solidarity among tribes had garnered national attention and within hours, the protest had gone viral.

"The Cherokee need the casino. The income will make a big difference to their community," Nora said. "Why not build yours elsewhere? You don't have ties to this area."

"People are moving here in droves. The housing and leisure markets are booming. I'd be an idiot *not* to build a casino here. My world-class resort will provide lots of jobs and revenue for the county." He shrugged. "There's always a winner and a loser when it comes to deals like this. I'm not a villain because I have more to offer than the next guy. Or, in this case, ten little Indians."

Nora wondered exactly when her ex-husband turned into a sexist, racist, megalomaniac.

"You were fiscally conservative when we were together. What changed?"

"The bigger the risk, the bigger the reward," he said.

It was a well practiced line. A conversation ender. But Nora couldn't let it go at that. She knew the casino deal was important, she just didn't know how it connected to the death of Lawrence's second wife or his current girlfriend.

"You've obviously had big wins. Have you ever lost big?"

A shadow crossed Lawrence's face, but their second round of drinks arrived, and he was saved from having to respond.

Direct questions weren't paying off, so Nora decided to switch tack.

"Between the casino deal and the murders of an ex-wife and a girlfriend, you must have the press breathing down your neck."

Lawrence dismissed this with the flick of his wrist. "Money buys me privacy. I have a team of PR people, drivers, bodyguards, consultants—you name it. Besides, I have an airtight alibi and no reason whatsoever to want them dead."

Because you didn't care about them at all. Women are disposable to you.

"I met Justine, you know. She came into the shop looking for book recommendations. She specifically wanted romance novels where the young, beautiful heroine gets the older, richer, savvier hero to marry her."

"Of course she did. Even though I told her on our very first date that I'm not into commitment. No more wives. No more kids." He used two fingers to mime a cutting motion. "I got snipped, so I can't be tricked."

Nora took a generous swallow of her drink and said, "You should have that made into a T-shirt."

Lawrence chortled in delight, and Nora was tempted to

throw her drink in his face. Instead, she took a deep breath and kept talking.

"Justine seemed angry. At *me*. Any idea why?"

"She flew here from Vegas to check you out. You *and* Kelly. She was trying to figure out what made you two special. The girl was desperate. She knew I was ready to move on. And she had the nerve to charge the flight and her hotel room to *my* Visa card."

Nora drained the rest of her drink and leaned forward in her chair. "You loved Kelly. It might not have lasted long, but you loved each other. Justine obviously cared about you, or she wouldn't have tried so hard to hold on. Kelly and Justine are dead. They both died in this town within days of each other. They're both connected to you, and *you're* here because of a casino. Does anyone else have to die for this deal, or are all the loose ends tied up?"

Though she hadn't seen Lawrence for over a decade, some habits never changed. He still ran his thumb over his watch face when he was uncomfortable. He did this twice before reaching for his cocktail glass, but it was enough to convince Nora that she was barking up the right tree.

The server stopped by to see if they wanted another round and Lawrence nodded in assent. A phone rang from the inside pocket of his jacket. He took a quick glance at the screen and got to his feet.

"I have to take this. I'll be right back. Don't go anywhere," he told Nora. He flashed her his trademark smile, but his body was tense. If he squeezed his phone any tighter, it would shatter.

Hurrying away from the bar, Lawrence took the path leading to the Japanese Zen Garden.

When he was out of sight, Nora entered the hotel and crossed the lobby to an alcove where the restrooms were located. Opening an unmarked door, she stepped out into the Zen Garden.

In three steps, she was facing the exterior rear wall of the teahouse. It was the only structure in the garden with a modicum of privacy, so Lawrence was likely to seek it out. The walls looked solid but were actually quite thin, which meant Nora could listen to his conversation without being seen.

"Thank you for stating the obvious, but it won't be a problem. I *will* get the damned papers." Lawrence's voice sounded like the snap of a rubber-band. "She'll lead me right to them. Sees herself as a fixer. She's got a Mother Teresa complex." Lawrence grunted. "Yeah, I don't miss a thing. Just gimme another day. Two at most. I've gotta go."

Since she couldn't beat Lawrence back to the table, Nora used the restroom and checked her phone for messages. She had a text from Estella, who still hadn't heard from her father, and a missed call from Kirk. He hadn't left a message.

"Where'd you run off to?" Lawrence asked when she returned to the table.

Nora didn't sit down. She held up her phone and said, "It's time for me to go, but thank you for the drinks."

"Just like that?" Lawrence was nonplussed. "Come on, the night is young!"

"But I'm not. It's been a long day and I'm ready to put my feet up." Nora wished him a good night and walked out of the bar.

She didn't feel the least bit tipsy. She wasn't sure if the food had soaked up the alcohol or if talking about Kelly and Justine or listening in on Lawrence's phone call had had a sobering effect on her, but she felt okay to drive.

Her moped's speed topped out at thirty-five, but Nora would slow down even more once she reached the dark, curvy road leading back to town.

She'd just passed the stone pillars marking the Lodge's entrance when she heard a motorcycle engine roar to life in the parking lot behind her.

The space above her pinkie tingled and she gripped her handlebars in fear.

They're following me.

Knowing she'd never make it to town before her pursuers caught her, she didn't turn left on Mountain Road but kept going straight. Pushing the moped to its max speed, she leaned forward, silently egging the little engine on, until she came to a steep driveway on her right.

She ascended the driveway and was soon hidden by a wall of trees and shrubs. Switching her engine off, she went very still and listened.

Within seconds, she heard the growl of the motorcycle. She didn't need to see it to know that its rider wore black clothes and had a spider web tattoo on his neck. He might even be carrying a passenger. A woman with a high, thin voice.

For a few, terrifying moments, it sounded like the bike was heading right for her. But as she pressed her chest to her handlebars, she realized that the noise was fading.

The motorcycle had taken Mountain Road.

Nora let out the breath she'd been holding and sent a text to McCabe.

She sat in the darkness for another ten minutes before turning the moped on and easing back onto the road. She assumed she was safe.

But she was wrong.

Chapter 17

A map does not just chart, it unlocks and formulates meaning; it forms bridges between here and there, between disparate ideas that we did not know were previously connected.

—Reif Larsen

There was no sign of a motorcycle at the bottom of Mountain Road, but Nora wouldn't breathe easy until she knew the Walshes were safe.

She wasn't foolish enough to take on a potential killer alone. The best she could do was look, listen, and call for help, so she parked her moped at the end of the block and continued down Maple Street on foot.

It was almost eight thirty, and the neighborhood was quiet. Porch lights sparked in the darkness and windows were illuminated by the bluish flicker of television screens and the buttery glow of lamps. It felt like every resident was curled up on a sofa with their feet up.

Sugarberry Cottage seemed peaceful and still, so Nora decided to walk past the house and go around the block to return to her moped. She was a hand's breadth from the Walshes' mailbox when she heard shouting from inside the house.

The shrill, angry voice belonged to a child.

Tucker!

Nora was about to charge down the front path when she remembered Tucker's outburst at the bookstore. He'd said his final farewell to his mother that day. As if that hadn't been enough emotional turmoil for the boy to grapple with, his father had suddenly materialized, demanding attention and a physical display of affection. Was it any surprise that Tucker was expressing his hurt and frustration right now?

Glancing up at the window of Tucker's room, Nora didn't know what to do. She didn't want to disturb Kirk and Val, but she needed to warn them about the motorcyclist.

In the end, she sat on the curb and dialed Kirk's number.

It rang for a long time before he finally picked up.

"I'm sorry to bother you," Nora began. As quickly as she could, she explained why she was sitting outside their house.

"A motorcycle? The way Tucker's carrying on, I doubt we'd hear a commercial jet landing in our front yard. We can't understand him, and I'm about to pull out what little hair I have left. I have you on speaker, by the way."

"Can I help?" Nora asked, and instantly regretted having opened her mouth. She didn't know how to calm a person with Asperger's. Her experience with kids was limited to the story-time regulars or teens seeking book recommendations.

Apparently, Kirk's thoughts ran along a similar line. "I'm not sure . . ."

"Let her try!" Val cried in the background.

Five minutes later, Nora stood in the upstairs hallway. As soon as she'd reached the landing, Val had grabbed her by the arm. She was still clinging to it like a vine wrapped around a tree branch as she led Nora to the first door on the right.

"This is Tucker's room," Val whispered, cracking the door a few inches.

Nora peeked in.

Tucker was sitting on the floor, talking in a low, rapid-fire voice. He held Derek's pen in his hand and was bending it back and forth in a steady rhythm. Though still agitated, he was clearly exhausted.

Glancing down at the papers protruding from the crack under the door, Nora said, "What are these?"

"He draws maps when he's upset. Even when he was really little, he could draw maps from memory."

Nora gently detached Val's grip on her arm and reached for a piece of paper. "May I?"

"Please. See if you can make heads or tails of it. I can't tell if it's a country, a county, or Neverland."

The first sheet Nora picked up didn't resemble a map at all. It looked like toddler scribbles.

The next sheet was similar, as were the third and fourth. However, when Nora pulled out the bottom-most sheet, she saw a definitive shape.

She knocked softly on Tucker's door and said, "Hey, Tucker. It's Nora from the bookstore." She pointed at the map in her hands. "Is this an island?"

Tucker went abruptly silent and cast his eyes down.

Nora mouthed "Sorry" to Val, who shook her head as if to say "It's okay."

Just as Nora was about to back away, Tucker grabbed another piece of paper from a loose pile on his bed and shoved it under the door.

This sheet was less rumpled than the previous ones, and the map had been drawn with more care. It was clearly the same island, but Tucker had added a bunch of elongated V's to represent water and a big, bold, red X marked a spot in the middle of the landmass.

"Looks like a treasure map," Nora said to no one in particular.

Tucker selected another paper from the top of his bed and slid it under the door.

This map was beautifully detailed. Every line was precise and deliberate. There was a rose compass in the bottom corner, mountains and trees dotted the island, and certain areas were carefully labeled. As Nora's gaze swept over names like "Spyglass Hill" and "Skeleton Island," she knew exactly what Tucker had drawn.

"It's the map from *Treasure Island*. Tucker, this is amazing."

Kirk got up from where he'd been sitting on the top step and joined the two women.

"Why does he keep drawing this particular place?" he whispered.

Another sheet appeared under the door. Val scooped it up and held it so that they could all look at it together.

This map was very similar to the previous one. The only difference was the inclusion of an impressive drawing of a schooner in the bottom left corner. The site of the ship and the map reminded Nora of the sailor's valentine—the one covered in her fingerprints. That map had shown a chain of Caribbean islands.

Are there other maps in Virginia Love's collection?

When she asked Kirk and Val this question, they gave her blank looks.

"Just on the valentine that went missing," Kirk replied. "And I don't know if you heard, but the thief broke it. They pulled the map part off the base, but they were too rough, and the base cracked in half."

What were they looking for?

"What about the books? Did any include a map?"

Kirk mulled this over for a moment before answering. "I don't think so. Folks from the sheriff's office checked every page for loose notes or clues but didn't find a thing. None of the other valentine collectibles had a map or nautical themes. Why do you ask?"

Nora wasn't sure. A string of words ran through her mind like a news ticker: *Valentine, treasure, map, ship, love, Tucker, casino, land.*

"What are you thinking?" Kirk softly prodded.

"Nothing cohesive. I just . . ." She shook her head and started again. "Did you know that Lawrence was behind the casino deal?"

"Not until today."

Val lowered her voice to a whisper. "He said that he came for the funeral, but I didn't believe him. We made the arrangements at the last minute and didn't tell anyone. We wanted it to be as low-key as possible for Tucker's sake. When I told Lawrence he shouldn't have come, he said he was in the area anyway. He could've jumped out of a plane right over the cemetery, and he still shouldn't have come! What kind of man shows up, uninvited, to the funeral of a woman he treated like dirt?"

For once, Nora was in complete agreement with Val. She nodded in solidarity before turning back to Kirk.

"Has Tucker ever drawn a map of North Carolina?" she asked, speaking too quietly for Tucker to hear. "Like this town, or someplace nearby?"

"Not that I've seen."

What are we missing? Lawrence must've said something to Tucker to incite the meltdown at the bookstore. Had he been cruel or demeaning? Had he insulted Kelly or tried to touch Tucker without the boy's permission? Because even though Derrick had helped Tucker through the meltdown, the boy was still distraught. That much was obvious. The reasons behind his distress were less clear.

Stepping into Tucker's room, Kirk said, "Buddy, I had no idea you could draw the map from *Treasure Island*. Did you and your mom read that book together?"

The three adults held a collective breath as they waited for Tucker to answer. Finally, he murmured, "Meemaw read it to me. We saw the movie too. Twelve times."

"Do you have the book in your room?" asked Nora.

"Meemaw said not to show it to anyone. Only Mom. I promised. And when you shake on it, that means you promise forever."

Val gave Kirk a nudge so that she could enter the room too. "Was your dad trying to get you to break your promise? Is that why you're upset?"

Suddenly words tumbled out of Tucker like stormwater from a gutter. "He said Meemaw's secrets were *his* secrets because she was his mom. But that's *not* what Meemaw said. She said I could only tell Mom. We shook on it! She told me everyone else was a pirate. And pirates steal people's treasure."

Kirk and Val exchanged puzzled looks.

"Did your mom know your secret?" asked Val.

After a lengthy pause, Tucker murmured, "She said I could tell you and Uncle Kirk after she died. She said I had to share the secret with one grown-up because I needed a grown-up to watch out for pirates."

Val leaned close to Kirk and whispered, "It's just a story. Let's get him to bed. Poor thing is totally worn out. We can talk about treasure and pirates in the morning."

Kirk held up a finger. "Give me a sec. Tucker? If I shut the door, and it's just you and me, will you tell me the secret?"

"Just you?"

"Just me."

"Okay."

Val stepped into the hallway and Nora retreated until she was standing at the top of the stairs.

Kirk closed Tucker's door.

As the women waited, time slowed to a crawl. One minute turned to two. Two minutes turned to five.

Since she couldn't hear a peep from inside the boy's bedroom, Nora was tempted to text Estella. She was worried about Estella and Gus and she felt guilty because she hadn't connected with her friend all day. She pulled out her phone but couldn't think of what to say. It was impossible to concentrate while Tucker's door remained closed.

When the door finally opened, Kirk stood on the threshold looking shell-shocked. He reached out for his wife, and she rushed forward to take his hand.

"What is it?" she demanded.

Kirk moved his mouth, but no words came out.

Val peered over his shoulder to where Tucker sat cross-legged on his bed, hugging a large book to his chest. "Please, Kirk. You're scaring me."

"There *is* a treasure." Kirk's voice was filled with awe. "It's a deed—to a huge piece of property. It's close to here. I think it might be where Lawrence is planning to build that casino. Virginia gave the land to Kelly and Tucker. I didn't go through all the legal paperwork, but I read enough to know that this happened years ago, long before Lawrence had Virginia declared incompetent. The bottom line? He doesn't own the land he wants to build on. It couldn't belong to him because it didn't belong to Virginia when he took over her finances. It belonged to Kelly and Tucker."

Nora gasped. "Is that why Lawrence came to Miracle Springs? To steal the deed from his own son?"

"Even if he did, it wouldn't make a difference. It was recorded by the county. I saw a copy of that record."

Val's gaze swept over the papers on the floor. "Where?"

"It's inside Tucker's copy of *Treasure Island*. The book pages were removed. Now, there are only legal documents between the covers. Affidavits testifying to Virginia's sound mind. References from physicians and influential members of Virginia's community. There's a letter from Virginia too. She wanted Tucker to have this land so that he'd always have an income."

"I don't get it," said Val. "Unless it's super rich farmland or has a gold mine, how can it guarantee him an income?"

Kirk smiled at her. "There's no gold, but there's plenty of copper."

Nora was confused. "Is copper valuable? When I think of copper, I picture pennies and pipes."

"I might not have Lawrence's business savvy, but I know that you need copper to make electric cars. And batteries. As the demand for electric cars increases, so will the demand for copper. Virginia had the ore tested, and she left Tucker a high-quality deposit. When he comes of age, he can sell the land or lease it to a mining company."

Kirk's face was radiant with relief. As Val took in her husband's words, the lines around her mouth softened and she smiled.

Though Nora was happy for the couple, she could see that Tucker was completely spent. What the little boy needed most right now was to change into his pajamas, brush his teeth, and go to bed. He needed a good, long, healing sleep. He also needed protection. All three of them did.

"We should call the sheriff," she whispered to Kirk and Val. "Whoever broke in before—they might come back."

Kirk instantly sobered. "I left my phone in the kitchen. I'll go down and call right now."

Val led Nora into the hall, where she took her hand and gave it a squeeze. "You've been such a friend to us. More than I deserve."

Up close, Nora saw the dark circles under Val's eyes that her concealer had failed to hide. She thought of everything Val had been through in the past few months. She'd moved, started a new business, and opened her home to her sister-in-law and nephew. These high-stress events were compounded by Kelly's murder and a break-in.

The woman had been through hell, and Nora instantly forgave her any past unkindness. She demonstrated exactly how she felt by giving Val a hug.

When she let go, Val said, "It's time for Tucker to go to bed."

"I'll show myself out. Goodnight, Tucker. You were very brave. Your mom would be proud of you."

As Nora turned toward the stairs, she heard a loud thump from the first floor.

"Kirk?" Val shouted.

The sound of heavy footfalls floated up from below. Nora pictured a pair of black boots seconds before a man with a shaved head peered up at her from the bottom of the stairs.

He wore dark clothes and a predatory grin. His thick neck was tattooed, and in his right hand, he held a hunting knife.

Seeing the knife, a lightning bolt of adrenaline coursed through Nora's body. She shoved Val into Tucker's room and told her to lock the door. As soon as she heard the click of the lock, she darted toward the room at the end of the hall, pulling out her phone as she ran. She pressed the red emergency button and managed to scream, "*Send help!*" before a meaty forearm snaked around her throat and she found herself caught between the python-like limb and a torso as solid and unyielding as a cannon.

"Hush, now." The man's gravelly voice filled her ear. His arm tightened around her neck, cutting off her air supply. "I don't want to hurt you. If I wanted to do that, you'd have a knife sticking out of your back. Right about here."

The point of a sharp blade bit into Nora's skin and she whimpered in terror.

"Give me the deed and I won't need to cut you. I don't have time to—"

Without any warning, Nora stomped down hard on the man's foot and then immediately slammed her fist into his groin.

He let out an "oof" and released his hold on her. Those precious seconds allowed her to twist away from him and make a break for the stairs.

She was about to descend when the man launched himself at her.

The impact of his body knocked her off balance and she launched forward like a kid bellyflopping into a pool. Only there wasn't water below Nora. There was only empty air followed by a flight of uncarpeted steps.

All Nora could do was raise her arms to shield her face. She came down hard, landing in the middle of the staircase. There was a snap of breaking bone and a searing flash of pain as her left arm took the full impact of her fall.

Gravity dragged her down the last few stairs. She heard the bump of her shoulders and knees as her body slid over the smooth wood and a dull thud as her head struck the floor, but it felt like it was happening to someone else. Nora felt detached from herself, as if she were watching the scene on TV.

Someone was shouting.

Nora tried to listen. She tried to fight against the fog closing in around her, but she wasn't strong enough.

She closed her eyes and sank into darkness.

Ten minutes later, smelling salts jerked her back to consciousness.

"It's okay," said a paramedic. "I'm Amanda. Can you tell me your name?"

As Nora answered, she stared up at the ceiling and suddenly remembered where she was. Then, she remembered the man with the knife.

"Are they safe?" she asked, trying to raise her shoulders off the floor. Pain shot through her arm, and she grunted.

"Whoa, there. You need to lie still. You had a nasty fall and I'm pretty sure your arm is broken. I put a sling on it, but you've earned yourself a free ride to the hospital."

"The little boy—is he okay?"

Amanda nodded. "He's in his room. His aunt and the sheriff are with him."

"And Kirk?"

"He'll have a cartoon-sized lump on the noggin, which has earned him a free trip to the hospital too, but he's going to be okay."

Nora shut her eyes and sent up a silent prayer of gratitude. When she opened them again, McCabe was kneeling beside her.

"We need to work on your wrestling moves." He pushed her hair off her forehead and smiled. "You're supposed to throw the *other guy* down the stairs."

"I was *trying* to run away."

"Glad to hear it." A crinkle appeared between his brows. "How bad's the pain?"

"My arm aches, but only when I move it. Same with my head."

McCabe's face went red, and his voice was choked with emotion when he spoke next. "When I saw you—God—my heart just stopped. You're my favorite person in all the world, Nora. You know that, right? I love my job, but the best part of the workday is when it's over and I get to be with you. I feel like we're just getting started, you and me, so you need to be more careful, because I want to end my days with you until I run out of days. Can we do that?"

"We can do that."

He bent over and brushed her lips with his. "You need to get patched up now. I wish I could come with you, but Andrews called Hester. She and June will meet you at the hospital."

Someone called for McCabe, but when he turned to go, Nora grabbed his shirt sleeve. "Did you get him? The man?"

McCabe nodded. "We got him."

Nora nearly melted through the floor with relief.

"I love you," he whispered before joining his colleagues upstairs.

Because of her injuries, the paramedics insisted on putting Nora on a gurney and wheeling it down the driveway to where the ambulance was idling at the curb.

Blue and red lights strobed the grass, making it look like a dance floor. When Nora saw the man sitting in the back of a sheriff's department car, she thought her eyes were playing tricks on her. The door was open, so Nora could see that the man's hands were cuffed behind his back.

A pair of deputies stood a few feet away. One was talking to a woman in a bathrobe while the other spoke into his cell phone.

"Wait!" Nora told the paramedics. "Please! You have to stop!"

Amanda peered down at her in concern. "You okay?"

"That man in the car. Is he under arrest?"

Amanda glanced at the car. "Looks like it."

Nora started shaking her head. "No, no, no! That *isn't* the man who attacked me. You've got to tell the sheriff. The man with the knife had a spider web tattoo on his neck. He came for the deed. Oh, God. The deed. He must be working for Lawrence. Please get McCabe. He can't get away! He's already killed two women!"

Amanda exchanged a pointed look with her coworker and Nora knew they weren't going to do as she asked.

"Give me my phone, then. I need to call him!"

"Listen, Nora. You hit your head pretty hard and—"

"I know what I saw!" Nora shouted. Despite the throbbing in her head and the aching in her arm, she tried to sit up.

Amanda put a firm hand on her shoulder and said, "Whoa, there. You need to calm down. Everything's under control. You'll see—"

"*No!* They've got the wrong man."

As Nora tried to kick her legs free from the blanket covering her lower half, she heard Amanda say something about ketamine. And before she could object, she felt the prick of a needle in her arm.

"Please," she cried as the drug surged through her blood-stream. "Tell McCabe. Tell him . . . he's got the wrong man . . ."

Her tongue was too thick to form more words and sleep was rolling over her like a wave.

The last thing she saw was Gus Sadler's agonized face, star-ing at her from inside a cop car. Then her vision faded and there was only oblivion.

Chapter 18

Better a broken bone than a broken spirit.
—Lady Marjory Allen

By the time Nora's mind cleared, she was lying on an exam table while a woman in scrubs wrapped her arm in strips of plaster.

"Where's my phone?" Nora asked the woman. A badge clipped to her front pocket identified her as Monique Anene, MD.

"Hey, there. You slept through all the boring bits—well done. I'm Doctor Anene from Orthopedics." The woman gave her a brief smile. "Your friends have your phone. They're out in the waiting area. As soon as we're done here, and I'm just about finished, you can see them. You had a nice clean break. No surgery required. You'll have this stylish accessory for six weeks and—"

Nora grabbed the doctor's hand. "I need a phone. The man who caused my injury is still at large. A child's safety is at stake, okay? The man who hurt me might go after him. *I need a phone.*"

"Use mine." The woman punched in her passcode and handed Nora her phone.

Nora tried McCabe's number first, but he didn't pick up.

She tried Andrews next. When that failed, she called the department's non-emergency number and explained the situation to the on-duty officer.

When he promised to relay the message to McCabe, Nora thanked him and hung up.

"Sounds like you've had quite a night," said Dr. Anene.

Nora half listened as the doctor explained how to care for her cast. Five minutes later, a nurse pulled back the curtain separating Nora's treatment area from her neighbor's and said, "Your friends are in the waiting room. Do you want to see them while we wait for Dr. Shah? He's your ER doctor."

"Yes. Thanks."

Dr. Anene left and the nurse returned with June, Hester, and Sheldon.

"We heard you were very anxious to have this," Sheldon said, handing Nora her phone.

The case was bent, and the screen was so badly shattered that tiny triangles of glass were missing. Though she knew it was futile, Nora tried to turn the phone on. It didn't work, of course.

"How are you feeling, baby?" asked June.

Nora couldn't hide her agitation. "I'm sore and my head feels like it's stuffed with cotton, but I'll be okay. I'm freaking out because I can't reach Grant. I borrowed the doc's phone, but I couldn't get through to him. Hester, can you call Jasper? They arrested Gus and he's—"

"I know. Estella called us from the station."

June sat on the edge of Nora's exam table. "You can relax. They got the bad guy. The one who took out Kirk and did his best to take you out? They got him."

"What happened to Kirk?" Nora asked.

Sheldon put an arm around June's neck. "Spider-Man got him in a sleeper hold. But he was in a rush, so he didn't hold it for long. Kirk was only out for a few minutes. By the time he came to, Gus had entered the house and grabbed a cast-iron pan from the drying rack. While Spidey was busy picking the lock to Tucker's room with his knife, Gus clocked him. I bet the guy had little cartoon birdies circling around his head."

"You watched too much Tom and Jerry as a kid," Hester teased.

Sheldon wiggled his finger. "Not Tom and Jerry. Wile E. Coyote got the biggest bumps. And if there was any justice in this world, the Road Runner would've been hit by a Mack truck."

Ignoring this exchange, Nora focused on June. "If they got him, then why did I see Gus handcuffed in the back of a cop car?"

"He's an ex-offender. He was in the house when the cavalry came. They had to take him in while they figured out what had gone down."

"Jasper called his parole officer on the way to the station," Hester added. "The sheriff needs statements from Kirk and Gus before he can let anyone go, and you know these things don't happen quickly."

Nora nodded. Her mouth was dry, and the exam table was uncomfortable.

As if sensing her need, June pulled a bottle of water out of her purse and pressed it into Nora's right hand.

"You need to hydrate and relax," she ordered. "Jack and Estella are both at the station. They'll take Gus home as soon as they can."

Nora drank the water, and even though it hurt a little to swallow, the aching was a reminder that she'd survived the attack. Kelly and Justine hadn't been so lucky. Gus hadn't been there to save them. No one had.

"Why was Gus at the Walshes' in the first place?"

Sheldon said, "Gus has been watching Spidey all day. Spidey is the man Gus didn't want to work with at Midnight Chicken. He was bad news in prison and hadn't changed one bit since he got out. Gus said he was involved in lots of shady deals when they were inside, but he wasn't the brains behind any of the schemes—more like an unstable minion."

"He must've been working for Lawrence."

Hester shrugged. "We don't know. We don't even know the guy's name. But the Walshes are safe. Fuentes and Hollowell will be watching their house for the rest of the night. Can you tell us why this guy was looking for an old deed?"

"I think Lawrence wants to build a casino on land that he doesn't own. The land belonged to his mother, Virginia, and she left it to Kelly and Tucker. With Kelly gone, it's Tucker's land—or will be when he comes of age. Lawrence showed up at Kelly's funeral just to be near Tucker. He must've asked him about the deed. That's why Tucker had a meltdown. He felt threatened."

June kissed her teeth. "Larry was going to steal from his own child! Lord, hell needs a new circle for that man."

"There's a big copper deposit on this land. If Lawrence opened the casino in one area and a copper mine in another, he'd really rake it in," Nora continued. "I told you that he took over his mother's finances against her will, right? There was a big court battle, which Lawrence won, but Virginia gave the land to Kelly long before he took over her finances."

"Was the deed inside a book?" asked Sheldon.

For the first time since she came to, Nora smiled. "It was in *Treasure Island*. Virginia read the book to Tucker many times. It was their favorite story."

Hester pressed her hands to her heart. "That is *so* sweet."

"She must've told him about the land and the copper. I think that's why Tucker wore a penny as a necklace and why he collected pennies. To him, pennies *are* treasure. They remind him of his grandmother."

Sheldon made a time-out gesture. "You're going to make me cry. This whole thing sounds like the plot of a Lifetime movie, starring Larry as a cliché villain. A rich, handsome womanizer who took advantage of his mama and neglected his children? Who'd play him on TV? Jared Leto? Christian Bale?"

A nurse bustled in to tell Nora that Dr. Shah was on his way. "I'm getting your paperwork ready, so you should be able to go home soon."

That was music to Nora's ears. She'd had enough excitement for one day. All she wanted to do was change into her pajamas, make tea, and climb into bed.

Unfortunately, Dr. Shah had other ideas.

"With a concussion, you'll need to rest for the next two or three days. Cut way back on activities. No driving. Do you share a living space with anyone? Because someone needs to check on you in the morning."

"She's going to stay with me tonight," said Hester.

Dr. Shah reviewed post-concussion symptoms and treatments before finally signing off on her paperwork. Nora agreed to see her primary care doctor for a follow-up visit in three days, and reluctantly accepted a seat in the wheelchair the nurse pushed into the room.

Ten minutes into the journey back to Miracle Springs, Nora was overcome by fatigue. She rested her head against the cool window glass and closed her eyes.

Sheldon, who was sitting directly behind her, rubbed her shoulder and said, "You doing okay, my little flying squirrel?"

Nora cracked a smile. "Yeah. But did you hear what that doctor said about reducing my activities? There's no way I can sit at home with my feet up when Family Fun Fest is this weekend. We have to switch out all the displays in the store."

"We could leave the bee and honey displays. I mean, what's more familial than a hive?"

June clucked her tongue. "If you want to be healthy enough for the rest of festival season, then you need to follow doctor's orders." Glancing at Hester in the rearview mirror, she said, "What kind of treats are you making for this fest?"

"I'm playing off two themes: the family tree and home is where the heart is. I'm making two kinds of tree-shaped pull-apart bread and mini sheet cakes decorated with trees. On top of that, I'm doing house-shaped cookies and cupcakes with hidden hearts inside."

"Nothing too crazy, eh?" Sheldon scoffed.

Hester laughed. "It's a little optimistic, I admit, but I might have some help. As soon as I have the chance, I'm going to ask Gus if he'll work at the bakery."

Even Nora perked up at this. "I love that idea."

"He won't have to deal with customers if he doesn't want to, but the man is a natural in the kitchen," continued Hester. "I think it would be great for both of us. Estella too. Gus wants to help out with the baby, so if he bakes in the morning, he can watch his grandkid in the afternoon while Estella's at work."

Sheldon whispered, "*Un bebe.* I still can't believe it."

While her friends discussed the many ways a child would change Estella's life—and theirs—Nora's thoughts kept returning to Tucker.

Twenty minutes later, June pulled in front of Nora's tiny house and kept the engine idling. Though Sheldon offered to accompany her inside, she insisted that she could throw pajamas, a toothbrush, and a change of clothes into a bag without help. She almost brought Tucker's origami along but didn't want to risk it coming to any harm.

Five minutes later, they arrived at Hester's to find an SUV with the sheriff's department seal parked in her driveway. For a moment, Nora thought McCabe had come.

"Jasper's here," Hester said in a bright voice.

June stopped at the curb and put the car in park. "Jasper might not welcome a crowd right now. You can fill us in tomorrow."

Sheldon hopped out and threaded Nora's good arm through his. "I'm not helping you. I'm just getting you out of the car so I can hug you good night."

Andrews was on the phone when Hester and Nora appeared in the kitchen. After wrapping up his call, he kissed Hester on the cheek. Turning to Nora, he said, "It's good to see you on your feet. For a second, I thought you and the sheriff might be sharing an ambulance. He was white as a sheet. Poor guy."

"Before I go to bed, can you tell me who he is? The man with the spider web tattoo?"

"His name's Colton Fieri. He and Mr. Sadler served time together, and when Colton learned that an old enemy was working the late shift at Midnight Chicken, he decided to pay Gus a visit. Colton's parole officer thought he was working at Midnight Chicken too, but he never fried a single piece of chicken. The manager put him on the payroll because he and Colton were involved in a grease theft scheme."

Assuming she'd banged her head harder than she thought, Nora just stared at Andrews.

Hester was equally baffled. "Why would anyone steal grease?"

"Believe it or not, it's a million-dollar business. Fat and cooking oil are used to make animal feed and biofuel."

"Ugh. The poor animals," murmured Hester.

Andrews went on speaking. "Most restaurants keep grease collection units near their other trash receptacles. The grease is collected by a service and sold to a biofuel company. People steal from the outdoor bins or take the whole bin. They sell the grease and pocket the money. It's not like the biofuel company can tell where the grease came from, and there are organized rings of grease thieves in almost every state. When Gus saw Colton emptying the Midnight Chicken grease bin, Colton threatened him. He told Gus to keep his mouth shut or he'd have him sent back to prison *and* make Estella's life a living hell."

Nora shook her head. "No wonder Gus quit."

"Mr. Sadler suspected Colton of killing Justine, but he didn't think his word would carry any weight. Especially since his manager was sure to defend Colton. When Estella told him that you, Kelly Walsh, and Justine were all connected to Lawrence, Mr. Sadler got worried. He figured Colton must be working for Lawrence."

"Where was Gus all day?" Hester asked.

"In the woods behind the Walshes' house. This town has changed a lot in the past fifteen years, but the woods haven't. It's still a nature preserve, so no one's been able to tear down the trees. The trailer park where Mr. Sadler used to live is on the other side of that preserve."

Nora was suddenly feeling more alert. "Is that where Colton lives now?"

Andrews pointed at her. "You guessed it."

"Was Colton on a motorcycle? I thought one was following me when I left the Lodge."

"Probably. We found his Harley parked two blocks over."

Hester moved closer to her boyfriend. "Is Lawrence behind all of this?"

Andrews put a comforting arm around her and squeezed. She rested her head against his shoulder and laid her hand over his chest. "I'm sorry, babe, but Colton isn't talking. We don't know who the other players are. Not yet anyway."

"What about the woman?" Nora asked. "The one from the video?"

"We're still looking for her."

If only Nora had seen the woman's face the day she'd gone hiking, but Colton and the mystery woman had been on the boulders above Nora. She recognized their voices but couldn't remember what they'd been talking about. Her memory refused to cooperate.

Interpreting Nora's faraway look as fatigue, Hester ushered her upstairs to the guest room.

"I'll make tea while you get changed."

Nora struggled to get her T-shirt off over her cast. Then she stretched out the neck of her pajama top trying to get her head and arm through the opening at the same time. Her pajama bottoms were another challenge. She had to sit in a chair and shimmy the pants up her legs, a few inches at a time, until the elastic waist was more or less where it was supposed to be.

After washing her face and brushing her hair, she returned to the guest room to find a steaming mug of chamomile tea and the latest edition of *TeaTime* magazine on the nightstand.

Nora flipped through the magazine. Page after page, her tired eyes were treated to a bounty of beautiful flowers, teapots, and food. She read an article about flowering teas and drank in the images of fruit scones and lunch salads. The dainty table settings, delicate porcelain tea ware, and menus soothed her. By the time she got to the Cozy Corner section, which featured a cozy mystery novel and a recipe inspired by the book, her eyelids were drooping.

As she reached out to turn off the light, she pictured the origami flower on her nightstand at home. It was a comfort object, as was the magazine Hester had given her. At the outset, things made of paper seemed so fragile. They could be ruined by fire or water. They could be torn, bent, or stained. Yet paper held such power. A single sheaf could be transformed into a crane, a fortune teller, or an airplane. Decorated with words, it could tell a story, represent ownership, seduce or repel, bind or separate.

Nora had always loved paper because books were made of paper. But at ten years old, Tucker Walsh understood its beauty far better than she ever had. He'd used it to draw maps from memory. He shaped it into works of art. Through the pages of *Treasure Island*, he'd bonded with his grandmother. And his grandmother had used paper to leave him a legacy.

Nora shifted her cast and tried to get comfortable. Since she normally slept on her side, she had to prop her broken arm on a pillow to get off her back, but no matter where she moved, she seemed to press down on a bruised body part. The drugs she'd been given had long since worn off, and she ached all over.

Muted sounds from the television downstairs mixed with the murmur of Hester and Andrews's voices, and Nora felt as safe and secure as she had in her childhood bed.

She thought of the room she'd had when she was about Tucker's age. She pictured the floral wallpaper and the white wicker chair that held her stuffed animals. She remembered her dollhouse, her wooden bookcase, and the little desk where she did her homework. She'd loved her colored markers and her stack of construction paper, but her favorite thing of all was a new notebook. Each sheet was a clean canvas, waiting to be transformed into something more. Something magical.

Caught in this memory of paper, Nora fell asleep.

When Nora slogged downstairs to the kitchen the next morning, Hester was already gone. She left coffee and an apple turnover on the counter.

Is this for me or for Andrews? Nora wondered.

Glancing out the window over the sink, she saw no cars in the driveway. She was alone in Hester's house with no way of getting home unless she walked. Her moped was still parked on Maple Street, and she didn't think she could drive it with one arm.

Nora had a few sips of coffee and then used Hester's landline to call McCabe.

He picked up right away. "Your voice is music to my ears. I was going to swing by and tuck you in last night, but Hester threatened to push me in the oven if I did. She knew you needed to sleep, but I'm a selfish man and I wanted to see you."

"It's a good thing you didn't come, then. It's better not to mess with Hester when she's channeling the witch from 'Hansel and Gretel.' It sounds like you're in the car. Are you heading to work already?"

"I'll go in later. For now, I'm your Uber driver. I'm about

five minutes from Hester's house and I haven't had any coffee. Any chance she brewed extra?"

"Yep. I'll have it ready when you get here."

McCabe appeared at the back door carrying a bouquet of sunflowers and a black Sharpie pen. He dropped both on the kitchen table and enfolded Nora in a hesitant but tender hug.

"My tough girl," he whispered, kissing her on the brow.

Smiling up at him, she said, "I wish I'd had this cast yesterday. I could've done some real damage to Colton's face. It feels like my arm is encased in a bag of rocks."

"I wanted to be the first one to sign it." McCabe grabbed the Sharpie. "The flowers are for Hester. Knowing she was looking after you gave me the headspace to focus on work, so I want to thank her."

Nora opened a cupboard and pulled down a vase. "I can pour your coffee, but you're on your own with the floral arranging."

McCabe took hold of her sling. "Any requests, like a literary quote or a tic-tac-toe board?"

"Whatever comes to mind."

A sly grin crept over McCabe's face as he bent over her cast. When he was done writing, he chuckled and pocketed the pen.

The big, block letters said, YOU SHOULD SEE THE OTHER GUY!

Nora laughed, which caused her sling to jiggle up and down, nearly catching the handle of McCabe's coffee cup. He grabbed it before it could slide off the counter and cried, "Careful, now! I have a day full of interrogations, attorneys, and paperwork. I *need* this coffee."

"If it had spilled, I would've given you mine."

McCabe's eyes shone. "I guess you do love me." He carried their cups to the kitchen table and pulled out Nora's chair. "We have about ten minutes to drink our coffee. After that, I'll drop you off at home and head into the office. Are you going to rest today? Wait—of course you're not. Forget I asked."

"The store will be open, but I'll spend more time sitting behind the checkout counter than usual. I just hope Sheldon doesn't have a flare-up today. I don't know what we'll do if we're both achy and tired. Speaking of which, how's Kirk?"

"He's okay. He let the paramedics look him over, but he refused to leave Val and Tucker to go to the hospital. I talked to Val this morning. She and Kirk are shaken, but coping. Of the three of them, Tucker seems to be doing the best. To him, Colton was a treasure-stealing pirate who got caught by the good guys. Val said he's been talking up a storm since he woke up. He hasn't been this lively since before his mom died."

"That's the best news you could've given me," Nora said as she blinked back tears. "I don't know what it is about that boy, but I care about him. Is he safe now, Grant? Really, truly safe?"

"Colton's partner is still out there. We have the deed, so she has no reason to go after the Walshes, but I won't sleep easy until we have her in custody."

Nora recalled the woman who'd left her jar of honey on the checkout counter. Was she also the woman with the blonde wig from the truck stop?

"What about Colton? Is he cooperating?"

"He wants to make a deal, but so far, he's not offering anything we can use. He won't name his partner or tell us who he's working for."

Nora unfolded the newspaper on Hester's table and pointed at the top story. "It all comes down to the casino, which means Lawrence has to be pulling Colton's strings. Even though the deed was recorded years ago, Lawrence has a team of attorneys. I'm sure they could find a way to prove that Virginia wasn't of sound mind when she left the land to Kelly and Tucker."

"There isn't a shred of concrete evidence linking Lawrence to Kelly's murder, Justine's murder, the break-in, or last night's business." McCabe pushed his coffee cup aside and reached for Nora's hand. "We both know there's a bigger fish at the end of this line, but I can't reel him in without proof. Colton is too re-laxed for a man facing a double murder charge, which means he expects someone with deep pockets to take care of him."

"And Gus? Is he in the clear?"

McCabe nodded. "He deserves a medal and a handshake from the mayor. Instead, we gave him bad coffee and kept him from his bed. But I owe him, Nora. He saved the day. When I told him as much, do you know what he said?"

The impish gleam in McCabe's eyes made Nora grin. "What?"

"That I didn't owe him a thing. He said that since he was get-ting a second chance at being a better dad and a shot at being the world's best granddad, he already had everything he could possibly want."

Nora squeezed McCabe's hand. "I have everything I could possibly want too."

"Do you? Are you sure about that?" he asked softly.

"I wanted kids when I was younger but not anymore. I don't feel unfulfilled because I'm not a mom. Or a wife. I have a rich and wonderful life, Grant. Nothing's missing. Except a car. I'd like to have a car."

McCabe laughed. "Okay, I'll drive you home now."

"When we get there, I could use your help with something."

Gathering up their coffee mugs, McCabe absently murmured, "Oh, yeah?"

"Could you help me shower?"

McCabe dropped the mugs in the sink and donned his cap. Touching the brim, he said, "At your service, ma'am."

Chapter 19

It's a universal instinct of the human species, isn't it,
that desire to dress up in some sort of disguise?
—Daphne du Maurier

After clearing off the front display table and shelving all the
black and yellow books, Nora felt like she'd run a marathon.
When Sheldon arrived, she was sitting in a chair with her eyes
closed.

"I see you're already overdoing it." He perched on the edge
of the coffee table and studied her. "I'm going to start the coffee. You stay. After I make you some magic elixir, we'll figure
out how we're going to survive the next few days."

As Nora listened to Sheldon run water and scoop coffee
beans, she relaxed even deeper into the chair's soft cushion. She
didn't open her eyes again until Sheldon told her to.

"Coffee and Tylenol—the second breakfast of chronically ill
hobbits the world over." Catching sight of her cast, he said,
"Oh, I want to sign it too."

A minute later, he returned wearing a mischievous grin. He
uncapped a marker and bent over Nora's cast. "Have you broken a bone before?"

"Just a finger," she said. "I slammed it in a door. I was nine,
so I barely remember it."

"Well, in a few days, you're going to understand why I wrote what I wrote."

Nora glanced down at her cast and frowned. Sheldon had written, IT ITCHES!

He gave her hand a pat. "You don't get it now, but you will. You'll trade your life's savings for a wire hanger. Now, let's get down to business. I know how we can get ready for the weekend without killing ourselves."

"Are we going to change storytime into a Dickensian workhouse experience?"

Sheldon's eyes gleamed. "How'd you guess?"

"You're joking, right? Please tell me you're joking."

"Look. Family members help each other. Our bookstore is a big family—especially when it comes to our storytime and book club regulars. My book club meets tonight, and I'm going to ask them to do the heavy lifting. I'll order a few pizzas, turn on the music, and make a party out of it. They'll be happy to decorate and swap out displays."

Nora was familiar with everyone in Sheldon's Blind Date Book Club and knew he was right. "How do the toddlers fit in? Are they climbing ladders? Using the staple gun? What?"

Sheldon pretended to mull over the question until she poked him in the side, eliciting his Pillsbury Doughboy giggle. "Okay, okay! Our beautiful bambinos will plant seeds. Lots of them. I bought a bag of multicolored craft sticks, and I'm going to write the name of the plant on the stick and put it in the soil. Whoever 'adopts' a book during Family Fun Fest will get a free plant. My book club can make a sign about how reading together is growing together."

"I love the plant idea. It goes with our window."

"*Exactamente!*"

Nora jerked her thumb at the Children's Corner. "Are you going to plant seeds back there? In soil? I'm picturing lots of dirty hands touching lots of clean books."

Sheldon shuddered. "No, no, this is an outdoor storytime. I called Kirk Walsh this morning and he's donating soil and a bunch of biodegradable pots. The hardware store is lending us a wheelbarrow and letting us use their hose to clean our baby gardeners' hands."

"Is there a story for this storytime?"

"That's the best part! We're having a guest reader. Davis Godwin is going to read Larissa Juliano's *Nana's Garden.* It's about a little girl who gardens with her grandparents. Both of our themes are covered. Gardening? Check. Family? Check. All the parents, nannies, and caregivers will love Davis."

Nora hadn't thought about Davis in days—not since she'd reconnected with McCabe—and she felt a little guilty about how quickly he'd fallen off her radar once she no longer needed his professional help.

"What made you ask him?"

The coffee machine beeped, signaling the end of its brew cycle, and Sheldon leaped to his feet like a dog responding to a training whistle. He answered Nora from inside the ticket agent's booth. "It was June's idea. Davis has told the knitting group how much he loves to read to his nieces and nephews. When I called him, he said yes right away. I don't know how he has the time with his caseload and court appearances, but then again, he *is* a saint."

"Are you jealous?"

Sheldon poked his head out of the pass-through window. "Why? Because he's smart, handsome, and charming? Not a bit. He can't rock a sweater vest like I can."

"No one can," agreed Nora as she headed into the stacks to rearrange the mystery endcap. She took down the mysteries with bee themes and replaced them with mysteries with the word *family* in the title, including Lisa Jewell's *The Family Up-stairs*, Sally Hepworth's *The Family Next Door*, Leigh Perry's

A Skeleton in the Family, *Fatal Family Ties* by S. C. Perkins, and more.

When she was done, she unlocked the front door, greeted her first customers, and started in on the YA endcap. She'd just slid E. Lockhart's *Family of Liars* into an acrylic shelf holder when a voice behind her said, "Sounds like the testimonies I heard in court yesterday."

Nora turned around to find Davis holding a basket of snack food.

"It's nice of you to volunteer. You didn't have to bring treats for the kids too."

Puzzled, Davis glanced down at the basket. Then he grinned. "This is for you! You can eat every snack in here with one hand. There's apple sauce pouches, granola bars, dried fruit, nuts, and beef jerky. And plenty of chocolate. Raisinets are my favorite, and they're so easy to eat. Just tear open the box and pour them straight in."

"Even if I didn't have a broken arm, this is a perfect gift for me. I can eat any of these things without having to put my book down. Thank you!"

Nora offered Davis a cup of coffee and the two of them walked back to the ticket agent's booth.

Because there was a fairly long line of customers, Nora ducked into the booth to pour Davis's coffee and to help Sheldon by plating book pockets and muffins. The storytime crowd was always boisterous, but this morning, it seemed like there were twice as many kids and parents as usual. The noise level rose until Sheldon and Davis finally ushered everyone out the back door.

Though Nora was relieved when peace descended over the store again, she soon realized that it was going to be extremely difficult to work the espresso machine with one hand. It took so long for her to scoop the grounds, attach the portafilter, and steam the milk that the next customer changed his order from a latte to coffee with milk.

"I'm sorry," Nora said. "It'll go faster when Sheldon comes back."

For the next hour, she moved between the ticket agent's booth and the checkout counter, doing her best to see to her customers' needs in a timely fashion, but by the time toddlers and their parents began streaming back into the shop, she was feeling winded.

Davis, on the other hand, seemed energized by his storytime experience. After leading a crowd of starry-eyed adults carrying books, and toddlers cradling biodegradable pots to the front of the store, he joined Nora behind the checkout counter.

"I thought I'd bag for you," he said. Then he focused his dazzling smile on an adorable girl with corkscrew curls. "Hey, Layla! What are you going to call your new plant?"

Adopting a serious expression, the girl said, "Potato. Nana says that all new babies look like potatoes."

As Davis roared with laughter, the girl's parents unloaded fourteen picture books onto the counter.

For the next thirty minutes, Nora swiped credit card after credit card.

"You're good for business," she told Davis after the last toddler was led out of the bookstore. "Really. You were amazing."

"It was fun. I seriously love kids. I'd like to have my own, but I'm not getting any younger and I'm *still* single."

Thinking of Estella, Nora said, "You have time."

"I want to adopt kids with the right person. I just don't know where to find that person." He shook his head as if to dismiss the subject. "Hand me that marker so I can sign your cast."

Davis had just finished writing when Sheldon came to the front. He gave Davis a big hug, told him he was now the official substitute storytime reader, and ushered him to the front door.

There, he whispered something in Davis's ear. Davis's eyes widened and he beamed at Sheldon. The two men fist-bumped and then Davis waved at Nora and left the shop.

"What was that about?" Nora asked.

Sheldon mimed zipping his lips. "I can't betray the bro-code, but Davis might turn into a reader after all. He's coming to book club tonight because there's someone I want him to meet."

Nora didn't know what Sheldon was up to, but she liked the idea of Davis joining the eclectic group of singles who made up the Blind Date Book Club.

"What'd he write on your cast?" asked Sheldon.

Nora said, " 'I do my own stunts.' "

The two friends dissolved into laughter.

As Nora headed home that night, she was sore but content. Her good day got even better when she saw McCabe's SUV in the parking lot behind the bookstore.

When she opened the door to her tiny house she was greeted by the scent of garlic and onions. McCabe was in the kitchen, sprinkling sesame seeds over a wok filled with stir-fry chicken and veggies.

Nora said, "What a lovely surprise. Can I kiss the cook?"

McCabe set aside his wooden spoon and reached for Nora. A few minutes later, he plated their food and carried it to the kitchen table where a bottle of wine was already waiting.

"I didn't know you owned a wok," Nora said.

"I borrowed it from Deputy Hollowell last week. She dropped it off one night after her shift, but I haven't had time to use it until now."

Nora remembered seeing the K9 vehicle in McCabe's drive-way. She'd been jealous and angry over the thought of McCabe and Hollowell hanging out together, and now she felt silly for having felt that way.

Raising her wineglass, she said, "To coming home to you."

They touched rims and sipped their wine. McCabe asked how her day had gone, and Nora told him some of the highlights before inviting him to share his news.

"Today was a good day," he began. "Colton realized that no one was going to rescue him and that his time for making a deal with the DA's office was running out, so he confessed to both murders. He also gave up the name of his partner—Dana Kopinski. This young woman has been committing misdemeanors since she was thirteen. Shoplifting, marijuana possession, reckless driving, trespassing, breaking and entering, and so on. She and Colton grew up together. She's a few years younger than Colton and idolizes him."

"Is she Bonnie to his Clyde?"

"I think so, but this Bonnie has gone to ground. We'll find her—I'm sure we will. According to Colton, she's low on funds because they didn't finish their job."

Nora lowered her fork. "Did Lawrence hire them to steal the deed?"

"No. Justine did."

"*What?*"

McCabe let out a dry laugh. "That was my reaction too, but Colton convinced me. He knew Justine's room number at the Inn of Mist and Roses. He knew that her relationship with Lawrence was on the rocks. He showed us the Reddit thread where he and Dana offered their services for hire. They even created a private Instagram account, which is how they initially communicated with Justine. The messages aren't very incriminating, and Justine insisted on using burner phones once she was in Miracle Springs, but we have it in writing that they met a few days before Kelly died."

"Justine hired them to kill Kelly?"

McCabe folded his arms and sighed. "Murder was never part

of the plan. Colton was supposed to get the deed. That's all. The night Kelly died, Dana hid in the Walshes' yard and watched the house. She waited until Kelly was alone in the kitchen and then knocked on the back door. When Kelly cracked the door, Dana explained that she was pregnant with Lawrence's child. She said that he wouldn't return her calls and she had no one to turn to for help. She told Kelly that she and Lawrence had met when Lawrence was in the area scouting for land to build a casino. She used a menthol stick like actors use to turn on the water-works."

"That's so low," said Nora. "Kelly was a good person. I'm sure she felt sorry for Dana. After she tricked me into touching that honey jar so she could get my prints, I'm definitely not her biggest fan. Obviously, she and Colton screwed up or they wouldn't have tried to pin their crimes on me."

"Colton claims that Kelly's death was an accident. He and Dana wanted to lure her away from the house by asking her to bring some food, spare clothes, and whatever cash she could spare to the laundromat across the street from the Inn of Mist and Roses. It was a public place that was open late and only a short walk from the Walshes' house, so that's why they picked it. The idea was to intercept her before she reached it and get her to tell them the location of the deed. When she refused and tried to scream, Colton had to shut her up."

Nora held up both hands. "Wait, wait, wait. *Justine* wanted the deed?"

"Yep. In one of her Instagram messages, she said that Lawrence would never leave her if she could get him the thing he wanted most. She referred to it as the 'magic paper' because it could save their relationship."

Though Nora's wineglass was still half full, her head was buzzing.

"It's a lot to take in," McCabe said softly. "And I have to

admit—I wanted Lawrence to be the villain in this story. I wanted him out of your life once and for all, but he didn't even buy plane tickets until he realized why Justine had come here. By the time he landed, she was already dead. He kept his mouth shut because he cares more about that deed than he ever cared about his girlfriend."

Questions were climbing over themselves in Nora's head, but she wanted to let McCabe explain things at his own pace.

He poured himself more wine and added a splash to her glass. Then he started talking again.

"After killing Kelly, Colton and Dana had to break into the Walshes' to search for the deed. Justine told them to focus on a book collection packed in rubber bins. She told them to take any loose papers or any maps. They didn't have time to fan the pages of every book, so they took the valentine with the map. They didn't care if they stole the right thing. Justine was going to pay them for their trouble. They weren't going to give her a choice."

"They damaged those beautiful books for nothing," Nora muttered angrily.

McCabe gave her an affectionate smile. "You would've clocked them both on the head with a frying pan, wouldn't you?"

Returning his smile, she said, "The heaviest one I could find."

"Unfortunately, Justine didn't have the money she promised Colton and Dana. She'd scraped together what she could, but it wasn't enough, so she padded the envelope with fives and tens. It was supposed to be a bigger envelope, and it was supposed to be stuffed with hundreds. Not only had Justine tried to cheat two criminals, but she also knew that Colton killed Kelly. Colton had to silence her."

Nora was stunned. "How could she have been so naïve? She hired a pair of thugs online and then agreed to meet them alone, at night, with the intention of cheating them?"

McCabe shrugged. "All I can say is that she didn't spend much time in the real world. She started cultivating her online image as a teenager and was fixated on amassing a following on social media. She earned lots of free products but had very little money in the bank. When she met Lawrence, she was living in her parents' basement."

Glancing to the right, Nora studied their reflection in the window. She saw a middle-aged couple having dinner. Their faces were etched with tiny lines, their hands had age spots, and they both looked tired. And yet Nora wouldn't have traded places with any other woman. She was exactly where she wanted to be, sitting across from the man she loved. This good, loyal, dependable man.

"She risked everything to impress Lawrence, and he didn't care. There's always another woman waiting, isn't there?" Nora mused aloud.

McCabe got up and walked behind Nora's chair. He put his arms around her and whispered, "Let's not talk about this anymore. How about dessert on the sofa? There's a new crime drama on BBC."

Smiling up at him, Nora said, "That sounds perfect."

The next morning, Nora was humming as she unlocked the delivery door. After eight hours of uninterrupted sleep, she felt like a new person, despite having a broken arm.

Her first task was to gather fiction titles for the front table display. Loading the book cart with one arm was slow going, but Nora was in high spirits. It was a sunny, springtime Friday and Main Street was festooned with bright banners and colorful balloons. Hearing the organ strains of carousel music, she peeked out the front window to see which rides were set up in the park.

This wasn't a full-scale carnival, as most of the activities were geared toward little kids, but the alligator coaster, flying elephants, and Wild West railroad were adorable. The petting zoo and pony rides were on the far end of the park, which meant the aromas drifting into the bookstore would come from the nearby food trucks. For the rest of the day, the air would be perfumed with candied nuts, funnel cake, and caramel corn.

When Sheldon arrived with a stack of bakery boxes, he was glowing.

"Guess what? This is Gus's first day at the bakery. He and Hester were jamming out to Fats Domino. They were singing and baking and having a grand old time."

"They're like us, minus the singing." Nora gave Sheldon a wink.

Sheldon put the boxes on the counter and jerked his thumb toward the Children's Corner. "My book club pulled the family titles yesterday. I'm going to make the most beautiful, diverse, and inclusive waterfall display ever. *After* coffee."

"After coffee," agreed Nora.

She added a few more titles to her book cart and pushed it to the front of the store. She loved arranging books on the large wooden table and had deliberately picked novels with colorful covers or fun titles. Her first row included Steven Rowley's *The Guncle*, Jade Chang's *The Wangs vs. the World*, Jami Attenberg's *The Middlesteins*, Stacey Swann's *Olympus, Texas*, and Laurie Frankel's *This Is How It Always Is*. The next row was made up of books by Kevin Wilson, Jonathan Tropper, Claire Lombardo, and Emma Straub.

Thanks to Sheldon's book club, the rest of the store was ready for the festival. The spinner rack of bookmarks had been moved next to the checkout counter to make room for the wheelbarrow holding the biodegradable planters. A table piled high with cookbooks and books on family gardening sat next to the wheelbarrow and an ADOPT ME banner hung from the ceiling.

The bookshelves of every section were draped with chains of interlocking paper dolls or hearts. The word *family* had been written on each chain in over twenty different languages.

At five minutes to ten, Nora glanced around the store and said, "I think we're ready."

"Let the circus begin!" Sheldon bellowed.

From the moment Nora flipped the window sign from CLOSED to OPEN, she felt like a ringmaster. She led people to certain sections, rang up books, gave directions to the restroom, bagged books, held the door open for parents pushing strollers, and asked customers of all ages to refrain from eating cotton candy, roasted corn, or funnel cake inside the store.

Around one o'clock, Estella breezed in behind a mother carrying a sleeping baby in her arms. She came behind the checkout counter and gave Nora a hug.

"God willing, that'll be me next year," Estella said in a dreamy voice. "And one day, my kid will be coming here for storytime. Isn't that crazy?"

"Crazy awesome. How's Jack?"

Estella cracked a smile. "Happy. And terrified. Ecstatic, but also terrified."

"Speaking of happy, Sheldon said that your dad was having a grand time at the Gingerbread House."

"It's all he could talk about at lunch. It was so delicious that I picked some up for you and Sheldon." Estella removed two takeout containers from her tote bag. "I remember how to work the register, so you can eat while I take people's money."

Nora thanked her and carried a box back to Sheldon. He opened the lid, inhaled, and grinned from ear to ear.

"Bulgogi chicken! What angel brought this?"

"Estella. I'm going to eat behind the counter while she rings. Go sit in the stockroom and put your feet up. People can survive without coffee for a few minutes."

When Nora returned to the front of the store, Estella was

chatting with a father and son as she bagged their books. The pair selected a plant from the wheelbarrow and left the shop.

"Are you working today?" Nora asked before digging into her Korean barbecue.

"Two root touch-ups this morning and a quick cut at three, but my one o'clock canceled, so I'm taking a very long lunch. I'm glad I got to see my dad. I've been worried about him, but I feel like I can stop worrying now." She sighed. "If only you could too."

Nora glanced up from her lunch. "Life will be back to normal soon. I know it. McCabe will find Colton's partner and then he can arrest Lawrence. If not, he can slither out of town like the snake he is, and I'll never have to think about him again."

Estella looked thoughtful. "About Colton's partner—you thought she had a wig on when you saw her in the video, right? What about when she was in here, getting your prints on that jar of honey? What was her hair like?"

"Dark brown and wavy. Came to here." Nora touched her collarbone. "Thick bangs too."

"Hmm." Estella took out her phone and started typing. Then she showed Nora the screen. "Did it look like this?"

Nora examined the photo. "It wasn't that curly."

Estella scrolled until she found another image. "How about this?"

The woman in the next photo looked like a younger, fresher Dana. "That's it! How did you find this?"

"Honey, I know hair, which means I know wigs. Several of my clients—I won't name names—suffer from hair loss. I help them find high-quality hairpieces or wigs and show them how to style and care for their bonus hair. If Dana's wigs are local, there's only one place where she could've found that brunette wig, and that's Angel Hair Wigs. Angel and I go *way* back. I'll give her a call as soon as I help these ladies."

A pair of women stepped up to the counter and handed Estella a stack of picture books. One woman had a toddler on her hip. The other carried a stuffed shoulder bag. Digging a credit card out of a zippered pocket, she said, "Your display in the Children's Corner made our day. We *never* see books about a kid with two moms, and you had *two*, front and center."

Estella invited the moms to attend next week's storytime, but the women weren't from the area. They promised to stop back the next time they were in town and headed over to the wheelbarrow to pick a potted plant.

Nora stood up. "I'm going to wash my hands and pass their compliment on to Sheldon. Be right back."

When she returned five minutes later, Estella was wrapping up a phone call.

"Thank you, Angel." She hung up and turned to Nora. "Got her! When Dana's short on cash, she dances at Miss Scarlet's. Over the past year, she bought five wigs from Angel. She gave me all the serial numbers. We already know what two of them look like, and the third is a bright blue bob. If she's trying to hide, she won't wear that one, so let's look up the others."

"*If* she's trying to hide," Dana said. "She'd only stick around if she was waiting to see what happened to Colton. According to McCabe, Dana's had a thing for him since they were kids. She visited him when he was in prison, gave him money, and did whatever he asked of her after he got out. Colton told McCabe that Dana gives him all of her money too."

Still gazing at her phone, Estella grumbled, "What a prince."

"She doesn't have any money or anywhere to go. She's in love with Colton, which is why McCabe thinks she hasn't left town."

The sounds of the festival faded in the background as Estella pulled up a red wig called "The Curly Fox." She sent the link to Nora's phone before searching for the next wig, which turned

out to be a short blond ombre wig named after an anime character.

"I bet she's wearing the red or the blond ombre. McCabe can
keep an eye on Miss Scarlet's and circulate photos of Dana
wearing these wigs. There's an app that will literally put each
wig on her head."

Nora gave Estella a one-armed hug. "You're incredible, you
know that?"

"I do, but I never get sick of hearing it. Now, call your man
so that he can find this woman. I want everyone I care about to
be as happy as I am."

Estella had barely left when the shop got so busy that it took
Nora ten minutes to send McCabe a text. As soon as she hit
send, she dropped her phone on the counter and rushed to open
the front door for a man pushing a double stroller. The wheels
were stuck on the sill, so Nora used her good arm to lift the un-
wieldy stroller over the metal bump while the man pushed from
behind.

With the door flung open wide, noise from the street poured
into the shop. Suddenly there was a sharp *bang*.

Nora went rigid in alarm and began scanning the sidewalk
for danger.

On the other side of the street, a child holding the string of a
popped balloon wailed as if his heart was broken. When his
mother bent to comfort him, Nora got a good look at the
woman standing directly behind mother and son. She was in
cargo shorts, hiking boots, and a blue T-shirt. Her hands were
curled around her backpack straps and her mouth was set in a
thin line. Despite her short, blond wig, Nora instantly recognized her.

"I need your phone!" Nora cried to the man pushing the
stroller. "It's an emergency!"

Dana took off running.

The man pressed the emergency button on his phone and passed it to Nora. She grabbed the phone and rushed outside.

The sidewalk was packed, and it took Nora several seconds to locate Dana. She was headed away from the festival. And she was moving fast.

Nora couldn't really hear the emergency operator, so she shouted her name and Dana's location into the phone as she pursued her quarry.

She tried to cradle her cast as she jogged along, but the jostling movement was uncomfortable, and her body was still sore from her fall. Her pace slowed and she knew she was in danger of losing Dana altogether.

"She just turned off Main Street toward the train station!" Nora shouted into the phone. She could no longer see Dana. She could only hope that someone from the sheriff's department was nearby. If not, Colton's partner would probably get away.

The festival was now two blocks behind her, and she could hear the operator calling, "Ma'am? Are you still there?"

Nora was about to answer when the space above her pinkie finger tingled. Seconds later, she heard the shriek of brakes followed by a loud, mechanical groan.

Then came the screams.

Hugging her cast to her chest, Nora hurried to the end of the block and turned right. She ran another hundred feet before coming to an abrupt stop.

A trolley from the Lodge was parked in the middle of the street, and people were racing away from it in every direction. Many were covering their mouths with their hands. Their eyes were huge, and their faces were twisted with shock. Some of them were crying.

Despite a sense of impending horror, Nora walked toward the trolley.

A man on the sidewalk shrieked into his cell phone, "She ran right in front of it! She didn't even look!"

Nora skirted around the man and a small group of ashen-faced bystanders until she had a clear view of the street.

A woman's body lay sprawled across the double yellow lines in the center of the road. Her arms and legs were bent at such severe angles that she looked like a discarded doll. A crimson halo of blood pooled around her head and her eyes stared upward. Her lips were parted as if her last breath had been an offering to the wide, blue sky.

The search for Colton's partner was over. The woman with the Minnie Mouse voice was dead.

Chapter 20

*Evermore in the world is this marvelous balance of
beauty and disgust, magnificence and rats.*
—Ralph Waldo Emerson

Nora stumbled to the curb and sank down. Her stomach began
to heave, but she fought the urge to vomit by breathing slowly
through her nose.

As she focused on her breaths, the din in the street increased.

Though she heard sirens, car engines, and more shouts, nothing penetrated the bubble of shock encasing her body. A single
thought lodged in her mind.

Dana is dead.

Nora knew she should be feeling something. The woman
had been an accessory to two murders. She'd stolen the little bit
of precious time Tucker had left with his mother. She'd seen to
it that Justine's life was cut short. She'd done terrible things to
people she didn't know. And for what? To prove to a bad man
that she was worthy of his attention?

That was all over now. She would never hurt another person.
But neither would she have a chance at redemption.

A man squatted down next to Nora and offered her a bottle
of water. She took it, mechanically thanked the kind stranger,
and drank a small sip.

The man walked off to help someone else, but Nora didn't notice because her gaze was fixed on the asphalt. Specks of mica suspended in tar winked in the sunlight.

When Nora reached out to run her fingers over the glittery silver bits, her shadow dimmed their sparkle.

Still, the texture of the road was strangely comforting. The composite of sand, slag, and crushed stone felt solid against her skin. The robust surface bore the weight of hundreds of vehicles every day. It was pummeled by rain and sleet, frozen by ice, and baked by the sun. Today, a woman's life had drained away into its cracks.

As Nora stared at the ground, her phone rang.

She didn't remember ending the call with the emergency operator, but she must have done so because Sheldon's name was on the screen.

"It's my fault," she whispered to her friend. "I was chasing her."

Sheldon was understandably confused. "What? Where are you? When I came to the checkout counter, the door was open, and you were gone. The gentleman standing next to me is wondering where his phone is."

Nora looked around. She could barely see the trolley now. It had been blocked by a fire truck, an ambulance, and two sheriff's department vehicles.

"What's all that noise? Where are you?" Sheldon cried.

McCabe hopped out of his SUV and strode toward the knot of emergency response officers.

"I need to talk to Grant."

Nora disconnected and dropped the phone into her pocket. She got up warily, but the shock and queasiness had receded enough for her to raise her good arm and call out McCabe's name.

He was at her side in a flash.

Pointing at the trolley, her words tumbled out. "I saw her in the crowd. I didn't think. I just chased after her. She was running away from me when—"

McCabe cut her off. "This is not on you. Andrews spotted her at the festival too. He and Hollowell were both in pursuit. Nora, she pushed a whole vat of fry oil over! She almost burned a bunch of little kids and the funnel cake vendor. Thank God no one was hurt, but she didn't care what she had to do to save her own skin. Andrews and Hollowell were going to head her off at the train station. Dana was looking over her shoulder because they were coming after her."

"And me."

Gently, he pulled her in close. "And you. My bad-ass book dragon. Running with a broken arm."

Nora rested her head against McCabe's shoulder for a moment. "Dana has a tattoo on her upper arm. I can't say for sure, but I think it was a crow."

"You're thinking of the dead bird you found in your flower arrangement?"

"Yeah."

McCabe's shoulders rose and fell. "I guess we'll never know if she put it there or not, but I wouldn't be surprised. She was clearly comfortable with cruelty."

Nora stepped out of his embrace and, after giving his hand a quick squeeze, gestured at the ring of rescue vehicles. "You need to go, and I've got to get back to the shop. I left Sheldon on his own and he has no idea why I rushed off."

"Just don't run. And make sure you take a breather this afternoon. Doctor's orders."

He turned and strode toward the chaos.

Nora watched him for a moment, her heart swelling with pride. Then, she started walking back to the bookstore.

Miracle Books wouldn't be a quiet haven. Not today. But it would be cool and welcoming. Sheldon was there, as was her comfy stool behind the checkout counter. If she could grab a few minutes alone, she could open a book and bury her nose in its pages. She'd inhale the scent of paper and escapism, of dreams and ink, and her equilibrium would be restored. She might have to wait a few hours until the crowds died down, but when she finally had a moment to herself, she would sit down and take comfort in the company of books.

Nora was on her sofa with her legs propped on her coffee table when someone knocked at her door.

"It's us!" June cried before letting herself in.

"I have corn chowder," said Estella as she crossed the threshold.

Hester was right on her heels. "I have a loaf of Gus's bread and some leftover desserts from the bakery."

June held out a bottle of tequila. "It's margarita time."

"You are *not* allowed to move," Estella commanded. "All you're allowed to do is talk."

"Is that your mom voice?" June teased.

"Might be. How did it sound?"

June considered. "Not bad, but you'll have to work on your glare."

Over the whir of the blender, June asked Nora how she was feeling.

"I'm looking forward to Sunday. I'm going to spend the whole day in my pajamas, drinking tons of coffee, eating a bunch of junk food, and doing nothing."

Handing Nora a margarita on the rocks, Hester said, "I could use a day like that too. And now that I have Gus, I can actually sleep in once in a while."

Estella carried in a bowl of soup and a plate with two slices of buttered bread. She then returned to the kitchen for her own food and settled onto the sofa next to Nora.

"This is Dad's Italian rustic bread. I'm on my third and fourth slice. At this rate, I'll be in maternity clothes in no time."

Hester and June sat at the kitchen table. They both praised Gus's bread and told Estella to thank Jack for the delicious soup.

"We sure have some talented men among us." June looked at Nora. "How's your man? Burning the midnight oil?"

"He's interviewing Colton again but getting nowhere. According to Colton, Justine was behind everything."

Estella tore off a piece of bread and dipped it in her soup. "Do you believe that?"

"I believe Justine was involved. And yeah, she might have initiated this whole scheme, but there's no way she could have known about the deed or Virginia's book collection unless Lawrence told her. He was just going to use her like he uses everyone. And I think she knew it. That's why she was nasty to me that day in the bookstore. She *knew* she was risking it all for a man who would likely leave her the second she gave him what he wanted."

"Will he get the land or will the original deed stand?" asked Hester.

June answered before Nora had the chance. "Davis says that it'll be decided in court. It's called a quiet title, which is a lawsuit to clarify property ownership. It's not the kind of case that's resolved overnight."

Nora let out an exasperated sigh. "I just hope Lawrence doesn't stick around. He won't be arrested—there's no solid evidence against him—so I hope he slithers back to Vegas and stays there."

Estella carried the empty soup bowls into Nora's kitchen. After loading them into the dishwasher, she wandered over to the bookshelves and pulled out a vintage edition of *Anne of Green Gables*.

"If only things ended as nice and tidy as they do in books," she said.

Hester's voice floated out of the kitchen. "What would be the fun in that?"

Nora took the question seriously. "If I'm reading a feel-good novel, it's a comfort to know that a happy ending is guaranteed. But I'm also okay with a messy ending. If books reflect life, and life is messy, then I guess endings should be allowed to be untidy too."

Estella put a hand over her stomach. "Forget about endings. Let's talk about beginnings. What are we reading next?"

Hester placed a bakery box in the middle of the table and said, "It's your turn to pick, but I was wondering if you'd switch with me because I'll be out of town the weekend of my pick."

"On a romantic getaway?" June asked as she peeked inside the bakery box.

"I'm spending the weekend with Lea. She called this afternoon." Hester paused to wipe a tear from the corner of her eye. "Sorry. It was just so amazing to hear her voice. I've loved getting her letters but talking to her on the phone is way better. I'm hoping this visit will be the first of many. I'll take off every weekend to see her if she lets me, but I need to take it slow at first. We're just starting to get to know each other, but I love her."

June took Hester's hand. "Of course you do. She's your child. No matter how old they get or how far away they move, our child is always our child." She smiled at Estella. "You'll see what I'm talking about soon enough, mama bear."

Estella rolled her eyes. "I am *not* responding to that nickname."

Giggling, June said, "Okay, back to our book pick. If we're going to switch, I'd like to read Brit Bennett's *The Mothers*. We loved *The Vanishing Half*, and I've heard good things about her first novel."

"I'll order copies in the morning." Nora pointed at the bakery box. "What's in there?"

Hester said, "Cookies, mini cupcakes, lemon squares, and brownies. What would you like?"

"After today? One of each."

"That's the spirit! I have another box in the car for the Walshes. Along with mani/pedi gift cards from Estella, socks from June, and a copy of the supper sign-up sheet from her knitting group. They're making meals for the family for the rest of the month, and Tyson's going to swing by once a week to mow their lawn." Hester gestured at Estella and June. "We can't give them Kelly back, but we can show them that they're part of a community."

Now it was Nora's turn to wipe away tears. "Thank you for everything. For feeding me, for taking care of the Walshes, for being kick-ass women with hearts of gold. For all the book club meetings that have turned into therapy sessions. Thank you for being my family."

Raising her glass, Hester said, "To book sisters."

"To book sisters!" her friends echoed.

Later, after the impromptu meeting of the Secret, Book, and Scone Society was over, McCabe called to check on Nora.

"When I said I'd see you today, I thought it would be at the bookstore—not at the scene of a fatal accident. How are you doing?"

Nora murmured in agreement and then said, "I'm fine. June, Estella, and Hester came over to spoil me. How about the trolley driver? Is he okay?"

"He knows he's not at fault, but he's understandably shaken. I'm just thankful he was driving an empty trolley and that he wasn't injured."

"Did you tell Colton about Dana?"

McCabe's exhale was heavy. "Yeah. He wasn't too broken

up by the news because he blames her for his arrest. They were supposed to go to the Walshes' house together that night, but since Dana tied one on earlier that day and was still drunk, Colton had to go by himself. When I asked him why she hadn't left town when she had the chance, he said that she didn't have any money or anyone to go to for help. He also told me that she's a talented pickpocket and would've risked going to the festival to get some cash."

"Is that what happened at the funnel cake booth? Was Dana trying to steal someone's wallet?"

McCabe grunted. "Not a wallet. She went for the vendor's cash box. That's when she drew attention to herself. Now she's gone and Colton will spend the rest of his life in prison. Kelly, Justine, Dana, Colton. All lost. And for what? Money. Ten years from now, when people play craps at the new casino or mine loads of copper, will they remember who paid the price for these ventures?"

"You will," Nora said softly.

She heard the whir of a printer in the background and the squeak of McCabe's desk chair as he leaned backward.

"Lawrence is leaving in the morning," he said. "His lawyers will handle the dispute over the deed. I know it's not a resolution, but you won't have to see him around town anymore."

Nora felt like a huge weight had just been lifted. With Lawrence gone, the story that had started with him could truly be over. It wasn't a happy ending, but it was an ending. Sometimes, that was enough.

Glancing out her kitchen window, Nora recalled that it was supposed to rain all day tomorrow. She was looking forward to hours of quiet, gentle, rain. It would wash the world clean and encourage new growth. And since she was lucky enough to be spending a rainy, spring Saturday in a bookstore, Nora decided that her ending was a happy one after all.

McCabe interrupted her musings by saying, "I'm sorry, Nora. Sometimes, justice is incomplete."

"Lawrence will get his due. He's rich, but he's as hollow as an old log, and he's rotting from the inside out." Nora waved a hand as if shooing away a fly. "I don't want to think about him anymore. I'd rather focus on tomorrow night. How does Chinese food, some cheap wine, and Netflix sound to you?"

"It sounds just right. Just like you and me."

Six weeks later, Nora sat in the Walshes' kitchen watching Val pour coffee into white mugs while Kirk opened a bakery box from the Gingerbread House.

"Scones!" he cried. "Hmm, they smell good."

"They're Hester's special comfort scones. She made them using flavors that might make you think of Kelly."

Val distributed the coffee cups and then poured a glass of orange juice for Tucker. As she sat down next to Kirk, she peered into the box with interest.

"I didn't realize that Hester knew Kelly so well."

"She didn't. These scones—it's a gift she has. She gets a sixth sense about people and flavors. When it works, she can bake a memory."

Kirk put a scone on Val's plate before selecting one for himself. He broke his in two and sniffed one of the halves before popping it in his mouth. As he chewed, he began to grin.

"What?" asked Val.

"I taste tea," he said. "And vanilla. Reminds me of Kelly working a puzzle first thing in the morning. She'd drink tea and burn a candle. It was usually some variation of a vanilla scent."

Intrigued, Val took a bite of her scone. "Wow. That's delicious. If we were still serving food at Tea Flowers, I'd want these to be on the menu."

Kirk and Val had decided that running two businesses at once was too much for them, so they decided to convert the café into a tea shop. Instead of serving tea and sandwiches, Val was now selling a wide variety of tea and teatime items.

"How have things been since you changed up the shop?" Nora asked.

Val's relief was obvious. "So much better. For all of us. Kirk gets to focus on his plants, and I get to sell tea without having to serve it. The best part is how much Tucker loves to organize the shelves. He doesn't mind coming to work with us now. We just finished his year of homeschool, and Derek found an incredible summer camp for Tucker. That man has been a godsend."

Kirk lined up three slices of bacon on Tucker's plate, which was divided into sections. After spooning scrambled eggs and strawberries into the other two sections, he picked up the walkie-talkie sitting in the middle of the table and raised it to his mouth.

"Breakfast," he said into the speaker.

After a moment's pause, there was a crackle and Tucker replied, "Okay."

Nora said, "That's a fun way to communicate."

"It was Val's idea to get them for Tucker's birthday, and he loves them." Kirk beamed at his wife, and she blushed prettily.

"I brought him something too." Nora pointed at her tote bag.

"Best give it to him after we're done. Otherwise, he might get too excited and forget to eat. Something that would never happen to me." Kirk chuckled as he patted his tummy.

Tucker appeared in the kitchen and shyly returned Nora's greeting. The adults talked for a bit while Tucker ate, and then Val asked if he'd like to spend the afternoon picking strawberries at a local farm or going for a walk in the woods.

"Ms. Nora told us about a trail that has a bridge going over a river. We could check it out and stop for an ice cream on the way home."

"Or pick berries and stop for an ice cream on the way home. I want ice cream no matter what we do," Kirk added.

They told Tucker that he could make up his mind after breakfast and use his walkie-talkie to relay his answer.

Nora studied the boy over the rim of her coffee cup and liked what she saw. He looked well rested and at ease with his aunt and uncle. By the end of the meal, he was chattering away to everyone, Nora included.

"May I be finished?" he asked his aunt when his plate was empty.

She nodded. "But before you run off, Ms. Nora has a surprise for you."

Tucker's eyes lit up as Nora handed him a blue gift bag and said, "Happy birthday."

After reaching into the bag and withdrawing a box with a Polaroid camera, a line formed between Tucker's brows.

Seeing his confusion, Nora said, "It's a camera, but not like the one on a cell phone. You can point this at whatever you want to take a picture of and press a button. This special paper comes out of the camera and, after you wait a few seconds, you'll see the picture appear right on the paper. It's pretty cool. Want me to show you?"

Tucker cried, "Yes!" with such enthusiasm that the adults laughed.

Nora loaded the film and then pointed the camera at the pitcher of sunflowers in the middle of the table. She pressed the shutter button and heard a satisfying click. This was followed by the whir of the film being ejected from the exit slot. She passed the film to Tucker.

As the image of the flower vase began to appear, Tucker's mouth fell open in astonishment.

"Can I try?" he asked.

Nora grinned. "Of course. It's yours."

"What do you say, Tucker?" Val prompted.

Tucker thanked Nora, picked up the camera, and hurried out of the room.

"He's going to burn through that film before our coffee's done," Kirk said.

Nora produced a box of film from her tote. "Then I'd better leave this with you."

"What a great gift," Val said as she cleared the breakfast plates. "He could take the camera along on our outing. Maybe we'll go to the park. I thought I saw something in yesterday's paper about a toy boat competition. Have you looked at today's paper, Kirk?"

"Haven't even taken it out of the bag. Why don't you check while I top us all off?"

Val had barely unfolded the paper when she let out a little cry and pressed her hand to her mouth.

Kirk put down the coffeepot and turned to her in alarm. "What is it?"

"It's Lawrence," Val said in a near whisper. "He was arrested. By the *FBI*!"

Nora stared at her in astonishment. "For what?"

Val's eyes raced over the page. "Fraud. He convinced people to invest in his company by promising them a high return rate within one year, but he couldn't deliver. He lost most of the funds through high-risk cryptocurrency trades and spent the rest on personal luxury items."

"That man . . ." Kirk shook his head in disgust.

"Listen to this!" Val's face broke into a smile as she read. "'Blue Leviathan, a Fortune 500 gaming company, has pulled out of the proposed casino and resort project in Maddie Valley, North Carolina, after parting ways with Lawrence Townsend's subsidiary, Shipwright LLC. Area residents can still anticipate the construction of a new casino as the Cherokee are expected to receive a green light following an emergency meeting by local officials.'"

Nora sank back in her chair.

"How will we ever explain this to Tucker?" Val whispered to her husband.

Taking the paper from her hands, Kirk stared at the photograph of Lawrence flanked by FBI agents. "We'll wait until he's older. That little boy doesn't need to know that his father's a crook. He needs to go to camp and make friends. He needs to chase fireflies, eat ice cream, and take pictures with his new camera. He needs books and LEGO and to sit down at this table for family dinner."

Kirk opened the cabinet under the sink and tossed the paper into the recycle bin.

Nora stayed for a few more minutes, but since the Walshes didn't feel like talking any more than she did, she thanked them for breakfast and left.

As she drove her moped through town, she exchanged waves or friendly smiles with neighbors and customers.

The moment she was home, she called McCabe.

"You saw the paper?" he guessed.

"Yes. It's good news for the Cherokee. And in some ways, for Tucker too. Lawrence won't be able to contest the deed now." After a pause, Nora said, "I thought I'd feel relieved when Lawrence's transgressions caught up to him, but I don't. I feel sorry for him. Actually, that's not quite true. I feel sorry that he ruined so many people's lives, including his own. I loved him once—enough to marry him. So, maybe I feel sorry for myself too. For making such a crappy choice."

McCabe grunted. "Come on, Nora. You went into a relationship hoping for the best. It didn't work out. People get together. People break up. Your story isn't that different than mine. I never wanted to get divorced. I never wanted to feel like a failure. But I wouldn't change anything that happened because all those forks in the road led me to you."

In the background, someone called McCabe's name.

"That's Hollowell. She's driving me to the softball game. But before I go, I want to tell you that it's okay to be sad. The past few weeks have been hard, so go to the flea market and find some cool stuff for the shop. When you do what you love—or spend time with the people you love—it helps to balance the scales. Which is why I'm coming over after the firefighters beat the crap out of us *again.*"

Nora laughed. "I'll put the ice pack in the freezer."

McCabe ended the call and Nora felt a twinge of annoyance. *Hollowell.*

Her dislike for the woman hadn't abated, but Nora wouldn't complain about her to McCabe. He'd forced the deputy to admit that she must've been mistaken when she said that she saw Nora hit Kelly. Hollowell had even apologized to Nora, but it hadn't been sincere. She was still Nora's enemy, and it was best to give her a wide berth.

Nora drove to the flea market and parked in front of the red barn. Bea was waiting for her in front of the locked entrance doors.

"I was just about to give up on you!" she chided. "Didn't you get my text?"

Nora explained that she'd silenced her notifications because she'd been having breakfast with friends and had forgotten to turn them back on.

Bea jangled her keys. "I wanted you to see what I found at an estate sale last week. I'll show you real quick. We can talk price later."

She led Nora to her Ford pickup and then unlocked the tail-gate and raised the window of the bed cap. Gesturing at a cardboard box, she said, "Take a peek."

Inside the box, Nora saw a row of thin books, packed spine-up. She pulled out a random book.

"*The Water Babies,*" she murmured, flipping to the copyright page. The illustrated hardcover edition was from 1990 and was in very good condition.

Bea tapped the side of the box. "They're all kids' books, and they all have something to do with water. Sailing, swimming, fishing—you name it. Perfect display for July, don't ya think?"

Nodding absently, Nora reached for another book. She smiled as she recognized Helen Palmer's *A Fish Out of Water*.

"Are they all in good shape?"

"A few need TLC. They'll go in your used book section, I know, but you'll still make a few bucks off each one. I'll leave you the keys if you want to look through them."

"That's okay. I just need to know how many are in here. Did you count?"

Bea shook her head. "Go ahead. I can wait another minute."

Nora counted thirty-six books and Bea closed the truck. The women were about to walk away when a horn tooted and a man in an adorable yellow truck stuck his head out the driver's-side window and yelled, "You doin' shady deals in the parking lot now, Bea?"

"Hey, Earl! What brings you here?"

Nora didn't hear the rest of their conversation because she was too riveted by the old yellow truck. As she examined the full-sized door on the passenger side, she wondered if it had been an ice cream truck in a past life. Her gaze traveled over the painted design on the rear panel. A smiling man with a trowel perched on top of a stack of bricks. Above the man's head were the words, MISTER MASON. There was a FOR SALE sign taped to the inside of the rear window.

Hearing her name, Nora snapped back to attention.

Returning to the driver's side, she said, "I love your truck."

"It's a 1973 mail truck, which was converted to an ice cream truck and then converted to my work truck. I used it whenever I was called out on an estimate. This baby never carried a single brick. She's got almost eighty thousand miles but still runs like a charm. She'll run for twenty more if she's treated right. You interested?"

Nora's mouth curved into a big, goofy grin. "I am."

"Wanna take her for a spin?"

"I do."

Bea chuckled. "Oh, Lord, Nora, you've gone all starry-eyed! Earl, you need to give her the family discount because she's not going home without this truck. She's already changing those bricks into books and painting the name of her shop over yours."

Earl saluted Bea and climbed down from the driver's seat. Gesturing for Nora to hop in, he said, "Did she read you right?" he asked Nora.

Nora slid behind the wheel and smiled. "Like a book."

Paper Cuts:
A Secret, Book, and Scone Society Mystery
Reader's Guide

1. The flower baskets for sale at Tea Flowers are arranged by theme based on the Victorian meaning of flowers. Have you ever looked up the meaning or symbolism of your favorite flower? What occasion might call for a deeper understanding of a flower's meaning?

2. Tucker Walsh is clearly into origami. Why do you think it appeals to him? Is there a hobby you love and feel you'll never outgrow?

3. Estella's father has finished serving a long prison sentence. If you were to put yourself in his shoes, what would be the most challenging adjustments to reentering society after fifteen years?

4. Were you concerned about the welfare of Nora and Sheriff McCabe's relationship when she became a person of interest in a murder investigation?

5. Estella sees Deputy Hollowell as a woman who has very few female friends because she views other women as competition. Have you encountered someone like Hollowell? What's the best way of dealing with this type of personality?

6. If you stopped by Miracle Books for bibliotherapy, what topic(s) would appeal to you? Do you believe books can be used to solve problems?

7. Paper is an important theme in the novel. Can you cite an example?

8. If you created a window display for the Family Fun Fest, what would it look like?

9. How does the community come together to help Kirk, Val, and Tucker? Have you ever been the recipient of similar kindness? What other kinds of help would benefit this family?

10. Every chapter in *Paper Cuts* leads off with a quote. Which is your favorite?

Bibliotherapy & Book Lists from *Paper Cuts*

Books for Young Origami Lovers
> Tom Angleberger, Origami Yoda series
> Mila Montevecchi, *Origami for Kids*
> Joel Stern, *My First Origami Kit*
> John Montroll, *Easy Dollar Bill Origami* (and many more titles from the Dover Origami Papercraft series)

Novels Featuring Chronic Illness
> Mona Awad, *All's Well*
> Loretta Chase, *The Mad Earl's Bride*
> Talia Hibbert, *Get a Life, Chloe Brown*
> Nasim Marie Jafry, *The State of Me*
> Adib Khorram, *Darius the Great Is Not Okay*
> Lisa Kleypas, *Seduce Me at Sunrise*
> Karol Ruth Silverstein, *Cursed*
> Nicola Yoon, *Everything, Everything*

Books for Job Seekers
> Octavia Butler, *Parable of the Sower*
> James Clear, *Atomic Habits: An Easy & Proven Way to Build Good Habits & Break Bad Ones*
> Ling Ma, *Severance*
> Haruki Murakami, *The Wind-Up Bird Chronicle*

Erich Origen and Gan Golan, *The Adventures of Unem-
ployed Man*
John Steinbeck, *Cannery Row*
Martin Yate, *Knock 'Em Dead Job Interview: How to Turn
Job Interviews into Job Offers*

Select Novels in Virginia Love's Collection
Raymond Chandler, *Farewell, My Lovely*
Francis Gribble, *The Love Affairs of Lord Byron*
Stephen King, *The Girl Who Loved Tom Gordon*
Ian Fleming, *From Russia, with Love*
Anthony Trollope, *An Old Man's Love*
Toni Morrison, *Love*
Erich Segal, *Love Story*
Evelyn Waugh, *Love in the Ruins*

Second Chance/Alpha Male Romance
Christina Lauren, *Beautiful Stranger*
Jodi Ellen Malpas, *This Man*
Lynda Chance, *The Mistress Mistake*
Jennifer Probst, *The Marriage Bargain*
Sylvia Day, *One with You*

Novels in Bees Display
Myla Goldberg, *Bee Season*
H. F. Heard, *A Taste for Honey*
J. A. Jance, *Kiss of the Bees*
Sue Monk Kidd, *The Secret Life of Bees*
Laurie R. King, *The Language of Bees*
Kathie Koja, *Kissing the Bee*
Christy Lefteri, *The Beekeeper of Aleppo*
Meredith May, *Honey Bus: A Memoir of Life, Courage, and
a Girl Saved by Bees*
Mobi Warren, *The Bee Maker*

Select novels in the Family Fun Fest Fiction Display
Jami Attenberg, *The Middlesteins*
Jade Chang, *The Wangs vs. the World*
Sally Hepworth, *The Family Next Door*
Laurie Frankel, *This Is How It Always Is*
Lisa Jewell, *The Family Upstairs*
S. C. Perkins, *Fatal Family Ties*
Leigh Perry, *A Skeleton in the Family*
Steven Rowley, *The Guncle*
Stacey Swann, *Olympus, Texas*